24 Hours of Trouble

Elise Noble

Published by Undercover Publishing Limited

ISBN: 978-1-910954-35-5

Cover designed by Abigail Sins

Edited by Amanda Ann Larson

www.undercover-publishing.com

www.elise-noble.com

For Ollie and Trev.

Chapter 1

I KNEW SOMETHING was wrong the instant I opened the door to our hotel suite. The air crackled with energy, the kind that shouldn't have been there if Antonio was on his own. A faint giggle drifted from the direction of our bedroom.

As I tiptoed through the lounge, resplendent in plush velvet and bawdy gold fittings, I felt as though even the furniture was mocking me. Because every throw pillow, every polished candlestick, and every hand-carved table belonged there, while I didn't. They'd been designed for a luxurious lifestyle, whereas I was just an impostor.

The closer I crept to the closed door, the louder the sounds got. A man's voice instructed, "Raise your hips," followed by a feminine sigh.

I hesitated with my hand on the doorknob. Did I really want to know what was going on inside?

The answer was no, but all the same, I felt compelled to look. I couldn't back away. In my heart, I knew Antonio had a woman in there, but a part of me, the part that had once fallen in love with the sly son of a bitch, tried to convince myself he could be watching pay-per-view television.

I twisted my hand, and the door swung open on silent hinges. A busty brunette lay on our bed, legs spread, hair flowing over my pillow as her eyes screwed up in ecstasy. She clutched at the thousand-thread-count sheets while Antonio pounded into her like a jackhammer on acid and attacked her neck in the manner of a rabid goat.

Her eyes popped open, and her expression of delight turned to sheer horror when she saw me standing there, arms folded.

She tapped Antonio furiously on the back. "*Mon cheri, il y a une femme!*"

He lazily swivelled his head until his gaze met mine. He didn't speak. He didn't need to because his eyes said it all: *What are you going to do about it?*

Good question. I had no idea.

When I didn't speak, he turned back to her and finished. He bloody finished. There was no mistaking the harsh grunt he always gave as he came. The woman, whoever she was (Party girl? Stripper? Prostitute?) tried to get up, but he put his hands on her shoulders and pinned her down. Just because he could.

Her eyes widened in fear as she turned back to me. In an odd way, I felt sorry for her. When she met him, she, like I, couldn't have realised what a monster he was. My eyes may have been green, but I didn't feel a shred of jealousy.

Rather than focusing on his naked backside, I concentrated on the trivialities. Had he mentioned me to her? I was betting not. My make-up was missing from the dressing table, and he'd even closed my suitcase and shoved it up against the wall. No, I didn't exist.

Satisfied with his performance, Antonio rolled to the side, dripping with sweat and bodily fluids. Vomit swirled in my throat. The girl tried to rise again, but he pushed her back to the mattress and knelt in front of her. With two fingers, he peeled off the now-limp condom, dropped it on the floor then thrust his hips forwards.

"Clean it."

She licked her lips nervously, and her eyes met mine in a cry for help.

But with Antonio, there was nothing I could do. Nothing but look away and allow her to preserve some shred of dignity. Time stopped, then I heard the squeak of the bedsprings as she scrambled away from him. A few seconds later, she shot past me through the open door, clutching her clothes.

I turned to face my boyfriend. I might have loved him once, but that feeling had ridden away on the breeze of the second summer we spent together. All my heart held now was hatred. A hatred that threatened to consume me if I let it.

So I turned it to ice.

He looked me up and down, his gaze condescending. His eyes stopped at my chest, and I knew he was comparing me to her and finding me lacking. Chicken fillets, push-up bras, even wadded up tissue—I'd tried it all to avoid his taunts, but none of it worked.

Finally, he stood up and stalked towards me.

"I wasn't expecting you back. I told you I'd pick you up when I was ready."

I braced myself, waiting for the sting of his palm on my cheek. Tempting though it was, I didn't shut my eyes. Like all the other times, he'd only make me open them again.

"I'm sorry. One of the other teams offered me a lift."

Antonio stood close, toe-to-toe with me, but the slap never came. "Next time, you should get back earlier. You can join in."

Bile rose in my throat. Surely, he couldn't be serious?

Mind you, I'd thought that when he suggested bringing my riding crop into the bedroom, but I'd ended up wearing the welts from it for weeks afterwards.

He stepped back and looked at his watch. "I'd take you now, while the bed's still warm, but we'll be late for lunch. I know how long it takes you to get ready."

Just had to get that one last barb in, didn't he? The asshole sauntered off to his bathroom and slammed the door, leaving me standing in the bedroom, barely able to process what had just happened.

Was it a surprise? No, not really. In my heart of hearts, I knew he had other women. I just didn't think he'd be so brazen as to bring one back to our bed like that. But then, he'd done so many nasty things to me over the years, what was one more?

One more on top of... I'd lost count now. My life was one long series of humiliations.

Why don't you leave him? I hear you cry.

Oh, if only it were that simple.

Some women daydreamed about meeting their prince and being swept off their feet. Others fantasised about hot, sweaty sex with some tattooed love-god. I dreamed of being free.

The problem was, I had nowhere to go. No home other than his palace of ice, and no family to turn to. And it wasn't just me. I had my two four-legged best friends to worry about as well.

They were the main reason I'd stuck it out. Harley and Murphy, the two loveable oafs I'd cared for since they were foals. They lived at the di Stefano family's country spread, and Antonio had told me over and over that if I tried to leave, he'd have them shot. And once he'd disposed of the bodies, he'd find me and drag me back where I belonged, anyway.

I had no doubt that he meant every word of it.

Back in England, living in our elegant home on the estate with the staff around, he toned his actions down so he didn't come across as a complete bastard. Life was bearable—just. And while Antonio and his father came out of the same mould, his mother wasn't too bad, and his teenage sister was a sweetheart. It was when we headed out on the road that my significant other became utterly unbearable.

But for the horses' sake, I sucked it up, and every day I died a little more inside.

In public, I was Amelia Stanbrook, one of show jumping's global success stories and girlfriend to a successful businessman. At functions, we certainly looked the part. Antonio charmed the world in his made-to-measure suits, his brown eyes twinkling. Women worshipped him. With dark hair, perfect teeth, and a chiselled jaw, he only had to flash his adorably crooked smile at them and they were ready to drop their knickers, as he'd just proven.

Once, I'd been one of them.

I had no idea why he chose me over the bevvy of beauties he left in his wake. Maybe he sensed my weakness? Whatever the reason, I'd cursed his decision every waking hour for years.

With the fancy grandfather clock ticking in the background, I rifled through the wardrobe for something suitable to wear. Elegant. Classy. Demure yet sexy. I picked out a knee-length black cocktail dress and held it up in front of me. The girl in the mirror looked pale and gaunt, and the dress was perfect for a funeral. Appropriate, as lunch would be about as enjoyable as a wake.

In my own bathroom, I found my make-up case where Antonio had tossed it into the sink and used Yves Saint Laurent's finest to add colour to my cheeks. I'd become an expert at that over the years. My dark red hair was flat from being under a riding hat, so I spritzed it with water and reached for the curling tongs to give it a bit of volume. I'd just finished pinning the last strands into place when Antonio knocked on the door.

He only gave a light rap with his knuckles, but I jumped all the same.

"Are you ready? The car's outside."

I pulled my shoulders back and stood up straight. Antonio always lectured me about my posture. "I just need to get my shoes."

He was waiting there when I scurried out, tapping his watch. "Well, hurry up. Tick tock."

I dug a pair of kitten heels out of my suitcase. Antonio was only two inches taller than me and had a complex about his height, which meant no shoes that put my head above his. Up-dos were out too, as was standing on a slope above him.

We'd almost reached the door when his hand closed around my wrist. Close, so close. I turned, swallowing the lump in my throat, and found him staring at my ass.

"I've changed my mind," he said, reaching for his zipper.

Today's lunch was a publicity event for riders on show jumping's European Championship Tour, a series of glitzy competitions taking place from Spain to Bulgaria to Ireland and another twelve cities in between. As my boyfriend and sponsor, Antonio was attending with me. I was expected to be on my best behaviour, and I couldn't even hide quietly in a corner because he'd invited a group of his clients along as well. Wonderful. His family's import and export business traded all over Europe, and as he never stopped reminding me, paid for my "bloody nags." He was the main face of the company while his father ran the di Stefano's property portfolio plus the hotel and casino in London.

I stared out of the limousine's tinted window while Antonio talked on the phone, something about shipments and merchandise. The sky had clouded over to match my mood, casting a grey pallor over La Croisette as we drove through Cannes.

My most recent penthouse suite hell played in my mind over and over on repeat. I'd always known Antonio had no respect for me, but now he was rubbing my face in it. I kept seeing that girl's expression, the way her rapture turned to fear. Still, I envied her. She'd got away.

Then afterwards... Afterwards. He hadn't even let me clean up. His mess dribbled down my inner thigh as

I tried not to squirm on the leather seat, leaving me as disgusted with myself as I was with him. How had I let myself get into this situation?

All too soon, the car drew to a smooth halt outside the Marriott hotel. Photographers lined the red carpet, and Antonio put on his public persona for the world.

Hidden was the demon lurking within as he opened my door, smiling sweetly at me. Once upon a time, when he gave me that look, my heart had melted. Now, it was frozen solid. With my fans and the media watching, I had little choice but to link my arm through his when he offered his elbow, the same elbow he'd used to pin me against the wall less than an hour before. Thank goodness for the flimsy layer of material that kept his flesh from touching me.

"Smile for the cameras," he murmured.

I plastered on a practised grin and faced the press. Could they see through me? Did they know how broken I was inside?

"Are you looking forward to the competition, Amelia?" someone shouted.

I turned in the direction of their voice. "Of course. Riding two horses in one of the most prestigious events on the show jumping calendar is a dream come true for anyone."

"What do you think your chances are?"

What *did* I think? Well, Harley would try her heart out, just like her full name: Harlequin's Heart. Murphy, well, he was another story. On a good day, he was unbeatable. On a bad day? Well, I might as well go around on foot.

"My chances are as good as anyone's, but the competition will be tough. Some of the best riders in the world are here."

"They haven't all had your form over the last few months, though."

"I've been lucky."

"I'll say," a female reporter piped up. "You've got one hell of a hot man on your arm."

If only she knew.

Beside me, Antonio preened in the spotlight. "Today is Amelia's day. I'm just here to support her."

The reporter practically swooned as Antonio bathed her in his aura.

How looks could be deceiving. I'd once thought Antonio was my dream man. I'd been nineteen when we met, scrimping and saving every penny to pay for my show entry fees and working every job I could find to pay for my horses' keep.

Antonio had offered me every budding show jumper's dream: sponsorship. Only I soon found I'd sold my soul to Satan. Years ago, my costs had far outweighed my winnings, but now I was bringing in the prize money, every penny went into Antonio's pocket. He said I owed him. My bank balance was a big, fat zero, leaving me and my horses totally dependent on a man who made my skin crawl.

The photographers turned to the next rider to arrive, and Antonio gave me a tug, snapping me out of my thoughts. I narrowly avoided stumbling and followed him inside.

The hotel ballroom was a spectacle of overstated elegance. Gilt fittings sparkled so brightly my eyes hurt, and a blurred reflection of my face stared back at me from the polished wooden floor. And the ceiling... Flipping heck—the artist who'd done the ceiling could have given Michelangelo a run for his money.

It seemed like every rider on the tour had turned up to the event, which hardly surprised me. Most of the horsey set grabbed any chance to dress up. There was nothing glamorous about mucking out, and we spent so long in jodhpurs, our legs rarely saw the light of day. Fake tan was definitely in order, even in the South of France.

In the days when I was single, I'd shared their enthusiasm. Those had been happier times, when I'd giggled with my flatmate, Holly, as we sorted out each other's hair and make-up before heading off in eBay's finest to whichever party had free booze. The fun had lasted until one fateful evening at the local polo club when Antonio arrived to present the trophy to the winning team.

Six years on, I barely saw Holly anymore. According to Antonio, she was badly bred and talked too much, leaving our friendship reduced to the odd coffee and a few snatched phone calls. Yet another thing I missed about my pre-Antonio days.

More than once as I lay awake at night, I'd wondered if I'd ever again get the opportunity for real friendship. Back then, I'd never appreciated the importance of an impromptu movie night or a late-night run to pick up fish and chips. Funny how the small things mattered so much more when I was no longer able to do them.

Sure, there were other riders on the tour, and we did talk, but Antonio saw to it that I never got the chance to form any bonds. Either he or Jerry, the thug he'd hired to drive the horsebox, constantly eavesdropped on my chats and interrupted if I discussed anything remotely personal.

As we meandered around the party, Antonio led the conversation while I nodded politely at my competition. Every time I saw a large-chested brunette, my nerves, already so close to snapping, stretched a little tauter.

"Aren't you going to eat anything?" Antonio asked, waving at a buffet table stacked with everything from caviar to foie gras.

"I'm not hungry."

"Suit yourself."

Wine was out as well, as I was competing later, so I just sipped a glass of orange juice and counted down the seconds until we could leave.

The tour director had no such problem with alcohol. He tripped up the steps to a small dais and waved his glass as he spoke, champagne slopping over the edges. "Thank you for coming, yadda, yadda, yadda..."

I tuned him out.

I didn't want to be there.

I didn't want to be with Antonio.

I barely even wanted to exist anymore.

CHAPTER 2

ANTONIO HOVERED OUTSIDE the stable door as I groomed Murphy. It was taking longer than usual because the big grey horse kept fidgeting. He hated Antonio almost as much as I did.

At least Antonio didn't come into his box anymore, not since Murphy bit him. I'd given my four-legged friend extra carrots for that, but for weeks after, as long as Antonio's bruise took to fade, I was terrified I'd go down to the stables and find out Murphy had been sent to the knacker's yard.

The temporary stables, put in especially for the event, buzzed with activity. Riders hovered, chatting, and grooms ran this way and that, getting their charges ready for their moment in the limelight.

Whether at a big show or a small one, I loved that kind of atmosphere. Nervous energy crackled in the air, but the positive kind, with everyone looking forward to the upcoming spectacle.

Well, not quite everyone. Jerry wheeled my tack locker over from the lorry and dumped it between my two stables before stomping off again. Antonio seemed to have gone out of his way to get me a groom who didn't actually groom. Jerry occasionally took the horsebox off somewhere and washed it, but he spent the rest of his time sprawled on the couch in the living quarters, watching satellite TV.

I'd often wondered why Antonio didn't pull Jerry up on his lack of work ethic, but came to the conclusion that my beloved boyfriend got some kind of perverse pleasure in seeing me do all the work.

Not that I minded. The horses were my passion. I finished pulling a few stray hairs out of Murphy's mane and stood back. Yes, it was straight. Both horses were clean and tidy, and I could tell by the way they paced backwards and forwards that they knew something big was coming up.

"Will you tell that nag to stop fidgeting?"

Antonio's voice came from outside the stable, and I sighed. He didn't understand horses at all.

"Murphy can't help it. He's just excited." I needed to keep Antonio away from him. The more time they spent near each other, the worse Murphy's mood got. "Why don't we go and walk the course?"

The organisers had certainly picked a choice spot for the temporary arena, just fifty metres from La Croisette, the world-famous avenue that ran along the seafront in Cannes. We'd be doing our thing in front of the world's super rich, who'd sip champagne and nosh on canapés as they watched from their yachts moored close by.

The freshly harrowed sand crunched under my boots as we headed in to take a look. Pristine jumps gleamed in the sun, almost as tall as me, each one artfully constructed with a French theme. Poles suspended between two miniature Eiffel towers, a scale replica of the Arc de Triomphe, and the red, white, and blue of the French flag. The twisty course offered several alternate routes, each presenting its own challenges.

At three of the jumps, I'd have the choice of cutting inside other obstacles to take a shorter approach or going the long way around. The shorter option was harder for the horses but faster, and we'd be running against the clock.

If we didn't complete the set of jumps within a certain time frame, we'd incur penalty points, which increased with every extra second. We'd also get penalised if our horses knocked a fence down or refused to jump over one.

The twisty options always suited Murphy. The smaller of my two horses, he was made for a course like this as long as he was in the right mood. Harley would have to go the long route or she wouldn't pick her feet up.

I ran through the course in my head as Antonio strode beside me, bestowing me with his pearls of wisdom, which drove me nuts because he'd never once sat on a horse.

"You have to go the quick route," he said. "The Whitaker brothers will, and you don't want to get beaten again." He emphasised the "again," and I gritted my teeth.

Antonio did this every time—put his two pennies worth in so if I didn't win, and I hadn't done things his way, he could blame it all on me. Trying to explain why I rode the way I did fell on deaf ears. Trial and error had taught me it was simply easier to suck it up after.

"Yes, Antonio."

As we traipsed around, I couldn't help but notice the admiring glances he got. It was a well-known fact that there were few straight men on the show jumping circuit, so Antonio got more than his share of attention from the ladies. I could hardly be seen to encourage it, but I lived in the hope that he would trade me in for a new model.

A pompous man wearing a bow tie marched into the ring waving a clipboard.

"The course is closed. *Fermé. Geschlossen.* Please leave the ring, people."

As they did every time, the words set off the build-up of nerves in the pit of my stomach. Would I win? Would I take home a cup, a sash, and prize money for my darling boyfriend? Or would I come second or worse, and return to England with bruises instead?

Talk about pressure.

Murphy had his head over the door looking for me when I got back. He put his ears back when he saw Antonio to inform everyone of his distaste. *Please, Murphy, don't get all grouchy.*

Jerry skulked around the corner and held out a fancy carrier bag. "The courier just turned up with the new jackets, boss."

Antonio snatched it off him. "About bloody time. They were supposed to arrive before we left England. At least the incompetent fools managed to get them delivered in time for the competition."

Appearances meant everything to Antonio. I cringed inwardly as his hand touched my shoulder when he helped me into the navy-blue blouson jacket, embroidered with the name of his company in four different places. Oh yes, I was so proud to represent ADS Enterprises.

I didn't even know what the sodding company did, not really. Over the years, Antonio had made vague mentions of buying and selling things, but women in the di Stefano family were second class citizens, and the men considered business dealings far too complicated for our tiny, little brains. But whatever Antonio's job involved, the work could hardly be taxing, could it? Because he spent most of his time tormenting me.

A couple of girls wandered past, and one of them sighed as Antonio straightened my collar.

"Ooh, look, isn't he a gentleman?"

Once upon a time, I might have rolled my eyes at her comment, but I'd long since learned that any hint at sarcasm was a bad idea. Far better to stay impassive.

Around us, the other riders were starting to get ready, and I didn't want to be late. If I cut my warm-up short, the horses wouldn't perform well.

"I'm going to change," I told Antonio.

"I'll come with you."

That was what I'd been afraid of.

In the living area of the horsebox, he watched me as I stripped off, his gaze cold and assessing.

"You're putting on weight. You need to take more exercise."

I weighed myself religiously every day, so I knew it was true. Three pounds had crept on, and I'd been praying Antonio wouldn't notice. I had an awful habit of turning to food when I felt down, and too often lately, I'd reached for the chocolate.

"I'll spend more time in the gym."

He leaned over me, running cool fingers up my side. "I'll give you a workout later."

That thought made me queasier than the world-class competition I was about to jump in. Because I knew he wouldn't give me a choice. He never did.

His eyes burned into me as I pulled on my shirt and did the buttons up as fast as I could, hands shaking as I tied my stock. My white jodhpurs, designed to fit me like a second skin, strained slightly at the seams. I'd have bought a size bigger if I were allowed.

"Have you seen the safety pins?"

He shrugged.

I rummaged around in the drawer under the sink and found a couple to attach my number to the back of my black jacket. Wonderful. Lucky thirteen. Somebody up there was having a laugh at my expense.

Finally, I pulled on my black boots, polished to a mirror sheen no thanks to Jerry, and got halfway out of the door before Antonio closed it on my foot.

"Trying to get away without your good luck kiss?" he asked, his tone mocking.

I looked at the floor. "Of course not. I've just got a lot on my mind."

He tipped my chin up and pressed his lips against mine. When I didn't immediately yield and allow him access, he bit my lip hard enough to draw blood. The metallic taste swirled around in my mouth with his tongue. I tried to show some enthusiasm, but my attempt had all the passion of a dead fish.

Finally, he pushed me away. "I'll be expecting a bit more effort this evening, Amelia."

I practically sprinted back to the horses, tears pricking the corners of my eyes. How was I supposed to ride properly when he got me so upset? Murphy in particular was very sensitive to my moods. When I got stressed, it transferred to him and he acted up. At least Harley was first to go. I only hoped I'd be feeling calmer by the time I had to ride the lad.

Harley, as always, did her best to cheer me up, snuffling at my hand as I tacked her up in case I'd brought any treats.

I showed her my empty palm. "I've got nothing, sweetie. Later, I promise."

Antonio opened the door for us so I could lead her out, while Jerry stood in the background, chatting to a couple of the other grooms. Female, of course. Most girls tended to be blinded by his muscles and didn't see through to his shitty personality.

"Jerry, tack Murphy up, would you?" Antonio said. "Bring him down to the warm-up ring when you're done."

He didn't look happy about it, but he nodded. "Yes, boss."

I groaned inwardly, as thrilled with that idea as Jerry. He and Murphy were *not* a good mix. In fact, Murphy hated him almost as much as he hated Antonio. This competition had "disaster" written all over it.

I led Harley outside, and Antonio gave me a leg up onto her. Immediately, I felt at home. Something about being on a horse soothed my soul, no matter how bad things might be. In the warm-up arena, we walked around the outside to loosen up Harley's limbs, then I urged her into a trot. She obliged beautifully, striding around the track like a dream. The organisers had set up a pair of practice fences in the centre, a high upright and next to that an oxer, which was lower but wider.

Harley cantered up to each in turn, popping over them perfectly. I knew she would. She was a big horse, and they were well within her capabilities.

One by one, the other horses got called through into the main ring, and soon it came to our turn. Antonio came with us, leaning on the fence at the edge with a look of expectation.

A bell trilled, letting me know that I had a minute to start my round. The giant gold wristwatch began its countdown, but I wanted to get it over with as soon as possible, so I set Harley thundering towards the start line, aiming for the first fence of ten.

We cleared the Eiffel Towers and turned towards a double. Harley took it in her stride. The next fence had poles painted like baguettes, and we went the long route to get there. Across the arena, Antonio's face clouded over as I disobeyed his instructions. A wave of panic ran through me, and I almost missed the turn after. Thankfully Harley pulled it out of the bag, and we cleared a mini Airbus fuselage.

Next up came a treble, and I had to slow Harley up a bit, otherwise her strides would have been too long to fit between the obstacles. The red, the white, then the blue flashed by beneath us.

As I was already in trouble, I steered us on the easier route again for the following jump. It was narrower than all the rest, and Harley wouldn't get over it if I approached it at an angle. That had happened before. She'd panicked, convinced she wouldn't fit, and demolished the whole lot.

But this time we flew over, and there were four obstacles left, the Arc de Triomphe flashed beneath us, as did a clapperboard advertising the Cannes Film Festival. A collective intake of breath came from the crowd as Harley's hooves rattled the top of the second to last, a collection of watch faces courtesy of the event's main sponsor.

One fence to go. I could see the finish line just beyond, and I let Harley have her head as we galloped towards it. The speed felt appropriate because it was shaped like a racing car. I'd heard a few of the other riders talking earlier—apparently one of France's other big sporting events, the twenty-four-hour motor race at Le Mans, would be taking place in a couple of weeks.

Harley kicked up her heels as she took off. We'd gone clear!

But what was our time?

The oversized clock glinted in the sun, and I squinted at the display.

Two seconds over.

My feeling of dread returned as I looked over at Antonio. No, he wasn't amused at all. I slowed Harley as we headed back towards the collecting ring, wanting to delay the lash of Antonio's tongue as long as I could.

It wasn't long enough.

"You just don't listen," he hissed. "I told you to take the short cuts."

"But she can't make those turns."

He grabbed the reins and pulled Harley to a halt. "I'm the one paying the entry fees. *I* pay for the horses' keep. You'll damn well do as you're told; do you hear me? On the other one, you take the quick route."

"Okay, I will."

I kept my eyes cast downwards while Jerry brought Murphy over. He was dancing around at the end of the rope, agitated already.

Murphy gave me a dirty look as I hopped off Harley and swapped horses with Jerry. Antonio was talking to some other woman by that point, so I led Murphy over to the mounting block to hop on board.

No sooner had my bottom touched the saddle than he leapt into a series of bucks. Clearly, he'd read the instructions wrong and mistaken this outing for a rodeo. I clung on until he ran out of steam, ignoring the concerned looks of the other competitors who hurried to get out of our way. There was no anger from them, just sympathy. Everyone had needed to deal with a difficult horse at one point or another, and it wasn't the first time Murphy had put on a show like that.

"Give him a wallop," shouted Antonio.

Oh, like that would help matters. He'd probably already had a thump from Jerry, which was what put him into this mood in the first place. I spoke quietly to him instead, telling him what an idiot the two men were.

He relaxed under me, enough for me to leg him forward into a canter. He popped over the oxer, and then we were called to go into the main ring.

Would this be a miracle or a disaster?

CHAPTER 3

I SLOWED MURPHY to a walk, and we headed for the arena. Outside, we paused as the rider before me finished her round. I recognised her—she'd only joined the tour this year, and her horse was young but a nice type. I took a quick look up at the screen. Four faults glowed yellow in the corner, and when I looked past, I glimpsed a giant baguette lying in the sand.

Her face relaxed as she slowed to walk past me. "Good luck," she whispered.

I sure needed that.

Pasting on a smile, I legged Murphy forward, only for him to go in the opposite direction. The little sod shot backwards and nearly ran the steward over in the process.

All eyes were on me, and I could feel my cheeks colouring.

"Make that damned animal behave," was Antonio's gem of advice.

What did he think I was trying to do?

Murphy kept reversing, the world's media scattering in his wake. As his backside touched the wall, he shot forward as if he'd been branded with a hot poker, and I hung on by the skin of my teeth.

Thankfully the bell rang as we galloped in, and not being brave enough to attempt a circle, I aimed Murphy at the first fence. As we got under the spotlights, his ears pricked forwards, and he switched to the bouncy canter he'd need to clear the fences. Show off.

And that was why I loved him.

At sixteen hands, he was four inches smaller than Harley, with a lighter build. We flew around the course, shortcuts included, and had eleven seconds to spare as we crossed the line.

"Wonders will never cease," said Antonio. "I'll hold off on sending him for dog meat until after the jump-off."

Because at that level of competition, a jump-off was inevitable. That meant we'd have to race against the clock over a shortened course. My opponents would be all those who went clear within the time limit.

I gripped the reins as Murphy danced sideways past his nemesis and headed back to the warm-up arena. Now my job was to keep my horse settled for the final part of the competition.

That was harder than it sounded because the nearer it got to the end of the show, the closer it got to the time when Antonio would take me back to the hotel room. A cold finger of fear ran up my spine at the thought.

My fear transferred to Murphy, and Antonio looked on, his jaw clenched as Murphy jogged along with my heart matching the staccato rhythm of his hooves.

The twenty minutes I had to wait were excruciating as Antonio glowered at my every move, and when the announcer called us back to the ring, I did my best to block my darling boyfriend out. As was to be expected, they'd left the five nastiest fences in—the baguettes, the treble, the stile, the clapperboard, and the car, in that order.

"Go inside the Arc to get to the clapperboard," Antonio told me as we walked up to the ring.

I looked at it. Even for Murphy, that turn bordered on the impossible.

"I can't. It's too tight. He won't have a stride to jump from."

"You'll lose otherwise. And you don't want to do that. Trust me."

He was right. I didn't.

Murphy and I were joined by a flock of butterflies flapping around my stomach as we cantered through the timing beam. He flew over the baguettes and the treble, giving a swish of his tail over the third part as if to say, "That was easy."

Then I had a split second to decide whether or not to heed Antonio's advice. Could I take the repercussions if I didn't?

The answer was no.

I wrenched the poor horse around to the right and kicked him on hard. His ears flicked back in confusion as he attempted to work out what he was supposed to jump.

He tried, bless him. He tried so hard. I closed my eyes as he launched himself as high as he could, clearing half the wing before the whole fence crashed to the ground around us. My beautiful Murphy tripped on landing, going down on one knee as I exited stage left over his shoulder.

And as I lay there in the sand, a thousand camera flashes going off above me, my thought wasn't for the pain in my ankle, or even for my beloved horse.

It was for what I knew would happen when Antonio got me back to the hotel.

"You should have used your stick on that damned horse," Antonio said as we sat in the car. "What do you think you carry it for? Decoration?"

The paramedics had iced my ankle and strapped it up. It was swollen, but they were happy I hadn't broken any bones. Just sprained ligaments, they said. And luckily, Murphy had trotted up sound for the vet.

"He tried, Antonio. He really tried, but the turn was too tight." Even to my own ears, I sounded like I was whining, and Antonio hated that.

"Excuses. You're full of them, aren't you? Every time you lose, it's always someone else's fault. Well, I'll tell you now, it isn't. It's all on you. If I decide to shoot that horse where he stands, it's your doing."

A tear rolled down my cheek, and I tried to look away so Antonio wouldn't see. He was having none of it.

He pinched my chin and turned me back to face him. "So, now you're a cry-baby. Grow up."

I didn't feel grown up. I felt like a naughty child under his gaze. What I would have given to have my mother's arms around me at that moment. I missed my parents so, so much, and last month, Antonio had even grumbled when I wanted to put flowers on their grave because the anniversary of their death clashed with one of his business meetings.

"We're at the hotel, sir," the driver said through the intercom. "Shall I open the door?"

"Yes." Antonio didn't take his eyes off me. "And

you, Amelia, will be making up for your abysmal performance when we get inside. I expect obedience, and you can put a bit of effort into it this time."

As we walked into the lobby, I looked around for someone, anyone, who might be able to help me. But there was nobody. The doorman stared studiously towards the pavement as Antonio gripped my arm so hard his knuckles turned white while he forced me into the lift.

My last thought as the doors closed behind us was that one day this man would kill me.

Maybe even today.

Upstairs, Antonio shoved me through the door to the penthouse suite, and I tripped down the step. A yelp escaped as I landed hard on my bad ankle.

"Now there's a sound I like."

He regarded me from above, imperious, as he strode towards me. The sound of blood whooshing in my ears drowned out the crack of his knuckles. Time slowed as he stopped a foot away from where I was supporting myself against the wall.

"Strip."

My hands shook as I wriggled out of my jacket. He snatched it off me and threw it on the nearby sofa next to his.

"Not like that." His lips curved up in an evil smile. "I want you to put on a show. The one you didn't manage earlier."

He strode over to the sound system and put on some music. Rhianna's "Russian Roulette." If I'd had a gun in my hand at that moment, I'd have aimed it at Antonio and pulled the trigger six times, just to be sure of getting the job done.

The prison sentence would have been worth it. I wasn't free, anyway.

Nor was I a dancer, and how was it possible to be sexy while peeling off a pair of sweatpants, for crying out loud? One of the other riders had donated them after the ambulance crew cut my jodhpurs off me. My fingers fumbled at the drawstring as I tried to undo the hastily tied knot, and Antonio tapped his foot as he waited.

Finally, I got it undone and dropped the trousers. The cuff got stuck on my bandage, and a twinge of pain shot through my ankle as I pulled it free. Swaying my hips in time to the music, I undid the buttons on my shirt, one at a time. Antonio had bought it, so they were sparkly, overly ostentatious, and totally impractical. I slipped the sleeves down my arms and past the bruises that were already forming from his fingers earlier.

That left me standing in my underwear—a lacy bra and a thong, which chafed when I walked.

He stalked around me, perusing what he knew was his, and twisted my hair around his fist to pull my head back. I had no choice but to meet his eyes.

"You won't disobey me again, will you?"

"N-n-no, Antonio."

"Good."

He reached down and popped open my bra. I'd say I spilled out of it, but there really wasn't enough of me to do that. He palmed one of my breasts, pinching the nipple hard between his thumb and forefinger.

"Maybe we should do something about these. I like the idea of a touch of enhancement."

Was he serious? He wanted me to go under the knife? I hated needles; he knew that. The thought of having someone cut me open was a hundred times worse, and I grew a little faint.

He held my eyes with his, daring me to challenge him.

I couldn't.

I didn't dare.

With his other hand, he reached down and tore my panties off. In books, that always sounds so sexy, but in reality, the elastic bit into my skin before it gave way, leaving me with an angry red welt.

"Fetch me a drink then get on the bed. Oh, and take your birth control pill, first. We don't want any little accidents, do we?"

He let me go and walked into the bedroom, unbuckling his belt as he went. I'd felt the lash of it before. I had to do as he said if I didn't want it again.

My handbag sat on the couch by the door where I'd left it after lunch. I rummaged through, trying to find the blister pack of pills. He was right about one thing. Having his child would be the end of my world.

Where were they? I fished through until my hand closed around a packet. No, that wasn't them. Those were the sleeping pills the doctor had prescribed me for when I lay awake, dreaming of my escape.

I looked at the packet.

Then I looked into the bedroom and saw Antonio walk past, now shirtless.

Did I dare?

Quickly, I found my other pills and swallowed the one for that day. Then I popped six of the Temazepam out into my hand. I usually only took one, so I figured that ought to do it.

My hands were shaking so much, I could hardly

unscrew the top of the bottle of single malt that Antonio was so partial to. When it finally came off, I poured a generous measure into the glass. The water in the bathroom flowed as I broke each capsule in half and tipped the contents into the glass. How considerate. Antonio was brushing his teeth before he raped me.

Dammit! The powder had sunk to the bottom. What if it wouldn't dissolve? I stirred it with my finger. Slowly, slowly, it disappeared. I just hoped it didn't affect the taste. If Antonio noticed something wrong, I'd be dead. Of that I was certain.

But it was worth the risk.

Every night he did this, he killed off another little piece of me, anyway.

I shoved the broken halves of the capsules back into my handbag, making a mental note to flush them later. Then I sashayed as best I could into the bedroom.

The man upstairs hadn't been too kind to me lately, but I said a silent prayer that he'd make Antonio drink his damn whisky before things went too far. Surely, he could do that one thing for me?

Antonio snatched the glass from me as I walked through the door. "About time."

He jerked his head at the bed and took a mouthful, just the one, then glared down at the amber liquid.

I held my breath.

"I don't like this brand. It's bitter. Remind me to have the hotel get something else in."

Oh hell, he wasn't going to drink it, was he?

CHAPTER 4

MY HEART BEAT so loudly, I was sure Antonio must be able to hear it.

Drink the whisky. Drink it!

He upended the glass and swallowed then wiped his mouth with the back of his hand. "Not going to let it go to waste."

Thank goodness.

But the ordeal wasn't over yet. I knew from experience I had about twenty minutes before the drugs kicked in. Twenty minutes of hell.

"Get on the bed," Antonio said, slamming the glass down beside the telephone. "On all fours. Face the mirror. I want to see your beautiful smile."

Could he be any more sarcastic?

He'd screwed me like that before, doggy-style, but today it somehow felt more degrading than ever as he forced himself into me and took what I hadn't willingly given.

I hate myself. I hate myself. I hate myself.

The words repeated in my head like a mantra.

But then his thrusts started to slow, and before he came, he keeled over sideways, and a glorious series of snuffle-snorts filled the air.

I opened my eyes, which I'd screwed tightly shut because I couldn't bear to see myself that way.

He really was asleep!

A happiness I hadn't felt in years blossomed inside me. Finally, something good had happened. It might only have been a brief respite, but I had at least six hours of freedom.

Freedom from his orders, freedom from his hurtfulness, freedom from his fists. Only my sore ankle stopped me from doing a happy jig as I hurried across the room to put some clothes on.

What to do?

I could go for a walk, well, a hobble, or sit in the hotel gardens or stand by the sea. Then I thought of the way Jerry had stuffed the two horses back into their stables earlier and decided to sneak out and see them. It wouldn't take too long to get there, and the pain would be worth it.

It was frowned upon, going to the stables so late at night, but there were no strict rules. Plus, with the competition over, there'd be a little more leeway. My class had been the last to jump. Now it was party time, and the complex would be awash with tipsy grooms desperately searching for their own bed in the sea of horseboxes. My presence wouldn't be deemed unusual.

I put on my jeans, the one pair Antonio had allowed me to bring. "And you're not wearing them anywhere but the stables, got it?" he'd said. Denim wasn't ladylike.

I topped them off with a jumper and boots, and as I limped out of the hotel room, I grabbed my handbag and jacket from the couch. It may have been the French Riviera, but it still got cold at night.

The guard at the gate to the stables recognised me from earlier, and I gave him a happy smile and a wave.

I was looking forward to spending a few snatched hours with my two best four-legged friends.

"Late tonight?"

I mimed a glass of wine. "You know how it is."

Only a couple of dim lights were on when I snuck into the stables. Peace reigned. The only noise came from the temporary plastic roof flapping gently in the breeze and the occasional stomp of a horse's hoof as some of the world's most valuable equines munched on their hay.

I headed for Murphy first. He was the most sensitive, and I felt I owed him an apology.

"Hey boy," I whispered. "How are you doing?"

He swung away from his food and nuzzled my arm then rested his head against my chest. It was his way of trying to comfort me. He'd done it ever since I'd realised Antonio was the spawn of Satan disguised in a Saville Row suit.

I kissed his forelock. "I know, Murph. Things aren't good, are they?"

And they were about to get worse.

Jerry's voice echoed through the barn, closely followed by the high-pitched giggle of a female.

"Fancy a roll in the hay, do you?"

Another giggle.

"Reckon I can oblige. We've got stacks of the stuff here."

Their footsteps came closer, and I shrank back against the wall. Murphy seemed to understand my predicament because he shielded me from view with his body.

The steps paused next to Harley's stable.

"Well, she's still alive," came Jerry's voice, followed

by another titter. "The boss makes me check the horses last thing every night. Bloody oversized status symbols."

A shadow moved on the wall as he peered over Murphy's door. "I'd rather this one was dead. A right bastard, he is."

"I saw him this afternoon," the woman said. "He was a handful. You're amazing, being able to deal with him."

"Years of practice, darlin'. And that's not the only thing I'm good at."

The shadow disappeared, but the voices didn't. Odd words were interspersed with slurping noises as Jerry and his lady friend got down to it on the other side of Murphy's wall.

I heard a snick of a zipper being pulled open, followed by a frantic thumping as he hammered her against the slats. I gave Murphy a sympathetic look. He looked as disgusted as I felt.

It would seem that Jerry got a little excited because he didn't last long. And either the girl faked it, or she had a thing for tall, dark, and grouchy because she let out a wail herself.

"Oh, Jerry, you're something else." She was right there. "Are you up for another go?"

He gave a throaty chuckle. "I could be persuaded."

Antonio would be furious if he found out. Jerry was supposed to stay with the lorry at all times.

"Your place or mine?" the woman asked.

"It'll have to be yours. The boss gives me hell if I bring women back to our horsebox. He says it smells like sex in the morning."

"It's because you're so virile, Jerry."

Oh, please. She was making me sick.

Their footsteps receded into the distance as they headed off for round two, and I stretched out my legs. They had pins and needles from crouching.

"Wonder if I could sleep in the box tonight, Murph? Anything's better than being next to Antonio, even if he is unconscious."

I got a whicker in return.

Well, the bed in the living compartment would be empty if Jerry wasn't in it.

Come to think of it, the whole horsebox would be empty.

I looked at Murphy, and he looked at me. He'd been my partner in crime since I was sixteen, when I used to climb on his back to go apple scrumping in the orchard of the old manor house down the road.

"No, we can't. It's a crazy idea. Isn't it?"

But the seed had been planted.

Would I ever have this opportunity again?

The answer was most certainly no.

I scuttled out of the barn and ran to the lorry park. Jerry had disappeared out of sight, and only one of the boxes near ours showed a faint glimmer of light through a crack in the curtains.

The tack locker next to the driver's door had a combination lock, and Antonio always kept a spare set of keys inside. He'd done that since the previous driver had managed to lock the keys in the cab one day while we were at a show in Spain. That had been the guy's last day on the job.

They were right where they should be. I opened the door and took a quick inventory. We were due to leave in the morning, and Jerry had already stocked up on enough food and water to get the horses back to England.

I went to the back and lowered the ramp on its hydraulic rams. My heart was beating so fast I worried it might give out, but with that came something I hadn't felt in a long time.

Hope.

I ran back to the barn and bandaged up the horses' legs as fast as my fingers would let me then threw on their travelling rugs. Harley was half asleep, docile as always, but Murphy danced around with a look on his face that said, "About bloody time."

I took him out first. If there were going to be any problems loading, they'd come from him, and he had a habit of leaping backwards when the mood took him. But someone was still smiling down on me because he walked on board like an angel and parked himself in his slot. Relieved beyond measure, I closed the partition and went back for Harley.

She followed me out of the barn, her shoes sounding like thunderclaps on the concrete. Why hadn't someone invented slippers for horses?

A voice came out of the darkness.

"Where are you going with that horse?"

A torch beam hit me in the face, and I squinted, trying to see who was behind it.

Quick, Amelia! Think of something. "I came to check on her before I went to bed, and I reckon she's got a touch of colic. I'm trying to walk it off. I don't want her rolling."

The light moved out of my face, and I saw a groom I vaguely recognised standing behind it.

"Sorry to hear that. Have you got the number for

the emergency vet?"

"I have, thanks, but I'm hoping I won't have to use it. She gets like this occasionally. Usually a good walk does the trick."

"Good luck, then. I'm gonna hit the sack. Got an early start tomorrow."

"Same here and thanks."

He tipped his cap and wandered off.

I gulped in air, having held my breath without realising.

"Shit, Harley, that was close. I'm not cut out for this thief-in-the-night stuff."

She pushed me with her nose, as if to say, "Get a move on."

I was only too happy to oblige.

She soon stood beside Murphy, and I raised the ramp, shutting them inside. Then I jogged to the cab and swung myself up into the driver's seat. I'd hardly driven this lorry—Antonio wouldn't allow it. But I'd worked as a polo driver for a season when I was eighteen, driving eleven horse teams all over the country, so at least I had the right licence.

I'd been dirt poor back then, but those had been happy days.

It took me three tries, but I finally jammed the key in the ignition and hit the starter. The engine rumbled to life. As with everything else in his life, Antonio insisted on it being meticulously maintained, and pity his poor mechanic if the engine ever hiccupped. I shifted into first gear and pulled forward.

"Early start?" asked the guard on the gate, looking at his watch. Thankfully, they'd had a changeover, so it wasn't the same guy who thought I was an alcoholic.

"We've got another event back in England in a few days. The sooner I can get them home and settled, the better."

"I don't know much about horses, but I guess that makes sense."

"It's the approach I've always taken."

He gave me a resigned smile and shuffled forward to pull the gate open.

In slow motion, it swung wider. Wider... As soon as the gap grew big enough, it was all I could do to stop myself from mashing my foot to the floor.

Instead, I kept my head and pulled off sedately down the road, waving a "thank you" to the guard as I did so.

The second we got out of sight, I couldn't resist letting out a whoop of joy. We were free!

Somehow, by a stroke of madness, all three of us were free!

CHAPTER 5

THE INITIAL EUPHORIA of our escape gave way to fear as I realised we had to get as far away as possible so Antonio couldn't find us. I'd driven through the night, chugging along quiet roads in the early hours without a clue where I was going, knowing only that I needed to put miles between the horsebox and Cannes.

And when I thought through my options, I knew I couldn't just run home to England. The first thing Antonio would do when he found I'd escaped would be to station people at the road and ferry ports, watching for me. I'd never beat them to Calais or Caen, and sneaking past in a twenty-six-tonne lorry would be nigh on impossible, especially one branded all over with Antonio's company logo and our team information.

Although that could play out in my favour if he tried to report it stolen. It would be harder to accuse me of nicking a vehicle when it had my name written on the side in foot-high white lettering.

I didn't intend to keep it forever, in any case. I just needed enough time to find a place for the horses to live, somewhere the di Stefano family couldn't track them down, then I'd find a way of getting it back to him.

Besides, when my old horsebox got sold, Antonio had kept the money. Okay, so mine had needed a new floor and the transmission was shot, but I must own at least a doorknob on the new one. I figured that entitled me to the use of it for a couple of weeks.

I kept off the *péages*, the French toll roads with their multitude of cameras, and steered clear of the *routes nationales* as well. Instead, I stuck to the country lanes, and more than once I'd had to back up while a Frenchman gesticulated irately from the driver's seat of his Peugeot 106. At least the French were fond of their picnic areas. It was relatively easy to find somewhere to park up for a few hours and get some much-needed sleep.

Cold reality began to set in the following afternoon. I'd got far enough away that Antonio and his minions wouldn't stumble across us by accident, but I was also alone, and that brought its own problems. The horses couldn't stay cooped up in the back forever. Murphy in particular had started to get tetchy. They needed exercise. Not only that, I could only stretch the food we had on board for another six days, no longer.

What to do, what to do...

Despite growing up in the horsey world, I couldn't contact any of my usual acquaintances because word would get back to Antonio. He had money, and he wasn't afraid to splash it around to get what he wanted.

In fact, I couldn't call anybody at all because I was terrified to turn my phone on. If I did, he'd surely find a way to track it. For the same reason, I'd been afraid to power up the lorry's navigation system. Instead, I was stuck using the large-scale map of Europe that was currently spread out on the passenger seat.

Or to put it more succinctly, I was lost.

The only plus point was the thousand euros I'd

found in the glove compartment—Antonio's emergency stash. At least I could buy more fuel and some snacks. And at the third service station I stopped at, I had a brainwave.

"Do you sell mobile phones?" I asked the youth behind the counter, miming with my hand to my ear.

He pointed down the road. "*Dans le supermarché.*"

"Er, *merci.* Can I leave the lorry here? Just for a few minutes?"

He shrugged, and I took that to mean "yes." I limped down the road to Super U and quickly located the electronics booth near the front door. There were a multitude of handsets to choose from, but my decision wasn't difficult. I pointed at the cheapest.

The assistant started speaking in French, but I didn't understand. I pointed at the top up cards and held up all my fingers.

"Would you like me to start it working?" she asked, thankfully in English.

I nodded gratefully.

Fifteen minutes later, I had a functional phone and a carrier bag full of budget groceries. At least I wouldn't starve. I'd treated the horses to a bag of carrots as well, and I slipped through the groom's door to give them one each.

"I'll think of something, I promise."

Harley looked insanely happy with her carrot while Murphy looked annoyed.

I needed to get them out, at least for a while. A little way up the road, I found a layby by some woods with enough space to get the ramp down and tie the pair of them up away from the traffic. That would have to do.

Harley walked off the ramp nicely, blinking in the

sunlight, while Murphy plunged out like a lunatic. I'd have to ride him first, or I'd never get him loaded again. I put Harley back inside to wait her turn then tacked up Murphy. He was on his toes the moment we set off, but at least today he refrained from doing handstands.

Sunlight twinkled through the trees as we set off through the woods, and the rustling of bushes in the wind made Murphy jump sideways on occasion. A deer crossed the path ahead of us, pausing for a second to eye up the intruders in his territory before disappearing back into the undergrowth.

I hadn't ridden like this for a long time. Back when I first got the horses, I'd take them out hacking, and even schooled them over cross-country fences, but Antonio had stopped all that. According to him, they were valuable animals, and I shouldn't risk injuring them by doing anything unnecessary.

Far better to let them die of boredom instead.

Murphy was alert but happy as I gave him his head for a canter. He bounced along the path, and when I spied a log up ahead, he hopped over that as well. He'd relaxed by the time we got back and had no complaints when I swapped him for Harley. She enjoyed herself too, and I figured I'd bought myself another day of travelling by tiring them out so well.

That was one job done.

Next up on the list was a call to Holly, the only friend from my pre-Antonio days who'd weathered the storm that our relationship had become. No matter how many times Antonio had tried to scrape her off, Holly had clung to the tatters of our past like a limpet to the bottom of a speedboat. It had been a bumpy ride for her, and even though we'd had little contact over the last couple of years, I had to hope she was still loyal.

"Holly, it's me," I said when she picked up.

"Who's me?"

"Amelia. I can't talk for long because I don't have much phone credit."

"Holy shit! Antonio said you'd had a nervous breakdown. He's got people looking all over Europe for you and the horses."

"He called you?"

"Must have been desperate, huh? He said he's worried you'll do something stupid."

I laughed hollowly. "Far from it. I did the first sensible thing I've done in years and left him."

Holly's round of applause echoed down the line. "About bloody time. Where are you? Are you coming home?"

"The answer to both of those questions is I don't know. Not yet, anyway. I can't get back at the moment because he'll catch me, so I'm stuck in Europe for now. I just wanted to let you know I'm still alive."

"When he said you were missing, I did wonder. I thought he might have bumped you off and been trying to cover it up."

"If I hadn't got away, that's how it would have ended."

"Thank goodness you did, then. Hey, what can I do to help?"

"Do you happen to know any generous French landowners with no connection whatsoever to Antonio?"

"Sadly no, but I could ask around?"

"Thanks. Just be really discreet, though. Please."

"I will, promise. Anything else? I wish I could send

you money, but I'm skint as usual. Maybe I could try and borrow a few quid..."

I teared up when she said that. Weeks had passed since somebody was nice to me in more than a superficial fashion, and it made me feel all emotional. "I'll try to manage for now, but if I get desperate, I'll let you know. I need to find a job, I think. Somewhere I can keep the horses."

"Good plan. They've got far more land over there than we do. Someone'll have a bit of field space."

"That's what I'm hoping. Look, I'd better go before I use up all my minutes."

"Okay. Even though you're so far away, it's good to have you back. I've missed you," she added quietly.

"I've missed you too. I'll come home as soon as I can."

I said home like I actually had one. But I didn't, not anymore. I wouldn't be welcome at Antonio's again unless I was six feet under in the woods out the back.

The next three days passed in a blur. We got into a routine. I'd find somewhere to park, stretch my legs to get rid of the pins and needles then take the horses out for a ride. After that, I'd let them graze in-hand on whatever grass I could find, just to eke out their food a little longer. I only had two days' worth left, three at a push.

I'd stopped at every stable I saw, looking for work, but in the small French villages, people were suspicious of a stranger turning up out of the blue. Nobody had wanted to take me on.

On the Thursday after I left, I rolled out of the hard-as-nails bed above the cab of the horsebox and stretched, my fingertips just inches from the ceiling in the luxury living area. I'd left the door through to the horse compartment open overnight, and I could see my steeds snoozing contentedly.

At least someone was getting a bit of sleep. I sucked my tongue, screwing my face up in disgust at the day-old fuzz that I'd been too tired to brush away the night before. Despite being exhausted, I'd lain awake for ages, worrying.

I caught a glimpse of myself in the mirror above the soft grey leather bench seat, and my hair wasn't in a great state either. Close to my head, it was lank and greasy, but the ends looked like they'd been styled with a Taser. I took a delicate sniff of my armpits. Euch! Even I didn't want to stand next to myself.

The silver-framed clock next to the mirror told me it was just after seven in the morning. I'd been in bed for eight hours, although I'd barely slept for half of those. Time to move on.

The temperature outside had already begun to rise when I clambered into the cab and rolled down the window. Amber shards of sunlight pierced the trees as their glistening leaves shook in the early morning breeze. The smell of damp earth permeated the air, mingling with exhaust fumes from a passing truck. As the rumble of the sixteen-wheeler faded into the distance, birdsong took over, the twittering insistent, as if it were trying to make up for the mechanical interruption. At the edge of the picnic area, a Styrofoam cup tripped along, end over end, another reminder of man's intrusion into the beauty of nature.

I started the engine and glanced back longingly through the cutaway at the state-of-the-art bathroom. After five days on the road, I felt disgusting, but I needed every drop of water on board for the horses. After all, I didn't know when I'd be able to get more. Even with some sleep behind me, I dreaded another day on the road. Having to drive as well as look after Murphy and Harley in thirty-degree weather had taken its toll. The cool night had been a blessing, but it wouldn't be long before an unseen hand lifted the sun higher in the sky.

According to the road signs I'd seen yesterday, we were near the town of Orléans. I'd taken a winding route on my way up from Cannes, but as the crow flew, I'd only driven a few hundred miles.

Where should I go next? Did I carry on heading north with a view to somehow crossing the Channel? Or should I try east or west and pin my hopes on getting a job?

At that moment, I couldn't even decide whether to turn left or right out of the car park. I spied a stray euro sitting on the centre console and flipped it. Heads for right, tails for left.

Light glinted on the coin as it tumbled back towards my hand. Heads. At least that was one decision made.

I released the handbrake and slid the gearstick into reverse. Would this be the day my luck would finally change? Fingers crossed. I depressed the accelerator, lifted the clutch, and the lorry moved smoothly backwards.

In an instant, the chirpy birdsong was replaced by the screech of crumpling metal.

I slammed my foot on the brake pedal.

What had I done?

CHAPTER 6

THE PAINFUL SOUND of grating metal echoed in my ears as I yanked the handbrake on and peered into the driver's side wing mirror. As if to add insult to injury, the tiny line of text at the bottom of the glass leapt out at me: *Caution! Objects in the mirror may be closer than they appear.*

"Well, I bloody know that now," I muttered under my breath.

A tall, blond-haired stranger unfolded himself from the driver's side of a shiny, dark-green car, the mangled nose of which sat askew behind the lorry. I wasn't sure what kind of car it was, but judging by its sporty looks and the furious expression on its owner's face, I suspected it was an expensive one.

The man slammed the car door, and I watched his reflection growing bigger as he strode towards me. Nope, definitely not happy.

I weighed up my options. Should I get out of the lorry to face him? Or lock the doors? Or lock the doors then drive away?

No, not the third one. Firstly, it wasn't fair and secondly, I'd never outrun anything in a horsebox, anyway. They were famed for their ability to create traffic jams.

Maybe I could bank on option four—pray that this

was all a terrible dream and I would wake up soon.

I pinched myself hard on the arm, and it hurt. Looked like option four was out, then.

Where should I even start? My experience with the French language had ended at age sixteen after having spent four years sitting at the back of Mme. Bernard's class desperately praying I was invisible and therefore wouldn't be called upon to answer any questions. When I finally achieved a C grade in my GCSE, I'd joyfully donated all my textbooks to the local charity shop.

Yes, talking would be a problem. I was contemplating option two and trying to remember which button operated the central locking when the stranger wrenched the door open.

Option one it was, then. This little accident really made the perfect end to a perfect week.

"*Je suis desolé...*" I started, desperately trying to remember what the French word for car was.

"You'd bloody better be," the man growled.

"You're English?"

"No, I just like to try out different accents when I get bored. What do you think?"

I slumped back in the seat. "Oh, thank goodness. For a moment, I was worried I'd driven into a French person."

"Well, you haven't. Does that make everything all right, then? Is the front of my Aston Martin magically going to fix itself?"

"No, of course not! I didn't mean it like that. It's just I can't speak French, and I didn't know how I was going to communicate. I mean, I've never had an accident before, and I've got no idea what happens now and... I'm rambling, aren't I?"

His face told me I was, and I shrank back further into the seat.

"Look, it's quite straightforward. We exchange insurance details, and you go on your merry way to wherever it is you're going while I wait for a tow truck. You'll be happy to hear your lorry's barely got a mark on it."

Insurance? Oh, hell. Ten to one I didn't have any. It wasn't like I'd ever planned to drive the bloody horsebox, was it?

"You've gone white," the man said. "Well, whiter. What's wrong?"

How did I tell him?

His voice softened. "Come on, it's not that bad. Everyone has a little prang now and then. The forms won't be that bad to fill in. You can probably do most of it over the phone."

He was still standing in the doorway of the lorry. I had nowhere to run.

"It's not that."

"Then what?"

"I probably don't have any insurance," I whispered.

"You what? How can you be driving around in a truck that cost at least a quarter of a mil and not have insurance?"

"It's not exactly mine. Well, maybe a doorknob."

His eyes widened. "You stole this thing?"

"I prefer to think of it more as borrowing."

"Holy fuck. It didn't occur to you when you did your 'borrowing' that a small family hatchback might have been more your thing?"

I straightened up. "I can hardly fit two horses in the back of a Renault Clio, can I?"

"You've got horses in there?"

"It *is* a horsebox. That's not exactly unusual."

"Well, shouldn't you be checking on them or something? In case they got scared by the noise?"

I bit my lip. "Yes."

Of course I should be, but he was blocking the way.

He took a step back. "Well, what are you waiting for?"

I popped open my seatbelt and looked warily at him. He took another step back and held out his hand.

"Come on, I won't bite." He gave me a grin, displaying a row of perfectly straight white teeth. "Not unless you want me to, anyway."

Not wanting to appear rude, I clutched the very ends of his fingers in mine as I hopped down from the cab then let go as soon as my boots touched the ground. Now that I was standing next to him, I got a better idea of his height—around six feet, four inches taller than me.

A wall of intimidation.

I scurried past him and opened the door to the living area. The steps flipped down neatly at the touch of a button, and I climbed on board. When I peered into the horse compartment, two faces stared back at me, completely unperturbed by all that had taken place. Harley was chewing on her hay, and Murphy looked bored.

Thank goodness.

I turned around and almost bumped into the stranger. I didn't realise he'd followed me on board. Heart thumping, I sprang backwards and tripped over the corner of a cupboard, landing squarely on my behind.

He winced as I hit the deck, and pain shot through my back as well as my bad ankle.

"Ouch, I felt that. What happened to your foot? It's all strapped up."

"I came off one of the horses a few days ago."

My ankle hurt a lot less now than it had then, but still sent twinges up my leg when I put weight on it.

"Should you be driving with it like that?"

"Probably not, but I don't exactly have a choice."

Once again, he extended his hand. This time I took a firmer grip as he pulled me effortlessly to my feet.

"Thanks."

A smile flickered across his lips for a second before he motioned to the seating that ran around a small table, and I perched on the edge of the bench at the end. Now I had to crane my neck to look up at him. He was even more intimidating from this level.

But he seemed relaxed as he leaned back against the sink unit, supporting himself with his hands on the edge of it.

"So, what are you running from?"

"Me? Running?"

"I'm not stupid. You're driving a 'borrowed' vehicle." He used his fingers to draw air quotes around the "borrowed." "And you're jumpy as hell."

How could I tell him he scared the crap out of me? In here, in this small space? It didn't seem big enough for his presence. I'd always thought Antonio had the power to suck the air out of a room but this man... I was struggling to breathe.

Keep calm, Amelia. Just keep calm. Don't show him how nervous you are. Antonio had fed off my fear. It turned him on. Once I'd realised that, I'd become almost robotic.

But the man in front of me knew something was up. He crouched down, resting one hand on my knee.

"It doesn't matter, all right? Let's just get this mess sorted out and we can both be on our way."

I froze at his touch, my eyes focused on his hand. What if he inched it higher? What if he moved closer? We were in the middle of nowhere. Apart from the horses, only the deer and a few birds would hear me scream. Holly was the only person who had an idea where I was, and she wouldn't be expecting to hear from me yet.

"What's wrong now? You've stopped breathing."

"Y-y-you're touching me."

He removed his hand like I'd burned him. "Shit, I'm sorry. I didn't think."

I gulped in air, trying to get myself under control. Tears pricked the corners of my eyes, and I willed them to stay put.

"W-w-what now?" I asked him.

"Can you ring the owner of this thing? See if they have any cover in place?"

I shook my head violently, as if it might somehow dislodge my brain and put me out of my misery.

He sighed. "Dare I ask why not?"

"He's my boyfriend," I whispered. "Ex-boyfriend. I'll be dead if he catches up with me."

"A lovers' tiff. I might have known."

"It's more than that. Is there any way I could pay off the damage in instalments? How much do you think it might cost to repair?"

He met my eyes. "Look, I'm sure we can sort something out. I'd guess about £10k."

"Ten thousand?"

The blood drained down to my feet, and I clutched onto the edge of the table so I wouldn't tip sideways.

"Astons aren't cheap to fix."

It would take me years to earn that much, even if I could get a job. Tears started to leak from my eyes and it was too late to stop them.

The stranger reached forward. I think his intention was to wipe them away with his sleeve, but then he remembered himself and dropped his hand.

"I'm guessing you don't have that kind of cash."

Give the man a gold star.

"I have five hundred and seventy-two euros, no home, no job, and two hungry horses."

I figured I might as well lay it all out. What was the point in trying to keep it to myself anymore?

He stood and paced up and down the tiny space. Five steps, turn. Five steps, turn. Five steps, turn.

"Sounds like you're in a bit of a bind."

If that wasn't the understatement of the year, I didn't know what was. "You could say that."

"I've got a small problem myself." He paused and chewed on his bottom lip, considering what to say. "If you're willing to help me out, then I'll cover the cost of the damage."

Was he serious? He'd write off ten thousand pounds, just like that? "What kind of problem?"

He gave me a sheepish smile. "Her name is Marianne."

I raised an eyebrow.

"I met her in a club in Paris a month ago. She was out for a good time, or at least that's what I thought. I spent the night with her, and then she turned into a raving lunatic."

"In what way?"

"She's convinced we're made for each other. She kept calling me, and when I didn't answer, the text messages started. I changed my number, so she found out where I was staying and bribed her way into my hotel room."

"But you're not in Paris now. Hasn't the problem gone away?"

"Unfortunately not. She knows where I'm working at the moment, and a couple of days ago, she turned up with three suitcases and an estate agent's brochure. The guys all thought it was hilarious, but it's got beyond a joke. Yesterday, we had to send out a decoy dressed in my uniform so I could get back to my house undetected."

I couldn't help it. I giggled at the thought of him being chased by some wanton female, complete with luggage.

"What? Women like me. I can't help it."

He looked so indignant, I laughed harder.

"Hey, it's not funny. This is a very serious issue."

I pinched my lips together. "Of course. I'm sorry. I just can't imagine that happening in real life. The movies, maybe."

He slid down the cupboard and sat on the floor in front of me. "It's like living in a nightmare. One with blonde hair extensions and breast implants. I don't know what I was thinking."

"So where do I come in?"

"When she showed up yesterday with a wedding dress catalogue, I told her I already had a girlfriend. It just slipped out. I was desperate."

"And you don't?"

"That's where you come in."

CHAPTER 7

THE MAN SAT on the floor looking up, waiting for me to say something.

"Well, I'm not for sale in that way."

I wasn't going to leap into bed with the devil again, even if this guy looked more like an angel with his blond hair and dimples.

His eyes widened and his mouth dropped open. "Shit, I didn't mean it like that. I just want someone to hang around with me in public for a bit. Maybe go out for dinner two or three times, enough for her to get the message."

"But I don't even know you."

He held out his hand again, this time for me to shake. "I'm Blake. Blake Hunter. You're Amelia, right?"

I jolted in shock then narrowed my eyes. "How do you know that?"

"It's written on the side of the truck."

Oh. Yeah. I reached out for his hand. "Yes, I'm Amelia."

He smiled, and this time it reached his eyes. "So, Amelia, what do you think?"

My name rolled off his tongue, and he made it sound playful. Whenever Antonio used it, I felt like a six-year-old about to get my knuckles rapped with a ruler.

I thought about what Blake said. A few dinners in return for him writing off ten thousand pounds? I'd had worse offers. And with both my provisions and my cash dwindling, any free food I could get my hands on was a bonus. How could I turn that down?

"Okay, I'll do it. On one condition."

He let out the breath he'd been holding. "Name it."

I jerked my thumb towards the back of the vehicle. "You'll need to find somewhere for the horses to stay. I can sleep in the lorry for a couple of weeks, but they can't."

He looked thoughtful. "Horses live in fields, right?"

"Yes."

At this time of year, they'd survive outside. It was only in the winter they needed to be tucked up in their stables with cosy rugs and plenty of hay. Harley in particular gave me dirty looks every time it got frosty.

"The farmhouse I'm renting has a bunch of fields out the back. They can go in one of those. Problem solved."

Really? That was almost too easy. We stared at each other.

"Can I park the lorry at your house as well?"

"Sure. There's plenty of space."

Hallelujah! By crashing into the poor man's car, I'd bought myself two precious weeks to come up with a plan.

"I promise I won't get in the way. I can stay in here most of the time. You'll barely notice I'm around."

"Sounds like we've got a plan?"

I nodded.

"In that case, shall we get going?"

"Okay."

An hour later, just after we'd waved Blake's sports car off on the back of a recovery truck, we had our first argument as a non-couple. I'd spent that time in with the horses, keeping them settled while Blake dealt with the driver and paced up and down on the phone.

But now he poked his head into the living area. "Okay, let's go. Where are the keys?"

"In my pocket."

"Hand them over, then."

"No way. I'm driving."

"I don't think so."

How could he be such a chauvinist? I put my hands on my hips and squared up to him before I realised what I was doing. "Yes, I am. Anyway, it's not your lorry."

"It isn't yours, either."

"It's got my name on the side. That gives me some sort of rights."

He let out a long sigh. "Look, I know you can drive it, and I know how precious your horses are to you. But I drive for a living, plus I'm insured to be behind the wheel. You're not."

"Really? You've driven lorries before?"

"With astonishing regularity."

Okay, so he did have a point about the insurance. Grudgingly, I handed him the keys.

He took the driver's side, while I shoved the map and a half-eaten packet of crisps into the footwell so I could sit down next to him.

"How far do we have to go?"

"In this thing? About an hour and a half. I take it you want me to stay off the main road if it's not entirely legal?"

"Please."

He stuck the key in the ignition.

"Don't use the SatNav, either. It's got tracking."

"It's a good thing I know where I'm going then, isn't it?"

The engine rumbled away, and he slowly reversed out of the rest area, taking me on a journey into the unknown.

Blake was right about one thing. He wasn't a bad driver. I'd given up complaining about Jerry's habit of accelerating and braking sharply as it fell on deaf ears, so I was pleased that Blake was giving the horses a smooth ride. I watched the villages drift past as he concentrated on the road, navigating us through the French countryside with a greater degree of success than I could have hoped for on my own.

It wasn't long before he turned into a winding driveway. A faded sign at the entrance proclaimed we'd arrived at *Ferme de Rive*.

"River Farm," he translated, as he slowed for the bumpy track. "I wanted to stay somewhere peaceful, and I found this place on the internet."

It certainly was secluded. The nearest neighbours had to be a quarter of a mile away, which I couldn't deny made me more than a little nervous. I desperately hoped he didn't turn out to be as much of a bastard as Antonio. Item number one on my to-do list: Call Holly and let her know where I was.

What with Blake being a lorry driver, I'd been

expecting something cheap and cheerful, a bit run down. River Farm wasn't it. As we rounded a bend, a two-storey farmhouse spread out in front of me, and when we drove closer, I saw it was impeccably kept. Flower borders added a splash of colour to the manicured lawns, and on the left, an orchard of neatly pruned fruit trees swayed gently in the breeze.

It was a world away from Antonio's modern monstrosity with its three-tier fountain of naked ladies installed outside the front door.

"It's beautiful," I said, unable to keep my thoughts to myself.

"I think that every time I see it. Plus, I like the swimming pool."

Blake drove on past the house, and the fields beyond opened up in front of us. The horses had definitely lucked out. In fact, once I let them loose out there, I wasn't sure I'd ever convince them to come back. Turn out at Antonio's had been restricted to one small paddock, three days a week, for an hour each time. Although he had plenty of other fields, he didn't like them getting muddy.

"Is this okay?" asked Blake, pointing.

"It's more than okay. It's horsey heaven."

He drew to a stop on the far side of a barn, set a hundred yards or so from the main house.

"What's in there?" I asked.

"No idea. Feel free to poke around if you want to."

I was curious, but it would have to wait. The horses came first. They'd spent long enough on board. When I lowered the ramp, Harley, who loved her grub, looked like all her Christmases had come at once.

"Do you need a hand?" Blake asked.

"Do you know anything about horses?"

He shook his head. "I rode a pony on the beach once when I was about five. These are a bit bigger, though."

I wasn't going to inflict either of these two on a novice. Harley was looking at the grass like she'd been starved for a year, and Murphy would definitely take advantage of him.

"Thanks for the offer, but I can manage."

As I thought she would, Harley dragged me into the field, and I only just had time to un-clip her rope before she took off. Murphy was next, and he must have been in a happy mood because he paused to give me a snort before he followed his friend. As they galloped around like equine versions of Usain Bolt, I kept everything crossed that they didn't slip and do themselves an injury. After a few minutes, the novelty of being free wore off and grass won the day. They put their heads down and started munching.

For me, the taste of freedom had receded into the distance on the breakdown truck along with Blake's car. I was trapped once again, only in different circumstances.

I turned to Blake, who'd stayed with me to watch the horses. "So, you've got me here. What do you want me to do now?"

His brow furrowed. "I don't know. Picking up a stray woman and bringing her home with me wasn't exactly at the top of my agenda when I went out for a drive this morning."

"I'll just keep out of your way, then. Call me if you want me."

I headed back towards the box.

He reached out and grabbed my arm, right over my bruise, which was still a delightful shade of green and yellow.

"Wait."

I winced as memories of Antonio flooded back but fought to maintain a neutral expression. Rule number one: Don't show weakness. Slowly, I turned back to him, expecting anger, but what I saw on his face was confusion.

"Why are you shaking?" he asked.

I tried to laugh it off. "I must have had too much coffee this morning."

"No. You didn't. He did a number on you, didn't he? That ex of yours?"

Only Holly knew any of what he'd done, and I'd kept most of it from her. I wasn't about to spill intimate details of my relationship to a stranger.

"That's none of your business."

"Suit yourself. I was only going to ask if you wanted a cup of tea."

I had to stop overreacting like that, especially if it was going to invite questions. So, I did the only thing I knew how to do and slipped back into my robot persona. Meek and compliant.

"No, thank you. It was very kind of you to offer, though. May I go now?"

He released my arm. "Of course."

I retreated to my sanctuary and lay down, longing for clean sheets because even after five nights these ones still smelled of Jerry's cologne. But without access to a washing machine, I was out of luck on that one.

I tried to get some sleep. I'd only managed a couple of hours each night since I left, and I'd turned into one of the walking dead, something that had probably contributed towards the accident this morning. It was no good, though. My mind wouldn't stop its rush. Thoughts tumbled like turbulent water in a shallow river.

I'd done it again, hadn't I? I'd got myself stuck in a situation I couldn't get out of. And worse, I didn't yet know how bad this one had the potential to be.

Right now, Blake seemed prickly but relatively sane. Would that last?

What were my alternatives? There was only one—running again.

Except I'd be back in the same situation, only this time I'd have two furious men looking for me instead of one. What I wouldn't have was more money, a place to stay, or suitable employment. After an hour of thought, I decided that my best option was to stick it out with Blake for as long as I could. At least the horses were happy here.

I was counting the circles in the pattern on the ceiling when a knock sounded at the door. The glowing hands on my watch told me it was just after two, and there was only one person it could be.

"Are you coming in for lunch?" Blake asked. "Or do you have a stash of gourmet meals in here?"

I thought about the cheese and crackers waiting for me if my appetite ever came back.

"My choices are a bit limited, but I'm not very hungry."

"I'm not going to make you eat, but do you want to come in anyway? We need to sort out what we're doing tomorrow. I spoke to one of the guys at work, and he said they've spotted Marianne hanging around. It would be useful to have you along with me."

Ah yes, my new "job." "Okay. I'll come."

The inside of the property was as stunning as the outside. The huge kitchen had a long, rustic table at one end, countered by modern stainless steel fittings and an enormous range at the other.

Blake stopped in front of the fridge. "Sure you don't want anything? I'm going to make myself an omelette."

I was about to say no, but my stomach rumbled loudly and gave the game away.

Blake turned and chuckled. "Two eggs or three?"

I managed a wan smile. "Two please."

In the six years we were together, Antonio had never cooked for me. Not one single time. Either I made dinner, or we dressed up and went out to one of the many places to see and be seen.

So when Blake laid a plate with a perfectly fluffy omelette and a lightly dressed salad in front of me, I stared at it as if little green men had landed.

"I'm not trying to poison you," he said.

"I didn't think you were. It's just... Nobody's cooked for me since my grandma, and she died when I was sixteen."

His hand was halfway to mine before he stopped it. "I'm sorry. Sorry that you lost your grandma, and sorry you had such a shitty boyfriend."

I hadn't started eating, but there was a lump in my throat. I turned away so he wouldn't see how wet my eyes were getting.

"I'll cook for you again," he said softly. "We can take it in turns, yeah?"

I nodded, unable to speak.

Blake sat down opposite me and started forking his

mountain of eggs into his mouth. Not wanting to waste something that looked so delicious, I tucked into mine as well.

Who was this man? He said he drove lorries, but he was living in luxury. Did he have family money like Antonio? How much did a lorry driver earn compared to the cost of an Aston Martin? And if he was wealthy as well as good looking—okay, I admit it, he was—why on earth didn't he have a real girlfriend?

I spent so long musing over those mysteries, I'd only got through two-thirds of my food by the time he finished his. Oh, hell. I dropped my fork with a clatter and sprang up to clear his plate away.

"What are you doing?" he asked.

I paused halfway to the sink. "Tidying up."

"But you haven't finished."

It hadn't even occurred to me to do so. He was done; therefore I was, too.

"Old habits die hard, I guess."

Blake stood up and took his plate from me. "If you want to finish, go ahead. I don't expect you to be my maid."

It was then that I felt a tiny piece of the ice that surrounded my heart chip away.

He was treating me like a human being.

"Are you sure?"

"Damn right I'm sure."

I sat back down and ate the last few mouthfuls before taking my plate over to the dishwasher he'd left open. When I straightened up, he was leaning against the table.

"So, tomorrow..." he started.

I smiled with a brightness I didn't feel. It was time

to earn my keep.

"I need to be at work by midday, so you can have a lie-in. We should be done by six."

"Will I need to ride in the lorry with you?"

"Lorry?"

"You said you were a driver. And you drove lorries."

He burst out laughing. "No, I said I *could* drive lorries. And I can. I move the team trucks around the paddock quite often."

"Team? What team?"

"The team I work for. I'm a racing driver."

CHAPTER 8

I SAT DOWN on one of the roughly hewn chairs with a bump.

"A racing driver?" I asked, as if by disbelieving it, it somehow wouldn't be true.

Blake grinned at me. "Yes. I'm driving at Le Mans in a couple of weeks. We've got testing this weekend."

"Oh, shit." I put my head in my hands.

He took a seat beside me, looking confused. "Most girls have a slightly different reaction when I tell them that."

I didn't know very much about motor racing, but I knew the race at Le Mans was a big one. Therefore, it would be attended by the media. It might even be on television. And if there were cameras there, that meant Antonio or one of his minions could see me.

My heart raced and I forced my breathing to slow. I mustn't get caught. I mustn't!

"Amelia, what's wrong?"

The humour had left Blake's voice.

"I can't... I can't... I just can't. He'll find me. If I'm out in public like that, he'll find me."

"Your ex. That's who you're talking about, isn't it?"

I nodded.

"Fuck."

Blake adopted the same pose as me, head in hands.

Seeing him like that, I felt so guilty. Although our situations were somewhat different, we were both being pursued by unwanted lovers.

"Your idea to have me put off Marianne would have been perfect if I wasn't at risk of being seen."

"How about if we made sure the cameras didn't get a good look at you?" His voice was tinged with desperation.

"How could you guarantee that?"

"A hat maybe. Sunglasses. A wig."

"I don't have any of that stuff. I only have this pair of jeans and some riding gear."

"If I could sort out a new look for you, would you do it?"

Despite our rocky start, I found myself wanting to help him. He'd been nothing but kind to me, and so far, all I'd managed to do was crumple his pride and joy. How dangerous would it be for me to go to Le Mans? On the arm of a driver at France's most prestigious motor race would be the last place Antonio expected me to pop up. He'd assume I'd hidden away, wouldn't he? Poor, spineless little Amelia, always letting life steamroller over her. I bet his men were out searching every equine establishment between here and Calais, which, let's face it, was where I'd have ended up if Blake hadn't taken me in.

"Okay, I'll do it as long as we can avoid the rest of the media as well as the TV cameras."

"I promise we will." He leapt up. "I need to call Lexi."

Before I could utter another word, he disappeared into the bowels of the house. Who on earth was Lexi?

Ten minutes later, he came back, and I could tell by

his grin he'd sorted something out.

"My little sister's agreed to help. She was due to arrive on Saturday, but she said she'd pick up some things this afternoon and come a day early."

"Lexi's your sister?"

"Two years younger."

"What did you tell her?"

"That she needs to bring a wig and clothes."

I rolled my eyes at him without thinking. Then froze, waiting for the repercussions.

He raised an eyebrow.

Was that it?

When he didn't explode, I relaxed a little. "I meant about me. What did you tell her about me?"

"That you were my secret weapon against Marianne."

"You told her about Marianne as well?"

"I tell Lexi most things. We've always been close. She thinks the whole situation's hilarious. She's been saying for years that my love-'em and leave-'em attitude would get me into trouble, and now it has, she's reminding me of that at every possible opportunity."

Lexi sounded like quite a character. What would she have to say about my situation? I supposed I'd find out soon enough.

"Does she know what to buy?"

"She's a model. She does clothes and make-up and all that shit. And she said she'll be here early, before we have to go to the circuit."

I suppressed a groan. A model? Great. That was just what I needed. Some stick-thin beauty to make me look like an elephant. I tried to appear grateful.

"That's fantastic. I can't wait to meet her."

"She said the same about you. She's thrilled to have someone to hang out with while I'm busy with the car."

"Is she staying for a few days, then?"

"Until after the race."

Suddenly, the two weeks I had to spend with Blake seemed an awfully long time. Surely he wasn't expecting me to hang around with Lexi every day? I understood equines, but what would I have in common with a clothes horse?

"What are your plans for the rest of the afternoon?" he asked.

"I need to clean out the horsebox."

Five days' worth of poop had built up in the back because I hadn't found anywhere convenient on my travels to toss it. It wasn't a job I was looking forward to doing.

Blake made a face. "Rather you than me. At least cars don't crap everywhere."

He had a point, but cars didn't offer you love and companionship, either. My two neds were worth every second I spent clearing up after them.

I spied an old muck heap behind the barn, neatly stepped but covered in weeds. Surely nobody would mind if I added to it? Now all I needed was a wheelbarrow and a shovel.

The barn door creaked as I pushed it open, and when I walked into the darkness, spiderwebs wrapped around my face like ghostly caresses. As I inhaled the musty air, I resisted the urge to run screaming and persevered until I found a light switch.

My heart leapt at the sight before me. Four large loose boxes bordered a central aisle, and at the far end sat a stack of hay and straw bales. I pulled out a handful of the hay and sniffed it. It was a little elderly, but still palatable enough if needs be. At least if the weather turned bad, the horses could come in at night.

I found the tools I needed and spent the afternoon mucking out so the back of the lorry was spick and span. Flipping exhausting. Cleaning out the lorry was the only useful thing Jerry had ever done. He used to take the rubber mats out and scrub them down, but they were too heavy for me to lift on my own, so I just swept as best I could. By the time I finished, I looked like I'd been in a brawl with Worzel Gummidge and come out the loser. Oh, if Antonio could see me now. I laughed out loud at the thought as I wiped my face and collapsed on the bed in the living compartment. Forget dinner. All I wanted to do was sleep.

Later, a tapping noise disturbed my slumber, and it took me a few minutes to get my bearings enough to work out that it was coming from the door. I threw it open. What did Blake want?

He wrinkled his nose as he took in my appearance.

"I know, I know—I need a shower," I said. "You don't have to say anything. But I found a hose in the barn, so I'll top up the water tanks tomorrow and then I can have one."

"Why don't you use one of the showers in the house? And more to the point, why are you sleeping out here?"

"It's where I live. At least at the moment."

"What's wrong with the three spare bedrooms I have?"

"Firstly, you didn't offer them to me, and secondly, I like having my own space."

"Well, I don't like the idea of you staying in the truck."

What was it to him? At least I wasn't getting in his way. Then it dawned on me.

"I get it. You don't trust me, do you?"

I stomped back inside and wrenched open the cupboard above the cooker. My hand closed around the keys I'd left in there, and I marched back over to Blake.

He winced as I shoved them at his chest.

"Here. Take them. I can't drive off now, okay? I wasn't planning to. I said I'd stay and I'm not a liar."

That prickle built up behind my eyelids again. Why did I have to be so flipping emotional?

His reasonableness didn't make me feel any better. "It didn't occur to me that you would run away. It's just that you're pretending to be my girlfriend, so it's only logical you should sleep in the same house as me. How many men do you think let their women sleep in a truck?"

Let? *Let?* It was going to be like Antonio all over again, wasn't it? I'd never get to have my own say in things. A tear leaked down my cheek and ran along my jawline, swiftly followed by another, and I sank onto one of the seats.

"What did I say?" Blake asked.

If I didn't know better, I'd have said he looked upset.

"You said you wouldn't *let* me. I'm just so, so sick of being told what to do. I'd rather have no life at all than be stuck under someone's thumb again."

The tears were coming thick and fast now, and I rubbed at my eyes, smearing dirt from my still grubby hands across my face.

Blake dropped to the floor in front of me and laid a hand on my knee. Then he realised what he'd done and swiftly removed it.

"I didn't mean it that way," he said, looking panicked. "Please don't cry. You can stay in here if you want. It's just..."

Just what? I watched through my tears as he turned and looked out into the twilight for a few seconds. At this rate, I'd need to buy shares in Kleenex.

"I don't like thinking of you on your own out here."

I tried to stifle my sobs and say something, but I wasn't sure what words to form. Before I could properly process what he'd said, he unpeeled my clenched fingers and pressed the keys back into my hand then stood up.

"I'll see you in the morning. Promise me you'll lock the doors, yeah?"

A blink of an eye later, he was gone.

CHAPTER 9

I SAT ON the bench seat for ages after Blake left. The feeling running through me had been unfamiliar until recently: guilt.

I'd snapped at Blake without thinking things through, and how had he reacted? By showing a trust in me that no man ever had.

Eventually, when my legs were ablaze with pins and needles, I struggled to my feet, knees cracking. The keys had grown warm in my sweaty palm, and when I dropped them on the counter, I found that as well as the ignition key and the keys to the tack lockers, I had an extra one.

Blake had given me a key to the house.

He'd given me a choice.

It was a funny thing, choice. When you didn't have any, you wanted it, but when you had it, it caused all manner of confusion as you tried to make the right decision.

What was the right decision for me?

Part of me craved a comfortable bed and a hot shower, but the little bit of pride I had left made me stick to my guns. Still struggling under the weight of exhaustion from the last week, I crawled back into the bed over the cab and pulled the duvet over my head.

By six o'clock, I realised I'd made the wrong choice,

but still I stayed, tossing and turning so much I almost fell out of bed. As the sun rose, I gave up on pretending to sleep. Remorse had been eating away at me, and I needed to apologise to Blake for the way I'd acted last night. And how could I do that? A simple "sorry" wouldn't cut it. After some thought, I decided to start by making him breakfast.

I caught a glimpse of myself in the mirror as I dropped out of bed. Ouch. My hair was even worse now I'd slept on it, and my cheeks were streaked with dirt. I splashed water on my face and cleaned up as best I could, but my hair was beyond help. Would it be acceptable to wear my riding hat in the house?

I came to the conclusion that it probably wouldn't be.

The key turned smoothly, and I slipped in through the back door and looked around. Apart from an old-fashioned cuckoo clock ticking on the far wall, the house lay silent. Blake must still be sleeping.

Every pore screamed out for a shower, but until Blake made an appearance, I didn't know where the bathroom was. I'd sort out the food then hope he woke up.

But what did he like to eat? I had no idea. After a quick rummage in the cupboards, I decided to go with pancakes. Everybody liked pancakes, right?

It didn't take long to mix up some batter and put the coffee maker on. I was just wondering what time Blake would be down when I heard the door behind me open.

"Oh good, you're..." I started then stopped dead.

It wasn't Blake.

A stunningly beautiful blonde stood before me. Her

skin looked like it had been airbrushed and her makeup photoshopped on.

Who was she? Blake hadn't mentioned anyone visiting apart from his sister, but she was a model. This girl was no stick insect. Her figure formed a perfect hourglass, and she had a chest I could only dream of.

And I was standing there looking like I'd had an argument with a hedge trimmer.

The blonde's eyes widened when she saw me standing at the kitchen counter, long eyelashes brushing her cheeks.

"Uh, hi?" she said.

I wanted to sink down through the flagstones, never to be seen again.

Blake chose that moment to turn up. He stumbled through the inner door rubbing sleep from his eyes, wearing a pair of boxer shorts and...nothing. Had it suddenly got hot in here? Antonio ate well and went to the gym, but Blake had *abs*. And pecs, and...

Look at his face, Amelia.

He gazed between us, blinking. "I see you two have met."

"Not exactly," said the blonde in a clipped British accent. "I just got here."

"Oh." He paused to yawn, forgetting to cover his mouth. The blonde gave him a disgusted look. "Lexi, this is Amelia. Amelia, this is my beloved baby sister, Alexis."

She looked me up and down. "I can see why you called me now."

I shrunk to the size of a Lego figure when she said that, but I couldn't disagree with her.

"We'd better get started. What time do you need to

be at the circuit?" she asked Blake.

"Eleven."

She rolled her eyes at him. "Nothing like cutting it fine, is there?" Then to me, "Honey, I think you need to wash your hair before we do anything. Blake, you can finish making breakfast. I'm starving. Are those pancakes?"

Before I could answer in the affirmative, she'd already disappeared through the far door. Her voice followed her up the stairs. "Blake, bring my suitcases up, would you?"

He paused by me on the way out. "She can be a bit blunt, but she means well."

I'd certainly noticed the bluntness. The sting of her words was still painful across my chest, but I smiled as best I could. "Thanks for the warning. Blake, I'm sorry about last night. I was really rude, and—"

He waved his hand and cut me off. "Forget about it. I can see you've had a rough time, and I need to try and remember to make allowances."

"But..." I wanted to tell him that I needed to make allowances, too, but he stopped me again.

"You need to take a shower, or Lexi'll be doing her impression of the Tasmanian Devil. And that isn't pretty, trust me."

Looked like the subject was closed, at least for the moment. "Where's the bathroom?"

"Closest one's at the top of the stairs, second on the left. It's full of that stuff you get in hotels."

That was a relief because I didn't have so much as a bottle of shampoo to my name. Jerry had left one solitary bottle of Lynx shower gel in the horsebox, and I didn't fancy using that.

The stairs were wide with a rustic bannister in keeping with the rest of the house. And like the kitchen, the bathroom had been fitted with no care for expense and an eye for design. From the claw-foot tub to the double-width shower stall at the far end, every detail was perfect. I longed to have a good soak, something I hadn't done for years, but with time marching on I jumped into the shower instead. I could have stayed in there for the entire day. Only the fear of using up all of Blake's hot water finally made me shut it off.

Wow, I felt almost human now, wrapped in one fluffy white towel with my hair bundled up in another. My skin was squeaky, and I smelled of vanilla rather than Jerry or week-old sweat. The only problem was I'd left my only clean-ish clothes in the lorry. I'd have to put my filthy ones back on to go out and get them, because I could hardly wander around in a towel, could I?

I was contemplating whether there might be a way around the issue when someone hammered on the door.

"Are you done in the shower yet?" came Lexi's not-so-dulcet tones.

"Er, yes, but I'm only wearing a towel."

My words seemed to form an invitation to Lexi, because two seconds later she barged in, carrying an armful of boxes and bottles. Out of habit, I hadn't locked the door. Antonio forbade it. I put that at the top of my list of things to do differently in the future.

But right now, I pulled the towel tighter around me as she arranged her goodies on the counter.

"Right, let's get started then," she said.

"What?"

"Blake said you needed a makeover. Hair, clothes, the works."

I looked at the array of lotions and potions laid out, most of which were foreign to me. The woman was like a walking beauty salon. I gave her a worried grimace.

"I thought we'd start by changing your colour," she said, and after perusing her wares, she picked up a bottle of peroxide and shook it.

I gulped. "Blonde?"

"No, we'll go with dark brown. It doesn't stand out so much. But I need the peroxide to strip out your natural colour first."

"Uh, have you done this before?"

She giggled. "Don't look so nervous. I was a hairdresser before I started modelling."

"Me, nervous?"

More laughter came as she pushed down on my shoulders until I sat on the closed toilet lid. Clearly, I wasn't getting a choice in this.

"You're probably wondering about that, aren't you? The modelling I mean? Because I'm not a twiglet."

Well, I had been, but it seemed rude to admit it. "Blake mentioned you did a bit."

"You're very diplomatic, but don't worry, my skin's made of elephant hide. I do plus size. I got spotted at one of Blake's shoots. He used to do the proper stuff—Calvin Klein."

Underwear? I harked back to him shirtless this morning. Oh yes, I could imagine him reclining on a bed, wearing only a pair of tight white briefs, and maybe a smile. No! I shook my head to clear the image. I shouldn't be thinking like that.

Oblivious to my dirty mind, Lexi continued.

"Anyway, next thing I knew, I was getting paid a fortune to prance around in clothes for catalogues. Then I started getting magazine work. Now I've done my own calendar, and I've got a lingerie and swimwear range coming out in the autumn. Crazy, huh?"

"Er..." I didn't want to agree with her, in case she thought I was demeaning her career choice.

"Oh, come on, you can say it. It's nuts. People pay thirty-five pounds for a signed calendar." She shook her head at the insanity of it. "Now, sit up straight, and I'll cut some layers in."

It looked like I wasn't getting a say in the matter. But as Lexi snipped away and chunks of red hair lay stark against the white tiles on the floor, I found some of my tension was being cut away as well. Antonio had always insisted I keep my hair long in the style of his choosing. It was liberating to finally see the back of it.

I tried to lean to the side and look in the mirror, but Lexi pushed me back again. "No, no cheating. That way you'll get a nice surprise at the end."

Once she was done with the scissors, she mixed up lotions and potions in little pots on the counter. A peculiar kind of alchemy. Then she brushed the gunk all over my head and looked at her watch.

"We have to give this forty-five minutes. I'll bring you some magazines."

By the time Lexi came back to rinse my hair, I'd flicked through every magazine in the stack she'd dumped at my feet and been rewarded with two articles on Blake. *Autosport* gave a brief history of his racing career. He'd come up through the ranks, starting off by working every job he could find to run a car at weekends, which reminded me a little of my own early career. Then he'd won enough races to earn a drive in the British GT championship. From there, it had been a short leap to world domination, and now he drove for the Aston Martin team. This year would be his first attempt at the Le Mans twenty-four-hour race.

And in *Dirty* magazine, Blake appeared at number seventeen in a feature on the world's hottest bachelors. As well as photos of him in his racing overalls, they'd dredged up some of his modelling shots. I may have leaned forward and squinted a bit at those. Had they been photoshopped? Or was stuffing involved?

As Lexi went to work with the blow dryer, I wondered what the day would entail. Hopefully nothing more than some standing around and throwing a few dirty glances at Marianne if she turned up.

"There, done," Lexi announced. "You can look now."

I was almost afraid to. There had been an awful lot of hair on the floor. But when she tapped her foot, I got brave and cracked one eye open.

Then the other.

"Wow! I like it."

My hair swung just past my shoulders, cut into choppy layers. A heavy fringe fell above my eyes, and the whole lot was a rich mahogany colour with golden highlights.

"Don't sound so surprised," she said, feigning indignation.

"Sorry, it's just I've never coloured my hair before. I was a bit worried."

"We got lucky. It could have all fallen out."

I swung my head around, eyes wide in horror. She cracked a smile and burst out laughing.

"Oh. You were joking."

She grabbed onto my arm and laughed harder. "I can't believe you fell for that."

She was still chuckling away as she led me out of the bathroom. Her good humour was infectious, and I was still giggling as I walked into Blake, who'd chosen that moment to hurry along the upstairs landing.

I clutched the towel around me and shrank backwards as his gaze travelled lazily up and down my body, but then he smiled.

"Nice hair."

That was it. He carried on past as warmth spread through me.

"He won't bite," said Lexi, upon seeing my reaction.

I recalled his words when we first met: "I won't bite, not unless you want me to."

For a fleeting second, I wondered what it would be like if he did. Then I gave myself a mental slap.

Two weeks, Amelia. Get the race over with, find a new home for me and the horses, and land a job. That was what I needed to do.

In one of the spare bedrooms, Lexi had assembled what looked like half a boutique. Clothes lay everywhere, and they were a far cry from what I'd usually wear. Antonio dressed me in black and neutral shades, nothing that would overpower his presence. In here, it looked as if the end of the rainbow and its pot of gold had got together and held a party.

I stepped forward and picked up a yellow T-shirt with a slice of watermelon printed on it.

"Very summery," Lexi said. "And cute. It'd go well with a pair of denim cut-offs or a little skirt."

I dropped the shirt back on the bed. "You don't

think it's too bright?"

"No way. And if you don't want people to look at your face, wear something quirky or a silly slogan. With that, they'll all be looking at your chest instead."

I wrapped my arms around myself. "Not much to see there."

"Nonsense." She appraised me with a critical eye. "Your boobs are perfect. And even better, you can get away without wearing a bra sometimes. I wish I could. I have to sleep in one."

Hmm, I'd never thought about it that way before.

Lexi threw the watermelon top at me and grinned. "Go on, wear it."

"Okay, okay. I will."

The top turned out to be the least of my worries. Half an hour later, I was struggling to walk in a pair of sky-high wedges that Lexi insisted would be perfect.

"I'm not sure about these. I'm not used to wearing heels this high."

"Then it's time to learn. Every girl should know how to look hot in heels. Besides, you'll have Blake to hang on to if you feel wobbly."

To be honest, that worried me as much as falling over did. And I was wearing a very short skirt. If I tumbled, everything would be on show.

"I think I should change..." I started, but Blake walked in.

"Time to go, ladies." He paused, staring at me. "Not bad. Better than the riding outfit."

"But..."

He tapped his watch. "No buts, we're running late."

Lexi slipped a pair of oversized sunglasses onto my face, covering up the eye makeup she'd expertly applied, and linked her arm through mine.

"Right, we're ready."

CHAPTER 10

A NEW CAR was parked outside the house, and I peered at the badge on the front. Another Aston Martin, this time a silver four-door. I paused next to it and turned to Lexi.

"Uh, how exactly am I supposed to get into that without, uh...?"

Blake stood there with a shit-eating grin on his face. "Flashing everyone?" he finished.

My cheeks heated. Lexi gave me a sympathetic look and opened the back door on the passenger side.

"Like this," she instructed, bending her knees, lowering herself elegantly to the seat, and swinging her legs inside. She made it seem so easy. My mouth went dry as I tried to copy her. All I could see was the smirk Blake wore as I settled into the soft leather. I sighed with relief as he closed the door for me then headed around to the driver's side.

My sense of accomplishment was short-lived, however, as he leaned over and whispered in my ear.

"Pink thong."

I couldn't meet his eyes as my face went a darker shade than my underwear. I definitely needed to work on my entry skills.

Blake started the engine with a roar and we were off. My only experience of his driving was in the horsebox, and I soon found out just how much of an allowance he'd made for the precious cargo. In the Aston, he was a monster. We roared off down the road, and Blake grinned as Lexi let out a whoop from the back.

I gripped the edges of the seat as he belted around a corner. Trees flashed past inches from the window, and I swear the wheels left the ground as we flew over a low bridge. When I saw a truck speeding towards us on a narrow road, I gave in and screwed my eyes shut.

Seconds later I opened them with a gasp at the feel of Blake's hand squeezing my leg.

"Don't worry, babe, I won't crash."

"Will you watch the bloody road!"

Laughter came from beside and behind me. I tried to turn around and look at Lexi, but the G-force as Blake accelerated held me in place. How could she be enjoying this?

While I panicked, Lexi chattered away. "If we're supposed to be keeping Amelia's identity a secret, shouldn't we give her a new name?"

"Not a bad idea," Blake said. "How about it, Amelia?"

"Yeah, okay, fine." I barely heard the question.

"How about something fun, like Mitzi or Chanel?" suggested Blake.

"Or how about something that doesn't make her sound like a porn star?" Lexi countered.

"Don't be crude. I dated a girl called Mitzi last year."

"And then we found out she was a stripper, remember?"

"Okay, you come up with an idea, then."

"What about shortening Amelia? Amie? Lia? Wait, I've got it! Mia."

"Mia sounds good," Blake said.

"That's settled then. You're called Mia now," Lexi told me.

And that was that. I was too busy praying to argue.

I was still breathing hard by the time we drew up at the circuit. As we slowed at the gate, Blake wound his window down and held out three passes on lanyards to the security guard. He scanned the barcode on each and handed them back. Blake put one on then handed one each to Lexi and me.

"Wear these. They'll get you in anywhere."

As long as mine got me into a taxi for the ride back, I'd be happy.

Blake drove slowly along a tarmac track, waving at the empty space on both sides of us. "Come race week, every inch will be full. This is the calm before the storm."

The storm. That was the part I was dreading, but I kept quiet as we pulled to a stop beside a couple of articulated lorries, painted in British racing green and covered in Aston Martin logos.

"We're in the pits. It's restricted entry, but somehow Marianne keeps managing to talk her way in." Blake sighed, gathering his thoughts. "Okay, let's do this. I'll introduce you to the guys and show you where everything is."

He came around and opened my door, which surprised me a little. Blake hadn't struck me as the type to display such manners. Then again, Antonio had always opened the door so he didn't appear like the asshole he was, so I figured it didn't mean much.

Blake held his hand out, and I hesitated. Yes, I knew I was pretending to be his girlfriend, but the logistics had been hazy, and we hadn't talked about what that might involve in the way of physical contact. I made a mental note to initiate that discussion this evening so we could put some boundaries in place.

Meanwhile, Blake raised an eyebrow at me, waiting. A small group of people dressed in green overalls hovered in the background, watching us. Wonderful. I wiped a sweaty palm on my skirt and put my hand into his, and he pulled me up effortlessly. I thought he'd let go once I was on my feet, but he didn't. If anything, his grip tightened as he pulled me into position beside him.

"Smile," he whispered. "You make dating me look like a prison sentence."

I gritted my teeth and gave a half-smile, half-grimace. "Well, in a way, it is."

He'd opened his mouth, no doubt ready with a biting comeback, when we were interrupted.

"Blake! You made it! I hope you got some sleep last night, eh? We've got a full day ahead."

I looked down at the speaker, an exuberant man with a shock of white-blonde hair and a strong Scottish accent. He gave me an exaggerated wink.

Blake grinned back at him. "She let me get a couple of hours."

He squeezed my hand in a warning to keep quiet, and I bit my tongue, but inside I was seething. How dare he announce something like that in public?

"Mia, this is Angus, our team manager. Angus, meet the lovely Mia."

Angus held out his hand, and I removed mine from Blake's grip and did the same, but instead of shaking it,

Angus took my fingers and brought the back of my hand to his lips. I glanced at Blake, who was staring daggers at his boss. If nothing else, I had to give Blake top marks for acting.

"Pleasure to meet you, Mia," Angus said, ignoring Blake's warning glare as he kept hold of my hand. "I hope you've sharpened your claws. You might need them."

Blake groaned. "Marianne?"

"Danny spotted her in the spectator area when he went out to do the croissant run." Angus shook his head, resigned. "It's only a matter of time."

"Mia's been remarkably understanding of the problem," Blake told him, claiming my hand back.

"Aye, she'll need to be. Still, no point dwelling on the inevitable." He jerked his head towards the replacement Aston. "How's the new beast?"

"Not bad, not bad."

Angus turned back to me and smiled wider. "He's a lucky bugger, that one. Good thing the PR bird at Aston Martin's got the hots for him. Some idiot trashed his promo toy in a car park, and she sent him out a better one before anyone could blink. If only I had that kind of appeal."

Blake squeezed my hand again, but this time I ignored it.

"So it wasn't his own vehicle that got damaged?" I asked.

Angus chortled. "Oh no, ducky. Hasn't bought a car for years, have you, lad?" He patted a panicked-looking Blake on the back. "Or clothes, watches, shoes, meals, or nights out. All these companies send him free stuff. Good publicity, you see."

I wriggled out of Blake's grip and took several rapid steps backwards.

"If you'll excuse me, I need to use the bathroom." I tried to smile at Angus, but it wasn't happening.

"Just along there on the right, ducks."

"I need to go too." Lexi scurried along behind me.

I managed to walk surprisingly quickly on my ridiculous shoes, and I'd locked myself into a cubicle before Lexi caught up. The seat didn't look so clean, but I closed the lid and slumped down on it anyway. Just when I'd begun to think that maybe Blake wasn't so bad, he proved he was a lying shit, just like Antonio. Okay, maybe not quite as bad as Antonio, but he was still an asshole.

Lexi rapped on the door. "What's wrong?"

"Nothing."

"Oh, don't give me that. I'm a woman too, remember?"

"Fine, Blake's an asshole, how's that?"

She sighed. "What's he done this time?"

Should I tell her or not? I didn't want to upset her by saying nasty things about her brother.

"Look, just tell me. It wouldn't be the first time he's been a jerk."

I grabbed a piece of toilet paper and wiped my eyes. The white sheet came away covered in black streaks, and I groaned. Lexi's careful makeup job had turned me into an extra from a horror movie.

"How did Blake tell you we met?" I asked.

"He said you bumped into each other one day and got talking. You needed somewhere to stay for a few weeks, and he needed a hand sending a message to Marianne, so you came up with a mutually beneficial arrangement."

I gave a hollow laugh. "That's not exactly how it was."

"What, then?"

"The idiot who crashed into his car? That was me. Only he didn't say it was a freebie. I kind of forgot to get insurance, and he told me it would cost him a fortune to fix the damage. When I told him I couldn't afford it, he said he'd cover the cost if I posed as his girlfriend. Except it turns out it didn't cost him anything at all."

"I'll be back in a minute," Lexi said.

"Where are you going?"

"To kick my brother in the shins. I can't believe he blackmailed you!"

I quickly unbolted the door and grabbed her arm. "No! Please don't."

She looked torn. "But he deserves it."

"I don't want to cause a scene."

"Fine. But I'm giving him a piece of my mind later. So, what do you want me to do? Shall I sort out a plane ticket to get you home?"

I slumped back down on the toilet. "I don't have a home. Not anymore." The sanitised version of my life with Antonio came tumbling out. "So, you see, I'm stuck at Blake's with the horses. I don't have anywhere else to go."

"Wow! That's some story. But it doesn't excuse Blake misleading you."

"So? There's nothing I can do about it. I may be cross at him, but I still need to apologise for running off."

"No, you don't. You need to wait here while I

inform my brother he's an idiot, then I'll fix your make-up, and after that, we're going for lunch."

"But..."

"No buts."

She pulled the cubicle door shut behind her as she stomped off on her heels, considerably more graceful than I'd been able to manage.

I put my head in my hands. Why did everything in my life turn out such a mess? Blake and Lexi were all I had at the moment—one intimidating girl and a guy who'd dented my trust. If only I could get back to England and Holly. I needed a hug from my oldest friend.

And I missed Alyssa too. Antonio's sister may only have been seventeen, but I'd felt closer to her than anyone else over the past few years, and although I'd never confided exactly what went on between her brother and me, I was sure she suspected things weren't all roses. What had he told her about my disappearance? I bet it wasn't the truth. Guilt ate away at me as I thought of her alone in the madhouse, sitting in the bedroom where she spent most of her time. Would I ever be able to send a message and let her know I was okay? And that I missed her?

Thankfully, the restroom was empty as I blew my nose and left the sanctuary of the cubicle. The facilities were basic, but I used hand soap and water to clean the worst of the mess from my eyes. I looked a far cry from the girl I'd seen in the mirror before we left for the circuit.

A few minutes later, Lexi came back, holding her handbag out in front of her like a prize. "I've brought emergency supplies," she announced. "Now, stand over here, under the light."

I shuffled to the side and positioned myself as she instructed. "What did Blake say?"

"He's realised the error of his ways, and he's crapping himself in case you back out of the deal. I told him I was behind you all the way if you decided to."

It was a long time since someone had taken my side like that, and I managed a small smile. "Thanks, that means a lot."

"So, what do you want to do?"

"I'll stay. I don't have much choice, what with the horses."

"And the girlfriend thing? Even if you say no to that, I won't let him kick you out of the house."

"That's sweet of you, but I'll stick to my end. I still feel I owe him. I'd have been in such a bind if he hadn't stepped in, blackmail or not."

She shrugged. "It's up to you. But let's leave him to stew while we have fun this afternoon. He deserves that much."

This time my smile was bigger. "That sounds like a good plan."

CHAPTER 11

"SO, WHERE ARE we going for lunch?" I asked Lexi as we emerged into the sunshine.

"I thought we'd head into Mulsanne. A friend told me about this wonderful little cafe that does a great steak and chips. He said it was nearby."

"Can we walk there?"

"I have no idea."

When Lexi searched on her phone, "nearby" turned out to be seven kilometres away. "And some of the roads might be closed," she said.

"You know a lot about this place."

"I came last year for a few days with Blake, just to watch. Race week's something else. It's like a seven-day party."

Well, she certainly made it sound like fun. But would I enjoy it? "It'll certainly be an experience, but I'm not much of a party girl."

She linked her arm through mine. "You'll have fun, trust me. I'll make sure of it."

"Do you know anywhere closer we can eat?" I asked, going back to my original question. I'd reserve judgement on the "fun" part for now.

"Nah, we'll just borrow Blake's car and go to Mulsanne."

"What, his Aston Martin?"

"Sure. I'm covered under my insurance, and anyway, if I break it, he can just flash his junk and get us a new one."

I had a sudden image of Blake showing off his bits and choked a little.

"You okay?" Lexi asked.

"Fine. All good." I wasn't about to admit to visualising her brother in Technicolor glory. "Never been better."

I almost broke an ankle walking to the car, but thankfully it was unlocked, so I waited in the passenger seat while Lexi sweet-talked Blake into giving her the keys.

"That was quick," I said as she slipped in behind the wheel.

"I'm his little sister. He loves me. That and I promised if he didn't hand them over, I'd tell you about the time he accidentally reversed his first car into the wall of grandma's house."

"Weren't you supposed to not tell me that?"

"Oh, yeah. Oops."

The key wasn't exactly a key, more a black plastic rectangle with a fancy glass end, and she stuck it into a slot in the dashboard to start the engine.

"Right, apparently I have to put my foot on the brake before I shift into first," she said.

"You've never driven one of these before?"

"Nope. I have a Smart car, and I only drive it about once a month. I normally take cabs."

Good grief. I said a silent prayer as the car lurched forward. Lexi had one eye on the road and one eye on the SatNav she was fiddling with as we trundled out of the paddock. I still couldn't get over the expanse of asphalt outside the pits being called a paddock. To me, paddocks were lush and green and full of ponies.

We brushed the kerb, and I poised ready to grab the wheel as Lexi narrowly avoided a rubbish bin. Whose driving was more terrifying? Lexi's or her brother's?

We managed to make it out of the circuit in one piece, and then we had the challenge of the French countryside. Lexi drove the two-hundred-thousand-pound supercar as if it were a bicycle, which was to say not very quickly and not very straight, either.

"Uh, weren't we supposed to take that turning back there?" I asked, trying to check the road and the screen at the same time.

She grunted. "Hmm, probably. Let's go the scenic route."

Twenty minutes later, we ground to a halt on a single-track lane as a farmer herded cows from one field to another in front of us.

"Maybe we'll make it for dinner?" I said.

Lexi looked at me and rolled her eyes, and we both started laughing. The farmer gave us a confused look as he ambled along behind the last few beasts and closed the gate.

"About bloody time. Let's have another go, shall we?"

Half an hour later, we pulled up outside the Bol d'Or cafe in the tiny village of Mulsanne. Lexi's friend was right—the steak-frîtes was fantastic. I had to discreetly pop open the top button of my skirt as I lowered myself back into the car.

"I think I'm going to eat lunch there every day," Lexi said as we prepared for the return trip.

"Please, no. I don't think my wardrobe could take

it."

"Okay. Maybe every other day."

Finding our way back was a bit quicker now we knew several of the routes not to take. A nervous-looking Blake was waiting for us as we parked up.

"Don't worry, all the dents are on the back," Lexi told him as she threw the key in his direction

He gave the car a wide-eyed glance before he realised she was joking. Even then, he didn't relax completely and stepped forward until he was a couple of feet away from me.

"Mia, I need to apologise. I shouldn't have misled you about the damage to the car. I don't expect you to forgive me, but can we at least try again?"

An apology? And a proper one? I hadn't been expecting that from Blake.

I was trying to think of a response when he looked over my shoulder and stiffened. "Oh, fuck." He closed his eyes for a second. "It's her."

I turned to see the French version of a Barbie doll walking towards us. Well, hello Miss Plastic Fantastic.

Seeing the look of dread on Blake's face, I couldn't abandon him to the vixen. I stepped right up to him and tentatively slid my arm around his waist. He reciprocated right away, and I caught his grateful expression before he faced up to Marianne.

"You're not supposed to be in here," he said.

"Nonsense. I 'ave a pass." She waved it in his face.

"Where did you get that?"

"A friend gave it to me. It should 'ave been you."

"Look, Marianne, for the hundredth time, I'm not interested. As you can see, I'm with someone else now."

He gave me a squeeze for emphasis.

She looked me up and down and wrinkled her nose. "You may 'ave temporarily lost your mind, but when you return her to the street corner she came from, you will realise that I am the only woman for you."

Did she just suggest I was a prostitute? The little...

Lexi stepped forward, toe-to-toe with her. "You're delusional, you Botox-faced bitch. Now go back to whatever gutter you crawled out of and leave my brother alone."

Marianne ignored her and addressed Blake instead. "Are you really going to let her speak to me like that?"

Blake smirked at her. "Yep." Then he turned to Lexi. "You should perhaps have added some four-letter words."

Marianne's face clouded with anger. "Clearly you are feeling unwell today. I will return when you 'ave come to your senses."

I stared wide-eyed as she strode off on a pair of platform Perspex sandals that made mine look like flip-flops, swinging her hot pants-clad butt. Dimples of cellulite rippled in the sunlight.

Blake groaned. "Look, I was really, really drunk when I tapped that. I haven't touched spirits since. She's enough to sober any man up in a hurry."

"She's quite a piece of work."

"I know, and she just won't take the hint." His blue eyes softened as they met mine. "Thank you for helping. It's the quickest she's ever left."

I broke the connection and stared at my feet. When he looked at me like that, I got a little confused about what my role in all this was supposed to be. And almost forgot that I was a bit peeved with him.

"It's okay," I muttered.

Looking past Blake, I found we'd gathered an audience. Half a dozen men in overalls had gathered to watch the show. Blake followed my gaze.

"I'd better introduce you to the rest of the team." He kept his arm around my waist as he led me over to the small crowd. "This is Patrick, our head mechanic."

I shook hands with the giant of a man, and Blake introduced me to a few more staff whose names I promptly forgot before waving at a handsome, dark-haired man standing near the garage.

"That idiot is Brandon, one of the other drivers."

Brandon wandered over, and I dutifully shook his hand then moved out of the way as Lexi stepped forward. Instead of shaking her hand, he stepped forward and kissed her on both cheeks.

"How have you been, Lex?"

She blushed before mumbling a reply. I glanced at Blake, but he was oblivious to whatever was going on between the two of them. And there was definitely something going on, of that I was sure.

Angus stuck his head out of the garage and hollered at the men. "Stop slacking, will you? This car won't set itself up."

The team scurried off, Blake and Brandon included. "So, what's going on between you and Brandon?" I asked Lexi.

"Nothing."

Except she'd gone bright red. I was dying to ask more questions, but then I thought of how I'd feel in the same situation. No, it was none of my business. I decided to change the subject instead.

"Do you fancy an ice cream? Or are you still full from lunch?"

She looked surprised yet pleased when I didn't push things. "I don't think I could eat another thing at the moment. How about we go for a walk and see what else is around?"

I was a bit curious about the place. I'd never been to a race meeting before, and here I would have the amazing opportunity to experience it from the side the public didn't normally get to see.

"Why not? Lead the way."

My stupid shoes, that was why not. We spent almost an hour wandering around, looking at the pits and paddock, before I admitted defeat.

"I can't walk any further. How do you do it?"

Lexi showed no ill effects from her skyscraper heels, while I was virtually crippled. I'd tried to put on a brave face, but I couldn't manage any longer.

She stopped beside me as I sank down on a handy bench. "Uh, practice, I guess."

I took off the wedges and gave them an evil look. My feet were covered in pink marks from the straps, and I had matching blisters on each little toe. For a moment, I considered tossing the shoes into the nearest bin and walking back to the car barefoot, but there was an awful lot of gravel to cross.

Lexi's phone rang. "Hey, Blake."

Oh, great. Blake.

"Yeah, we're on our way back. We might be a little while, though. Mia's having trouble walking... No, she hasn't been drinking. It's her shoes... Okay, yeah, good idea. We're by the entrance."

I clenched my fists. "He thought I was drunk? It's only five o'clock."

"Last year, he accidentally ended up dating an

alcoholic. She used to keep a pair of hip flasks in her handbag. That was a fun three months for all of us."

"He sure knows how to pick them, doesn't he?"

"Yeah. When she threatened to jump off a building if he didn't marry her, he finally went to her parents and they arranged for her to go into rehab."

"Wow. Should you be telling me all this?"

She shrugged. "Probably not, but I don't want you always thinking the worst of him. Sure, he's an idiot a lot of the time, but he's also had a fair amount of shit to wade through."

With that in mind, when Blake turned up in a golf buggy five minutes later, I returned his nervous smile and climbed in beside him. Lexi clambered in behind, and it wasn't long before we were back in the Aston Martin on our way to River Farm.

CHAPTER 12

BACK AT THE farm, I trekked out to the field to see how the horses were doing. Harley was asleep, flat out, making the most of the last few rays of sun. Murphy gave me a dirty look and sidled away.

"It's okay, boy. I'm not going to take you away from the grass. I only came out to check you're all right." He took another step backwards as I showed him my empty hands. "Look, no headcollar."

After a couple of minutes, he got the message and allowed me close enough to check him over for any lumps or bumps. There was no damage, thankfully.

When I got back to the kitchen, Lexi had already started dinner. Her jaw was set rigid as she chopped carrots like a woman possessed.

"What's up? You're going to take a finger off in a minute."

"Blake invited Brandon over."

"So?"

"So? *So?* It means I have to make something spectacular!"

"I thought you said there was nothing going on there?"

"There isn't," she said through gritted teeth.

"Ah, but you want there to be." I suddenly understood.

"It doesn't matter what I want, does it?"

She finished the carrots and slammed a cucumber down on the chopping board. I gently took the knife from her before she did any damage.

"Do you want to talk about it?"

"No."

She walked to the fridge and grabbed a bottle of white then started opening drawers and slamming them shut.

"Are you looking for this?" I held up a corkscrew.

"Yes!"

She uncorked the wine and poured us both a large glass before I could blink.

I thought I'd better finish the salad before I touched my drink, so I carried on with the cucumber where Lexi had left off. She hopped up on the counter next to me and began talking, even though she'd said she didn't want to.

"Blake and Brandon have been besties since they raced karts together when they were thirteen. Except then Brandon grew up into this...this...god. But I was still just Blake's kid sister. Except then I got the modelling gig, and last summer we were both at this party and we ended up in bed together."

"But that wasn't a good thing?"

"Well, I thought it was going to be, except just as we were about to do the deed, he looked down at me and got this horrified expression, mumbled something about it being a mistake, and bolted."

Wow. I could see how that would make things a little awkward. "So, did you discuss it with him?"

"No! We avoided each other for six months, and then when Blake insisted we both go out for his birthday dinner in January, we both just pretended it never happened."

"Except it did."

"Yeah. And now I've seen him naked. Every time I get within three feet of him, it's all I can do to stop myself from ripping his clothes off and licking him."

I'd just taken a sip of wine, and I choked. "Uh, could you try not to do that over dinner?"

"I'll be keeping my tongue to myself tonight. Blake'd go mental if he found out what went on. He hates to think of me seeing men, and Brandon? Well, even though he was a shit to me, I'd like him to keep his teeth."

"I won't say anything, I promise."

"Cheers."

Lexi drained the rest of her glass and poured another. And another.

Oh heck. When she tripped over a chair, I confiscated her wine glass and sat her on the sofa in front of the TV. Whoever designed the kitchen obviously intended it to be more of a family room because they'd included a small seating area between the counters and the dining table. Thank goodness, the BBC World Service broadcast in English. Lexi's head lolled against a cushion while I went back to shredding lettuce.

Poor girl. Brandon had upset her terribly, and as Blake didn't know, the chances were he'd keep inviting his friend over and making the problem worse. All I could do was attempt to minimise the damage with the seating arrangements. If I put Lexi opposite Blake and Brandon next to him—

"Mia!" Lexi shrieked. "It's you! You're on telly!"

"What?"

"On the news. There's a picture of you in your horsey gear."

My heart sank as I dropped the knife and hurried over, hoping with all my heart it was simply an old show jumping feature they'd rehashed on a slow day. But of course, I wasn't that lucky.

Antonio faced the camera, face solemn as he explained to the world that his beloved girlfriend had disappeared from their hotel room in the middle of the night.

"We had a nightcap and went to bed, but when I woke up, Amelia had gone. Her handbag was missing, but all her clothes were left behind. We know she drove off with her two horses, and I'm terrified she's met with an accident."

The interviewer nodded solemnly. "She gave no indication of where she was going?"

"None at all. But she fell off earlier in the day and hit her head, so she could have been confused. And she's been under so much stress lately with her riding."

"The doctors have suggested she could be suffering from some sort of breakdown?"

"It's entirely possible, yes."

A light touch on my arm made me jump. "Is that him?" Blake asked. "Your ex?"

"Yes. Antonio."

"Prick."

Blake watched beside me as the camera panned out to reveal Alyssa standing at her brother's side, large as life on the flat-screen TV. Her red-rimmed eyes showed she'd been crying. The interviewer held a microphone in front of her.

"And Alyssa, I understand you haven't heard from Miss Stanbrook since before she left for France?"

"No, and I miss her. She's my best friend."

Oh, Alyssa. I longed to give her a hug.

"This must be a very difficult time for your whole family, Mr. di Stefano. Do you have anything else you'd like to say?"

He gave a sad smile, one I bet he'd been practising for the occasion. "Amelia, if you're listening, just call me so we can sort this out. We all love you, and we want you to be happy. And if anybody else sees Amelia, please let the police know so we can get her safely back home where she belongs."

The camera zoomed back in, but before she disappeared, Alyssa looked into the lens and gave her head a tiny shake. A coincidence? Or was she trying to warn me off?

I couldn't tell, and the news anchor switched to an exciting article on sheep farming in the Outer Hebrides as I leaned back against the counter for support.

"He's got everyone searching for me."

Blake tucked a lock of hair behind my ear. "You look totally different to those photos now. I wouldn't recognise you, and I bet nobody else would either unless they knew you well. And the horses are out of the way. Nobody but the landlord's visited since we've been here, and he only came to fix a leaking tap."

My voice dropped to a whisper. "I'm so scared."

"Those newscasts won't be on for long. Tomorrow, they'll be talking about the merits of dry stone walls or tourism in Guernsey."

"Antonio won't stop looking for me."

"Mia, it's fine if you don't want to come to the

circuit. Back when I asked you to help, I didn't realise what a nasty situation you were in."

"I don't know. I mean, the thought of staying here by myself isn't exactly appealing either."

"Think about it. If you do come, you can just stay in the motorhome. None of the team'll say anything. I promise."

"Okay. I'll sleep on it." Or rather, I'd lie awake panicking for hours.

I left the TV on low as I went back to making dinner. Thank goodness I'd finished with the knife, because my hands were shaking so much I might have lost a finger if I'd picked it up. Blake stayed nearby too, shooting me a concerned glance every so often, but Antonio didn't appear on screen again.

Brandon turned up half an hour later in an Aston Martin that was the twin of Blake's. He stepped into the kitchen, and there was an awkward moment where he presented Lexi with an obviously expensive box of chocolates.

She stood clutching them while he thumped Blake on the back then announced he needed to use the bathroom. Okay, he didn't put it quite that politely. A little of the tension followed him out of the kitchen, and Lexi let out a long sigh.

"Thank goodness that part's over. Just the meal to get through now."

I finished searing tuna steaks and served them up with the salad. The boys were apparently on a health kick before the race. Blake grimaced as he took a swig of alcohol-free beer.

"This stuff's worse than rat piss."

"How do you know?" Lexi asked.

"Well, I don't for sure, but it's hard to imagine anything more disgusting."

I took my seat next to Lexi, leaving Blake and Brandon to do their male bonding on the other side of the table. Thank goodness it was wide enough that they were almost in the next county. Did France even have counties?

Brandon and Blake talked about car stuff, while Lexi pointedly ignored them both and chattered away about anything and everything, getting louder and louder, interspersed with knocking back glasses of rosé.

She'd made Blake stop at a patisserie on the way back so she could buy a selection of pastries for dessert, and it was only when she started her second and missed her mouth completely I realised just how drunk she'd got. I peeled her fingers from the stem of the wine glass in her other hand and set it down on the table. She looked at me like I'd just murdered her puppy.

"I wash drinnnnking that."

"I think you might have had a little bit too much."

"No shuch thing. More wine ish alwaysh good."

She tried to reach for the bottle, lost her balance, and fell off the chair. Brandon leapt into action, and between us we hoisted her up. He held one arm and I gripped the other as she flopped around like a rag doll in the middle.

"What now?" he asked as Blake laughed in the background.

"I think she needs to go to bed."

"I'd agree with you there." He picked her up, one hand behind her back and the other under her knees. "Where to?"

"I'll show you."

I led the way up the stairs, heading for Lexi's room at the front of the house. We'd just got past the bathroom when she started to struggle.

"Lemme down. I'm gonna puke," she garbled.

Brandon dropped her so hastily she ended up on her knees with a face full of his crotch. Her eyes lit up, but then she clapped both hands over her mouth and started crawling for the toilet. I just had time to yank her hair out of the way before she hurled into the bowl.

Brandon stood leaning on the doorjamb, the edges of his lips quirked up in amusement.

"Could you get me a damp cloth?" I asked.

Anything to get rid of him. Lexi wouldn't want him seeing her like that.

"Sure."

He sauntered off.

Lexi carried on heaving until there wasn't anything left then sat back against the wall next to the toilet, eyes unfocused. Brandon still wasn't back, so I dampened some tissue and wiped her face. By the time he returned, she'd slumped sideways and started snoring, and his previous smirk turned into full-blown laughter.

"It's not funny," I snapped.

"I know, but still..." he said. "She's been so uptight lately; it was about time she let go with a bang."

I nearly said it was the lack of a bang that caused the problem in the first place, but I stopped myself. I probably wasn't supposed to know that little detail.

"Could you help me get her into bed?"

He stepped forward and scooped her up again, and once I'd pulled her quilt back, he laid her gently on the mattress. When I'd tucked her in, he was still there, and this time the humour had been replaced with concern.

"Do we need to do anything else?" he asked.

"No, she just needs to sleep it off. I'll check on her later."

He followed me out of the room, pausing to give the sleeping Lexi one last lingering glance. Whatever may have happened between them, I could see from that look he still cared about her.

When we got back downstairs, I found Blake had been busy clearing up the kitchen. The dishwasher was going, and he'd even wiped the counters. Wow. With Antonio, I'd had to do everything.

Brandon clapped Blake on the back and picked up his keys. "See you tomorrow, guys."

"Do you have far to drive?" I asked.

"Only half an hour. My godparents moved out here a few years back and I'm staying with them."

So much for the debauched parties I'd imagined him having. I gave him a finger wave as he headed out the door.

"Do you want a drink?" Blake asked. "Kettle's on. Or there's something stronger if you want it?"

"A cup of tea wouldn't go amiss."

He waved me over to the sofa while he busied himself with the cups, and I sank into the cushions, grateful to take the weight off feet that were still aching from earlier.

I couldn't help watching Blake as he made our drinks. He moved with an easy grace that spoke of an awareness of his body. As he reached up to get the teabags, his shirt rode up, and I got a glimpse of his toned abs. A flush of heat blossomed somewhere it shouldn't, and I mentally castigated myself.

Two weeks and I'd be gone. No point in complicating this arrangement with feelings.

Blake came over and pressed a steaming mug into my hands then sat down beside me.

"Thanks," he said quietly.

"What for?"

"For helping with Lexi. She can be a handful sometimes, and my parents have never been much use. Usually, it's all down to me."

"Does she do this often?"

He frowned. "Not for ages. As a teenager, she was terrible. I lost count of the times I had to pick her up off the pavement outside some club or another, but once she hit nineteen and got a job, she behaved a lot better."

"It's probably just a blip," I said, trying to set his mind at ease. Although I had my doubts whether the whole Brandon situation would be resolved anytime soon.

Blake gave a long sigh. "I hope you're right." He swallowed a mouthful of tea. "We need to go to the circuit at the same time in the morning. Are you okay with that?"

I nodded. "At least I won't need to fit in a haircut tomorrow. I'm not sure I'd want Lexi going at me with scissors while she's got a hangover."

Blake smiled then reached over and tucked a few strands of hair behind my ear like he had earlier. I was growing used to the way he touched me now, and it no longer made my insides clench.

"It looks nice. The colour suits you." He paused. "Again, I'm sorry about the car thing."

"It's okay. This isn't a bad deal, really. At least I

have somewhere to stay until the end of the race. I don't know what I'd have done otherwise." And the fact that Blake seemed genuinely sorry made him go up in my estimation.

"Are you sleeping outside again tonight? I'll walk you out if you are."

No, not such a bad guy. "Can I stay in here? The bed in the lorry's like sleeping on builder's rubble."

"I'll show you where the spare rooms are. Now Lexi's here, you've got the choice of two."

He pushed himself up off the sofa then held out a hand to me. I took it, trying to ignore the heat between our palms, and got to my feet. He didn't let go as he led me to the door, and I looked down at where we were joined.

He gave me a grin. "Just practising for tomorrow."

Now logically, I knew he was talking rubbish, but the part of me that felt rather than thought decided to give him the benefit of the doubt. My heart thumped in time to our footsteps as we walked up the stairs together.

"I need to look in on Lexi before I go to bed," I told him.

"I'll come with you."

She was still sleeping, blissfully unaware of the drama she'd created earlier on. I pulled the door closed behind us.

"She'll be okay in the morning," Blake said. "Which room do you want?"

I picked the one next to Blake's. It was the smallest, but it was also where Lexi had left all the spare clothes for me, so it made sense.

Blake let go of my hand, seemingly with a degree of

reluctance. I couldn't help but feel a pang of emptiness, but then he squeezed my shoulder and leaned down to give me a soft kiss on the cheek.

"Night, Mia," he whispered.

My new name rolling off his tongue made my insides do a flip.

"Goodnight, Blake."

I quickly stepped back as I got a sudden urge to turn my head to the side and capture his lips with mine. What was wrong with me?

Whatever it was, the feeling wouldn't leave. Even as I lay in the dark, hoping for sleep, I could still feel the touch of his lips on my skin, burning strong.

Chapter 13

I WAS RUDELY awakened the next morning by a zombie walking into my bed. I shuffled up the mattress and rubbed my eyes. Oh, no, it wasn't a zombie. Lexi just hadn't taken off her eye make-up last night, and it was smeared all over her face.

She flumped down on the edge of the bed. "What happened?"

"You don't want to know."

"Tell me."

"You *really* don't want to know."

She groaned and slumped forward, head in hands. "What did I do?"

"Well, first you drank a lot of wine."

"I think I got that part. The Russian dance troupe in my head told me."

"Then you fell off your seat."

"Oh shit, did Brandon see?"

"He picked you up. Then he carried you upstairs and you got sick."

"Noooooooo! What? When he was there?"

"Unfortunately, yes."

She pulled out her phone. "That's it. I'm booking the next flight out. I don't care where it's going, and I'm never coming back. I'll get a job as a waitress or something. Somewhere they don't serve alcohol."

I pried her fingers away from the travel app she'd just opened. "Running away isn't a solution."

"You ran away."

I froze. What was I supposed to say to that?

"Mia, you've gone white. What's wrong? I didn't mean to upset you."

She clutched my arm, looking like she was about to cry.

"I ran because I had to. I wouldn't have survived if I'd stayed."

With the distractions of the last night, I'd managed to block Antonio out for a little while, but now memories of him flooded my mind again.

Lexi's eyes went wide. "Was it that bad?"

I nodded, and to my shame, a tear rolled down my cheek. "It wasn't so much the bruises; it was the way he controlled me. I wasn't allowed to do anything unless he agreed to it."

"He hit you?"

I nodded. "And worse."

She knew what I was alluding to. I saw the pity in her eyes when she realised. After a second or two, she wrapped her arms around me and squeezed me tight.

"Did you tell the police?"

"They wouldn't have believed me. I was Antonio's girlfriend, and he was good at putting on an act for the world. Women adore him. It's only once you get to know him that you find out who he really is."

"I'll help you," she declared. "After the race, we can fix up your life. You deserve to be happy."

I hugged her back. Nobody had truly been on my side before, and although I hadn't known Lexi long, it was clear that what you saw was what you got with her.

It felt good to have a friend.

"I'd like that," I whispered, swallowing down emotions that threatened to make my tears fall harder.

Blake broke into our thoughts by knocking on the door. "Lex, you in there?"

"Yeah."

"How are you feeling?"

"Like a class of middle-graders decided to use my head as a trampoline."

"I'll bring you an aspirin. Are you still coming today?"

She stiffened. "I can't," she whispered to me.

"It's okay. Just stay here. We'll be fine."

"I think I'm going to go back to bed," she called out to Blake.

"Suit yourself. Have you seen Mia?"

"She's in here too."

"Uh, are you...?"

"I'm coming."

"Are you sure?"

No, I wasn't, but Blake had been so sweet last night I didn't want to let him down. "As long as it's still okay to hide out in the motorhome."

"You're a lifesaver. I'll make sure nobody disturbs you."

I put yesterday's clothes back on and went out to check the horses. They were grazing side by side, the sun warming their backs. I'd never seen them look so content, and that alone made my decision to stay with Blake worth it.

Once I'd ensured the automatic water trough was filling properly and had a quick check around the fencing, I headed back inside. I'd need to start riding again in the week to keep the horses fit, but for now, a few days' holiday would do them good.

Lexi had picked an outfit for me, another quirky T-shirt and a pair of cute shorts. I noticed she'd gone with flats today. Ballet pumps were my friend.

"Good luck," she said as she did my make-up. "Don't forget to poke Marianne in the eye."

I giggled. "I'll try my best."

It was a quiet day in the end, and I was grateful for the handful of magazines Lexi had put in the car for me. The motorhome was like a Tardis. Bigger than my lorry, the sides slid out and the roof raised up to give even more space, and I was quite comfortable as I kept well away from curious eyes. Blake had spent most of the time talking to his mechanics, and there was no sign of Marianne.

"That worries me," Blake said on the drive back. "I can't see her giving up so easily. She's planning something, I know it."

"Hopefully she's too empty between the ears to come up with much."

He grinned at me. "Let's hope so, eh?" He took a right turn. "We could do with stopping off at the supermarket. Brandon's like a hoover when it comes to food."

"Brandon? He's coming over again?"

"He loves his godparents, but they're driving him round the twist. When he got back yesterday, Edna insisted on measuring him up for a knitted onesie. And they've got another karaoke evening tomorrow. After the last one, he had to spend two hours hunting for some old dude's false teeth."

"So he's coming over tomorrow?"

"Tonight. Well, and tomorrow. I said he could stay until after the race."

Shit! Who was going to break the news to Lexi?

It turned out to be Brandon himself. When we got back, he was already hauling a suitcase in through the back door as Lexi looked on in horror.

"What's he doing here?" she hissed at Blake as he got out of the car.

"I invited him to stay. It'll be nice to have another bloke around. I was feeling outnumbered." He grinned as Brandon walked back out. "All right, mate? The room next to Lexi's is free. I'll show you where it is."

Lexi sank back onto the car bonnet. "What am I supposed to do now? I'll need to try and find a hotel."

"Do you not think Blake might find that a bit odd? I thought you didn't want him to know what happened between you and Brandon?"

"Yes, you're right. Of course you're right. Where's the wine?"

She went to get up, and I pushed her back down again.

"No more wine, not after last night. You don't want to make things worse."

"He saw me puking," she shrieked. "How could things possibly get any worse?"

"Why don't we just keep out of their way?" I suggested. "They can do whatever it is that guys do, and we can sit in one of the other rooms. Just act as if nothing ever happened, like he does."

"Fine." She set her mouth. "But I'm still having a glass of wine."

A glass of wine turned into a glass for me and the rest of the bottle for Lexi. The stars she attempted to paint on my nails turned out more like Christmas trees, but at least she didn't end up hugging the toilet again. I tucked her into bed just after ten then went to get rid of the empties.

Only to find Blake sitting alone in the kitchen, staring at the wall.

"All alone?"

He broke out of his thoughts. "Brandon turned in early. His godparents kept him up most of last night watching a rerun of *The Sound of Music*."

"You okay?"

"Yeah. Just thinking about tomorrow. It'll be the first time I've driven the full circuit."

"Nervous?"

"I could give you the bullshit I give the media, 'no, just excited, blah blah blah.' But I won't. Yeah, I'm nervous."

I sat down next to him. "I get like that every time I jump at a new venue. No matter how much I practise at home, I can't replicate the atmosphere. Everywhere's different. Cannes buzzes; Monaco has this air of quiet dignity. In London, the crowds are always louder for the home riders."

"You're quite a serious rider, then?"

"I'm ranked thirty-six in the world right now."

He gave a low whistle. "I had no idea."

"Don't worry about it. I had no idea who you were either."

We both laughed. There had to be some irony in

that.

"So when's your next competition?" Blake asked.

"At the moment, never. When I left Antonio, I left that world."

"I'm not sure I could turn my back on racing like that."

Tears threatened again, and I blinked them away. "I'd rather spend my life living alone in an igloo than have to spend another minute with that sadistic bastard."

"Do you want to talk about it?"

"No." Unlike Lexi, I meant it.

Blake gave my hand a squeeze. "I'm here if you ever do. I won't judge; I promise."

He didn't push, and I appreciated that. But I didn't know if I'd ever be able to put into words what Antonio had done to me. Just thinking about it made my guts clench. If only I could rip all the bad memories out of my head and bury them for good, I might have a chance at happiness.

"Thanks for looking after Lexi," Blake said, changing the subject. "She's not been herself for the last couple of days. I don't know what's up with her."

"Maybe it's hormones?" That was a suitable excuse to make to a man.

Blake nodded knowingly. "You're probably right."

"I need to get some sleep. Are you going to stay down here?"

"No, I'll come up with you. I should get some sleep, too."

He didn't let go of my hand as we walked up the stairs, side by side. It was a revelation to find I didn't want him to. This time, his lips lingered on my cheek, and his other hand touched the small of my back.

My heart was beating faster when he stepped back, and his voice was a little hoarse as he said, "Goodnight, Mia."

Chapter 14

"WHERE'S LEXI?" BLAKE asked me the next morning.

"She overslept. Her alarm didn't go off."

Then she'd insisted she needed to take a shower, do her hair, and sort out her make-up. When I'd come downstairs, I'd left her staring at the six different outfits that were laid on her bed, trying to come to a decision. She may have pretended she wasn't interested in Brandon anymore, but she sure seemed to be going to a lot of effort when he was around.

Blake looked at his watch. "I told her we needed to leave at five sharp. I'm first in the car, and I've got an interview with a German TV channel before that."

"You go with Mia, mate. I'll bring Lexi," Brandon offered.

"Er, I'm not sure..." I started, but Blake was already halfway out the door.

"Come on. I can't be late."

Crap, what should I do? I didn't want to abandon Lexi, but a part of me thought that if she was stuck in a confined space with Brandon for an hour, they might be able to talk things out. In the end, I dashed after Blake.

He was halfway through his interview by the time the second Aston turned up. Lexi's face was red as she emerged from the car wearing a pair of hot pants and a top that left little to the imagination, while her hair looked artfully dishevelled.

Brandon leapt out of the other side and ran into the garage, but not before I caught the smirk on his face.

I hurried over to Lexi. "What happened?"

"I can't believe you left me behind!"

"I'm so sorry. Blake was going to be late for his interview if we waited any longer. You survived, though."

Lexi blew out a thin stream of breath. "Barely."

"What happened?" I asked once more.

"I tried to stay behind again, but Brandon picked me up and stuffed me in the car. Then before I could get out, he drove off."

"Then what?"

"We talked. Well, Brandon talked and I listened."

"What did he say?"

"That he was sorry for what happened last year, and that he hadn't been able to stop thinking about me. But he was worried what would happen if things went further because I was his best friend's sister, and he didn't want to risk his friendship with Blake."

"Well, that's progress. And didn't you say the same? That Blake might be upset if he found out something went on between the two of you?"

"Yeah. So, we agreed to put it behind us, and then we chatted about random stuff the rest of the way. It was like old times again."

I breathed a sigh of relief. Maybe the tension at the house would ease a bit from now on. It had been a little uncomfortable. "So, no need to pile into the wine tonight, then?"

"No." She looked around. "I'm starting now.

Where's the nearest bar?"

She marched away from the car.

"What? Why?"

"Because when we were just outside the circuit, Brandon pulled over at the side of the road and kissed me."

I caught her arm and stopped both of us. "What!"

"Yeah, exactly. I need wine."

"Lexi, it's six in the morning. Nowhere's going to be open."

She sank down onto a bench. "What am I supposed to do?"

"Did you kiss him back?"

"Of course I did. It was Brandon. A rock would kiss him back."

"Holy crap! So now what?"

"I don't bloody know. I lost the ability to speak, and before I got it back, we were here."

"Okay, I understand why you want the wine now." I gave her a hug. "But the bar's still closed. How about we get pancakes instead? With chocolate sauce?"

That earned me a smile. "Go on, then."

Blake had given me money before I got out of the car that morning. I hadn't wanted to accept it, but he'd tucked it into my pocket.

"I don't like the idea of you wandering around without a few quid on you," he'd said. "What if you get hungry?"

"I've still got some euros left. I'll be okay."

"No, you're keeping that. When you're here with me, I'm paying."

I hated the thought of being beholden to a man again. It made me think back to how dependent I'd become on Antonio. But rather than argue, I stuck what Blake gave me in the back of my wallet and vowed to only spend my own cash.

It was my money I used to buy Lexi and me a stack of delicious-smelling crêpes each from a stall at the edge of the paddock. We sat on plastic chairs outside to eat, which we did in silence because the crêpes tasted every bit as good as they promised.

I'd just forked the last bite into my mouth when Lexi's phone buzzed.

She looked at the message. "Uh oh, Marianne alert."

We threw our plates into the bin and ran back to the pits, slowing to a seemingly casual stroll as Marianne came into view. My jaw dropped. I'd thought Lexi was dressed rather daringly, but Marianne made Miley Cyrus look modest.

She turned around briefly to speak to someone, and Lexi and I both gasped at the heart-shaped cut-outs over her butt-cheeks. The dimples of her cellulite did add a certain something.

"Oh my..." Lexi said, before losing the power of speech for the second time that day.

We found Blake hiding at the back of the garage.

"How close is she?" he asked. "One of the mechanics said she was two garages away."

"She's right outside now, scaring the kiddies," Lexi said. "When you said you had beer goggles on that night, I think it was more like a beer blindfold."

He dug his fingers into his scalp. "They should have her coach Alcoholics Anonymous meetings. No one would ever drink again."

"You nearly ready, Blake? We need you in the car

soon," Angus called from the far side of the garage.

Blake groaned. "I need to go to the motorhome to change into my overalls. Will you run the gauntlet with me?"

I slipped one hand into his, and Lexi took the other side. Marianne stumbled on one of her heels as she tried to get to him, so we made it to the motorhome unscathed. Just as we were about to step inside, Blake eyed up Marianne, dipped his head, and gave me a soft kiss on the corner of my mouth.

"Just for emphasis," he murmured as we walked through the door.

My face blazed as he led me into a smaller room at the back. That one had various sets of clothing hanging on hooks on the wall, and before I could gather my thoughts, Blake had whipped his shirt over his head and dropped his trousers.

From the initial spark, my whole body ignited. My mouth dropped open as my brain lost control of the muscles to close it. Blake reached over and did it for me as Lexi laughed.

"Don't forget he used to be an underwear model," she said. "He has no shame."

I could clearly see that. Most probably because there was nothing to be ashamed of. I checked Blake was looking away then couldn't resist dropping my eyes downwards. Holy shit! The boxer briefs he was wearing left nothing to the imagination, and there were definitely no socks required for his photoshoots.

I had just enough time to burn the image into my retinas before it disappeared under a set of overalls. I couldn't manage to stifle the giggle that escaped as he zipped them up.

"You're sponsored by Trojan?"

He grinned unashamedly. "Yup. And they give me all the free products I want."

I was still processing that when he said, "Ready?"

Marianne was right outside, lying in wait. Or rather, teetering. Her shoes had to be at least six inches high.

This time, Blake didn't hold back. When he was sure we were in full view of her beady eyes, he pressed me back against the wall and kissed me. Properly.

His hands twisted in my hair, his tongue gentle as it ran along the seam of my lips. They opened of their own accord, allowing him free access, and I felt him smile against me.

"Good girl," he whispered, pulling back for a second.

The relief wasn't to last, though. He leaned into me, holding me in place.

I'd thought that if I ever ended up in that position with a man again, I'd feel scared. Antonio used to trap me with his body and dominate me with his mouth. But as my pulse raced, it wasn't with fear, but with want.

I gave Blake a small push, just to see what would happen. He yielded immediately.

"You okay?" he murmured.

I managed a nod and got a sexy smile in return.

"See you later, Mia," he said before he strolled back to the garage, leaving Marianne and I both frozen in place. When I came to my senses, I stumbled back inside.

"Looks like I wasn't the only one to get surprised with a kiss today," Lexi giggled from the other side of the room.

"What was he playing at? I'm pretty sure that wasn't what I signed up for."

"Blake likes to put his all into things." She peered out of the window through the slats of the blind. "Have you seen Marianne? She looks furious."

She'd moved out of my sight by then, and I shook my head as I sagged onto the sofa at the back of the room. My heart was still going faster than Blake's Aston Martin, and I hadn't quite remembered to breathe.

Lexi plopped down next to me and felt my forehead. "You're all hot."

"No kidding."

She tilted her head to one side and studied me. "You like him?"

"What? No!"

"Yes, you do. This is awesome!"

I met her eyes. "Sorry to disappoint you. He might have caught me unawares, but that's all it was. I've just got out of one totally unsuitable relationship, and there's no way I'm going to jump into another one."

"How do you know Blake's unsuitable?"

"Well, we haven't got anything in common. He likes cars; I like horses. My home is in the country; he travels the world. He seems to thrive on one-night stands, and I'm not that kind of girl."

Only even as I said the words, I thought back to our talk the previous evening. Our careers hadn't been all that different to date. And wasn't there more than one kind of horsepower?

"Well, I'm still going to keep my fingers crossed," Lexi said, getting up. "Shall we go and have a look at the cars?"

I followed her rather than staying on my own. At

least with the noise from the engines, it would be difficult for her to keep asking me questions.

CHAPTER 15

I WASN'T EXPECTING the cars to be as loud as they were, or as fast. I jammed my fingers in my ears until Angus came out and handed Lexi and me each a pair of ear defenders.

"Thanks," I said, tugging mine on.

Lexi grimaced as hers flattened down her hair, but she wore them anyway. We were joined on the pit wall by Brandon, who stood behind Lexi. Close behind her. So close, in fact, that there was a mere sliver of daylight between them. A few seconds later, he pointed as Blake's car came into view. In an instant, it had disappeared.

"How fast is he going?" I yelled over the noise.

"Top speed's about 205 miles an hour, over on the Mulsanne Straight."

Woah. That made Blake's driving on the roads look almost sensible. "How long does it take for him to go around once?"

"Roughly three and a half minutes. A lap's eight and a half miles long. Thirty-eight turns, and most of the time we're at full throttle."

Suddenly, what I did felt like child's play. One of my show jumping rounds on a horse took about a minute, and I'd do maybe four in a day. Blake and Brandon would keep it up for eight hours each over the twenty-four-hour period.

Blake had explained on the way that they had a third teammate, a Le Mans specialist called Tom Christian. He'd driven the race eight times already and won on half of those attempts. Angus had hired him to help with strategy and advice as well as to put in some quick lap times.

The first test session ran from nine o'clock in the morning until one. Blake was driving for half an hour first, followed by Brandon, who was also a Le Mans virgin. Then Tom would drive for an hour to work on the setup of the car, followed by Blake and Brandon for another hour each.

It wasn't long before Brandon was donning his helmet for his turn in the cockpit. Blake punched his fist in the air as he got out.

"What a rush!" he shouted, his grin nearly splitting his face in two.

In his enthusiasm, he picked me up and spun me round. "Now that... That was the most amazing thing I've ever done!"

His joy reminded me of the first time I'd gone clear around a big track in an international competition. Only that time, it had been me saying those words, and Antonio spinning me in the air.

My face must have betrayed my memory because Blake's face reflected my anxiety.

"What's up, Mia?"

He put me down but kept hold of my hands.

I couldn't meet his eyes. "Nothing."

"Everything," he translated. "It's him, isn't it? You're thinking of him."

I nodded. "I'm sorry."

He tipped my chin up so I had to look at him. "You've got nothing to be sorry about. Everything he did, that was him, not you. But it's your choice whether you let him control your future as well."

"Blake," one of the mechanics called. "Can you come and look at this telemetry?"

He waved him away. "Two minutes." He gave me his attention again—a strange concept after being relegated to second place by Antonio so many times. "Don't let him keep hurting you," he whispered.

The way Blake looked at me, it was as if he could see right into my soul. Like he saw my pain and all my secrets. Fully clothed, I felt naked.

Yet I couldn't break his gaze. Silver flecked his blue eyes, and in the darkness at the centre, I could see something else smouldering. Despite the heat, I shivered as he pulled me closer.

"Blake, we need you over here," Angus shouted, and the spell was broken.

Blake leaned forward and kissed me on the forehead. "Stay strong, beautiful," he murmured, then he was gone.

I was in a daze as I walked back out to join Lexi on the pit wall. She was bouncing up and down, whooping with excitement as Brandon went past. Every pair of male eyes was glued to her, and some of the women's as well. One poor guy tripped over a tyre and landed on his knees.

"Ouch," I muttered.

"What was that?" Lexi asked.

"Nothing. Have you noticed everyone's looking at you?"

She glanced around and the owners of the eyes

immediately pretended to be doing something else. "That happens all the time," she said, matter-of-factly. "It's good, though, helps me sell more calendars."

Well, that was one way of thinking about it. "How's Brandon doing?"

"That car's just increased his hotness factor by, like, a million percent. And it was off the charts before."

"I meant with his lap times."

"Oh. I have no idea."

It turned out they weren't too bad. By the end of the second practice session, which finished at six, the guys were fourth fastest overall. Several interviews and a team meeting meant it was dark before we were able to leave.

Brandon finished his commitments first. "They're just making some adjustments to the seat for Blake. He said for me to take you guys home, and he'll see us back there."

I didn't like that idea. Lexi and Brandon needed to talk, and they couldn't do that with me sitting in the backseat. Well, knowing Lexi and her frankness, they probably could, but I didn't fancy being privy to that conversation.

"You two go on ahead. I'll wait and go with Blake."

He gave me a suspicious look, and Lexi mouthed "thank you" from behind him.

"Are you sure?" he asked.

"Oh, yes. Marianne might still be lurking."

He put a hand on Lexi's back as he guided her over to the car. I hoped they'd still be speaking by the time they got back.

In the garage, I sat down on a toolbox and waited for Blake. He looked surprised to see me there when he emerged from the race car.

"I thought you'd gone back with the others?"

"I've never been in a car with Brandon driving before. I thought I'd be better sticking with a known quantity."

He smirked. "I give a much better ride than Brandon."

"You know, sometimes I think you might not be a complete idiot, but then you go and prove me wrong."

I sidestepped, but not fast enough, and he swatted me playfully on the ass.

"Admit it, you're curious."

"Not enough beer in the world, Blake," I said, but I couldn't help smiling.

"I'm going to pretend I didn't hear that."

Oh, Blake. Always the charmer. He yawned as he opened the car door for me, covering his mouth.

"Do you want to grab a coffee before we go?" I asked.

He fished a can out of the pocket of his overalls and popped the tab. "Another sponsor."

I peered more closely and recognised the logo of a well-known brand of energy drink.

"You want some?" he asked.

I held out my hand, and he passed me the can. I took a swig, and I couldn't help thinking that his lips had been on the metal just seconds ago. *Naughty, Amelia.*

"Tastes disgusting."

"Doesn't it? Keeps you awake, though," he said as he started the engine.

We drove back quite sedately. I guess Blake had worked all his speed out on the track earlier on. We didn't talk much, but the silence between us was comfortable, and I kept my hands folded in my lap. My mind fought a battle with them as I longed to slide the fingers nearest over Blake's thigh, getting closer to his... *Stop it!*

I know Blake said I should live for the future, but I needed to imagine one without him in it. Why was that so difficult?

Maybe because he was the first person in a long time to treat me like a human being. That was it. I was just using him as an emotional crutch. Nothing at all to do with the fact that I wanted to strip him naked and run my hands over those tanned abs.

I gave myself a mental slap for even thinking those thoughts. What was wrong with me? A little freedom and I'd lost my mind.

"Why is the house dark?" Blake asked. "And where's Brandon's car?"

"Er..."

"Didn't they leave before us?"

"Maybe they stopped off for coffee?"

"No chance. Brandon's been knocking back those energy drinks all day. I'd be surprised if he sleeps a wink tonight. The dude was wired."

"I'm sure they'll be back soon."

He pulled his phone out and tapped on the screen. "Lexi's not answering." More tapping. "Nor's Brandon." His forehead crinkled in worry. "Do you think they could have had an accident?"

Not unless one of the Trojans failed, I almost said, but I managed to keep my mouth shut.

"Why don't we go inside and give them a bit longer?"

Blake looked at his watch. "They've got until eleven then we're going out to look for them."

He paced while I perched on the sofa, wondering if I should say something. In the end, I decided not to. It had to be Lexi and Brandon's decision.

It was two minutes to eleven and Blake had the car keys in his hand when they pulled up outside. Brandon walked in first with Lexi behind him. She was tugging her skirt down and the buttons on her teeny shirt were done up wrong. I rushed over to give her a hug and surreptitiously fixed the problem.

"Thanks," she whispered.

Her eyes were dancing.

"About bloody time," Blake said to Brandon. "What the hell took you so long?"

"I realised I left my phone charger at my godparents', and we stopped off to pick it up."

"You could have called."

"Sorry, didn't think."

"So where's the charger now?"

"Lexi, you picked it up, right?"

She shrugged. "I thought you did."

He rolled his eyes at her. "We'll have to go back tomorrow, now."

Yeah. Right. I was guessing that trip would take three or four hours.

Lexi kicked off her shoes and practically ran up the stairs with Brandon not far behind, and Blake sat back on the sofa.

"Phone charger? I'm surprised they didn't come up with something better than that."

I joined him, unsure of what to say. Had Lexi's secret come out?

"I don't know whether to congratulate Brandon or warn him off," he continued.

"You know, then?" I ventured.

"It was inevitable, really. They've been dancing around each other for years. I just hope it doesn't end in tears. Lexi'll end up drinking a vineyard, and Brandon'll fuck his way through the phone book."

"If it helps, I think Lexi really likes him."

"I know. It was sweet, by the way, you trying to cover for her. I mean with the shirt. She could do with a good friend. Too many people have used her in the past."

"I won't do that, I promise." I paused, thinking of the people who'd used me too. Now I had the space to reflect, I realised that even before Antonio, I'd always been too quick to say "yes," preferring to suffer inconvenience rather than stand up for myself. "I could use a friend or two as well."

He twined his fingers in with mine, brought my hand to his lips, and kissed it. "You've got some friends now. We'll try our best to look after you."

See that little puddle on the upholstery? That was me. How did Blake manage to reduce me to such a mess? My legs still didn't feel like my own when he got up, pulling me with him.

"We'd better go to bed ourselves. I bet you five quid that if we listen carefully, we'll hear floorboards creaking as Brandon sneaks into Lexi's room later."

I giggled. "No way I'm taking that bet."

"Smart lady."

There was no sign of the two lovebirds when we reached the top of the stairs. We continued until we were outside my room, and when we stopped, Blake stepped close and caged me in. Only this time, I didn't feel trapped. All I felt was a delicious anticipation as his lips hovered an inch from mine.

Move closer, I willed him, even though it was dangerous. My heart could end up seriously damaged. Slowly, so slowly, he did, his eyes connected with mine.

Heat radiated from his skin, and small puffs of his breath caressed my cheeks. At that moment, all I wanted was his mouth.

Then we heard the squeak of hinges. Blake laughed first, and I joined in. Silent laughter, our shoulders shaking as the creaks continued along the landing away from us.

"So not taking that bet," I whispered in his ear.

He kissed my cheek, leaving me feeling like I'd just had a fence down in the biggest competition of my life.

"Goodnight, Mia," he said before he slipped past me into his room.

Chapter 16

THE NEXT DAY was Monday, and I knew from talking to Lexi that there was a week's break from racing until the pre-race scrutineering the following Sunday. That gave the teams time to make last-minute tweaks to the cars as well as catch up on some much-needed sleep.

"What do you have planned for this week?" I asked Blake as I sat down opposite him with my first cup of coffee of the day.

"There's some setup work to do on the car, plus our daily team meetings. And we've got a photoshoot on Wednesday."

"A photoshoot? What kind of photoshoot?"

"Advertising pictures for the team's merchandise, mainly. Plus a few calendar shots."

I couldn't help laughing.

"Don't look at me like that."

"So, these calendar shots, will they involve clothing?"

"To some degree. At least, I hope so." He looked a little sheepish.

I needed to remember to stock up on ice on Tuesday. Enough to fill the bath, because I'd have to sit in it if I watched Blake parading around in his undies for several hours.

"Do I need to come with you for all that?"

He gave me a pleading smile. "I'd be very grateful."

"Okay."

"And there's another thing..."

"What is it?"

"There's a dinner on Friday, a celebration of Aston Martin. Will you come?"

"You think Marianne will manage to get a ticket for that?"

He shook his head. "I've had her banned from the guest list. I just... I guess I just hoped you'd accompany me. Not because you have to, but because you want to."

Like a date? I was afraid to put a label on it. The sensible part of me screamed that it was a bad idea. That I'd just escaped from Antonio, and it was too soon to think about seeing another man. But when I opened my mouth to decline, what came out was, "Okay, I'll come."

Blake managed to look both pleased and relieved at the same time. His shoulders sagged as the tension left them, and he reached out and squeezed my hand. Then we heard footsteps on the stairs.

Brandon came into the kitchen first. "Morning," he said, scratching his unmentionables. I averted my eyes as he sat next to me.

Not two minutes later, Lexi barrelled in, grinning like she'd just won the lottery, and took the vacant seat next to Blake. "Good morning, brother. Good morning, Mia. Isn't it a beautiful day!"

Blake looked out of the window. "It's raining."

Her smile faded. "I was speaking metaphorically."

"In what way?"

"Uh, because it's the start of a new week. It's always good to be positive."

Blake glanced my way and smirked. "Whatever you say, Lexi."

I don't think she caught the sarcasm. She was too busy trying to play footsie under the table. I say trying, because she misjudged slightly and her foot ended up in my crotch. I kicked her, only my sense of direction was off as well, and I got Blake.

"Ow," he said, glaring at Brandon.

"What?" Brandon asked, oblivious.

I quickly feigned a coughing fit, and Blake leapt up to get me a glass of water. I smiled as he handed it to me, not because I was thirsty, but because he'd shown once more that he knew how to do sweet. Another piece of the ice around my heart chipped away.

"When are you going to tell them you know?" I whispered to Blake a few minutes later when we both got up to fetch cereal. Muesli for me, Coco Pops for him.

"Soon. You have to admit it's entertaining watching Lexi try to cover it up. She's terrible at it."

I stifled a chuckle. "Isn't she?"

Just then, Lexi piped up from the other side of the kitchen. "We're going out to pick up Brandon's mobile charger."

Blake caught my eye, and you know when you get the giggles? Well, I felt them welling up inside, and I knew I wouldn't be able to stop them.

I blurted, "I just need to check the horses," and ran out the door.

Blake was right behind me.

As soon as we got out of sight, we doubled over, tears of laughter mixing with the rain that was pelting down.

"Phone charger..." Blake spat out, and that sent us off again.

We clutched at each other, unable to stop ourselves from cracking up at something so silly. I couldn't remember the last time I'd genuinely laughed, and that was the thought that sobered me up.

Blake realised I'd calmed down and let go of me. "You okay now?"

"Think so."

"We should go back inside."

"The others are probably wondering where we ran off to."

"Nah, five quid says they took the opportunity to have a quickie over the breakfast table."

That was it. Laughter reigned again. Even the horses thought we'd gone mad. They'd wandered over to the fence to stare at us, ears pricked in confusion.

We were soaked through when we finally calmed down enough to go back into the house, and judging by the state of Lexi's lipstick, Blake's guess wasn't that far off the mark.

"Horses okay?" she asked.

"All good. I'm hoping the rain'll stop so I can ride today."

"We'll keep our fingers crossed, won't we, Brandon?"

"Sure. You ready to go?"

Lexi giggled. "Yes, ready."

"See you at the team meeting later," Brandon called as they sped out of the door.

Then it was just the two of us. Blake brushed past me to pick up his cereal, and it wasn't just Lexi who had a problem with her hormones.

Blake seemed unaffected. "Rain's supposed to stop in an hour," he said, fiddling with his phone as he spooned cereal into his mouth.

"Let's hope so. The horses are going to be full of themselves when I get back on them. I'd rather not leave it an extra day."

In the end, I went out while the rain was still falling to fetch them in. I think the weather helped—they were grateful to come into the dry barn where I'd laid down a straw bed for each of them.

I gave them a groom and tacked up Murphy. Might as well get the worst over with first. The rain had slowed to a drizzle as he plunged out of the barn with me hanging on and took off for the rainbow at the far end of the field. At one point, he was bouncing so high I thought he might actually try to jump it.

It was only once he'd calmed down that I noticed Blake standing by the fence, his knuckles white as he gripped the top rail.

"Do all horses behave like that?" he asked, once I was in earshot. "He looks as if he's trying to kill you."

"Murphy can be a little quirky."

"If that's him being quirky, I wouldn't ever want to get on his bad side."

I walked Murphy over and stopped him in front of Blake. The horse took another step forward and nudged Blake with his nose. Blake didn't look too comfortable with his proximity, but he gingerly reached out and stroked him. Murphy responded by snorting.

"Is that noise good or bad?"

"I think he likes you."

I got this ridiculous grin on my face. Murphy had always been a good judge of character, if his hatred of

Antonio was anything to go by, and the fact that Murphy tolerated Blake made me deliriously happy for some reason I didn't quite understand.

"Maybe I'll give him sugar cubes later," Blake said.

"He shouldn't really have those. Sugar sends him silly. Carrots are okay, though."

"I'll try to remember that."

Blake trailed me back into the barn when I went to untack Murphy.

"Anything I can do to help?"

His offer was so foreign, it took me a few seconds to think of an answer.

"Uh, could you take this saddle back to the tack locker on the passenger side of the lorry? There's an empty space on the left, and I need the one next to it for Harley."

"You don't use the same one for both horses?"

"No, they're like people; each of them's a different shape. Their saddles are made to measure."

"I never knew that." He took the saddle from me and carried it off.

I led Murphy into a stable and put Harley's bridle on. Blake came back with the second saddle, and I was soon on board. Things went faster with his help, something I wasn't used to having.

"Do you need to jump over things? For practice?" he asked as we walked back out to the field.

The sun had decided to show itself, and steam rose from the grass, giving the place an eerie appearance.

"Not today. I don't know if I'll ever compete again, so it doesn't matter much anymore."

"Don't think like that. One day you'll have your life back. Stay positive."

If only he was right. At that moment in time, I didn't see how he could be.

Harley was a little sluggish, no doubt feeling the effects of her full belly. She grudgingly did as she was asked, but she looked far happier when I returned her to the field along with Murphy.

Blake had gone back inside by that point, and I found him typing on his laptop at the kitchen table.

"Horses done for the day?"

"Yes, all finished. What time's the team meeting?"

"Two o'clock. I've made sandwiches for lunch— yours is in the fridge."

"Thanks."

I wasn't used to this type of service, and when I glanced down at my watch, I found I had just enough time for a quick shower to get rid of the *eau de cheval* that I was sporting.

While I stood under the water, I started thinking about the future. Blake was right. I needed to stay positive, but I knew nothing good would happen unless I made it. I might have bought myself a bit of time, being here at River Farm, but I couldn't afford to waste any of that.

"Do you think I could borrow your laptop later?" I asked Blake as I walked back into the kitchen.

I worked on smoothing down my hair, which had gone a bit frizzy under the drier. Even though it was shorter now, I wasn't a patch on Lexi when it came to making it behave.

"Sure. What for?"

"I need to look for a job and somewhere to live. I've only got two weeks."

"Three," he said.

"Three?"

"I've got this place for a week after the race. I was planning to go home, but you're welcome to stay."

"Are you sure?"

He winked at me. "Just promise you won't have any wild parties. I want to get my security deposit back."

I couldn't help it. I flung my arms around him. "Thank you," I whispered, my lips brushing his earlobe. It was so damn tempting to nibble the edge of it, and I drew back reluctantly.

Oops.

"You're welcome."

"Er, I'd better eat my sandwich."

I hurried to the fridge, needing to keep myself occupied with something other than thinking about the way Blake felt pressed up against me.

We took the laptop with us in the car to the hotel where the team meeting was being held, and Blake settled me at a table in a quiet corner of the bar. We deliberately picked one behind a pillar so I couldn't be seen easily.

"Order what you like; the team's got a tab," he told me.

"Will you be long?"

"A couple of hours, probably."

I got myself a diet coke plus the Wi-Fi password and started researching stable yards in France. The trouble was, I wanted somewhere small and out of the way, and that sort of place didn't tend to have a shiny website. Maybe forums would help? People with local knowledge tended to hang out there, and a handful of them were international. If I found anything of interest, I could always create a new username to reply, even though I was sure Antonio didn't know my old one. Internet gossip wasn't his thing.

Where to start? Horse and Hound wasn't much help, so I logged on to Show Jumping World. A number of the French competitors used the site, that much I knew, although I hadn't ventured onto it for months. Only when I entered my password, the red message icon in the corner began flashing at me.

I looked around the bar. Stupid. Nobody knew I was here. *Relax, Amelia. It's probably just spam.*

But it wasn't. MyLittlePony wanted to talk to me. My heart thudded as I recalled the day I'd sat next to Alyssa, giggling over horse memes and tales of dodgy livery yards. It had been a rare happy afternoon for both of us as Antonio had gone to a meeting with his father.

"Look at that horse—I can't believe someone dyed his mane pink," she said.

I could. It was all the rage, along with glittery hoof oil. "Purple would be more his colour. Pink doesn't bring out his eyes."

Alyssa snorted then covered her mouth in horror. "I'm gonna write that. Hang on, I need a username. What's yours?"

"DoubleTrouble."

"I feel like an imposter, seeing as I've never owned a horse."

Her parents wouldn't even let her sit on one. Apparently it was fine for me to ride "those dangerous animals," but not Alyssa.

"You had a My Little Pony, didn't you?"

She grinned. "I did."

And that was where her username came from. My

fingers trembled as I clicked on the message. Please, say it wasn't bad news.

Amelia, it's me, Alyssa.

I don't know if you know, but Antonio's really angry with you. He says you stole something from him, and he's got a whole team of men out looking for you. Honestly, I've never seen him so furious. I overheard him tell one of them he didn't care whether you came back alive or dead. He's scaring me, and I don't know what to do. I just hope you see this. I couldn't send you an email because he's monitoring your account, and your phone as well, so don't use them. If I hear anything else, I'll leave another message here for you.

Please stay safe.

I slammed the lid shut, wishing I hadn't seen those words, but I had. They were burned in my brain. It didn't matter whether I was alive or dead? A chill ran through me. Antonio had money and connections, resources I could only dream of. How was I supposed to survive this?

Chapter 17

BY THE TIME Lexi showed up half an hour later, I'd taken a leaf out of her book and knocked back a large glass of wine. Things didn't look much better with a rosé tint, but at least they were a little fuzzier.

While I was glum, Lexi's happiness bubbled over.

"Oh my goodness, Brandon's every bit as hot as I knew he'd be. Although I wish he had a different car. Do you know how difficult it is to wedge two people into the driver's side? My ass kept beeping the horn."

It wasn't a problem I'd ever experienced in an Aston Martin or anything else, and once I'd let myself visualise it, I couldn't get the image out of my head no matter how much I wanted to.

"Too much information, Lexi."

"Oh, sorry. But he's fantastic. Not only is he hung like a horse, he knows what to do with it as well."

"That's still too much."

"Oops. I'll shut up now. I need wine. And food. I must have burnt off a million calories last night, and I forgot to have breakfast."

I passed her the menu, and she ran her finger down it. "I'm gonna have a burger. And fries. What do you want?"

The very thought of eating made me feel sick. "I'm not hungry."

"Did you already have lunch?"

I shook my head.

"Then you should eat something."

"Really, I don't feel like it."

"Are you okay?"

"Physically, yes."

She reached over and clasped my hands. "What happened?"

I turned the laptop around and showed her Alyssa's message. "That's what happened."

Her eyes widened as she read. "Holy crap! You have to go to the police."

"And tell them what? That a seventeen-year-old says my ex-boyfriend's got it in for me? It's all hearsay, and that message came via a semi-anonymous account. They wouldn't be able to do anything. And if I did contact the police, I'd have to show myself, and Antonio would have more of a chance of finding me."

"So what are you going to do?"

"Stick with my original plan. Get the race over with then find somewhere to hide with the horses."

She looked worried, and I couldn't blame her. I was terrified myself.

"I'll help you. We'll all help you. You know that, right?"

"I can't ask you to do that. This is my mess, and I'm the one who needs to get myself out of it."

"Tough luck, sister. You're stuck with us."

She was so sweet. In some ways, me reversing into Blake's car had turned out to be the biggest stroke of luck I'd ever had.

"Thanks, Lexi. I mean it."

"I know you do." Her mind flipped off onto a

different tangent, as I'd noticed it had a tendency to do. "Are you coming to the dinner on Friday? I was going to go with Blake, but I'd like to sit with Brandon instead if you'll go in my place."

"Blake already asked if I'd go with you guys."

She clapped her hands together. "Awesome. I'll do your make-up so no one'll ever recognise you, and we need to get dresses. Are you going to the party after the race as well?"

"He didn't mention that."

"He probably just forgot. You're coming; it's decided. We can go to Paris for the day and shop!"

"Lexi, I can't go out, not somewhere like Paris. Who knows how many people Antonio has looking for me?"

Her face fell. "You're right. We're still having kick-ass dresses, though. I'll think of something."

She caught the eye of a waiter, and he was instantly at her side. She had that effect on men.

"How can I help, *mademoiselle?*"

"Two burgers with fries. And two more glasses of wine."

I sighed. Looked like I was eating whether I wanted to or not. Lexi was a force to be reckoned with.

I'd picked at my fries, my burger had got cold, and I'd downed three inappropriately named cocktails by the time the guys had finished their meeting.

"I'll ride with Brandon," Lexi informed Blake. "I get car sick when I go in the back, and it's not fair to ask Mia to sit in there either."

"Love sick, more like," Blake muttered to me as he opened my door.

He wasn't wrong there.

He was quiet on the way back. Occasionally he'd

mutter to himself, things about gears and turns and throttles. I think he was going through laps in his head. Thankfully it wasn't echoed in his driving.

Meanwhile, I was lost in my own thoughts. Should I tell Blake about Alyssa's message? If I did, it would only worry him, and he had quite enough on his mind already. And what would it truly change? Nothing. He already knew I needed to hide from Antonio. In the end, I decided to keep quiet and concentrate on phase two of my plan, which needed to be executed in a little over a fortnight.

How on earth was I supposed to hide with two horses? My heart seized at the thought of having to sell them. Harley might do okay with a new owner, but Murphy was a one-person horse. He'd only ever jump for me.

Just thinking about it made me crave another cocktail.

Despite having left before us, Lexi and Brandon once again turned up late. This time Lexi's shirt was on inside out. There wasn't much I could do to fix that.

"Did you get the phone charger?" Blake asked.

"What?" Lexi asked.

"The phone charger? The one you went to pick up this morning?"

Cue a panicked look between the guilty pair. "Uh, no, uh, we sat down for tea with Edna and clean forgot about it," Lexi mumbled, looking anywhere but at Blake.

"Was that before or after you tested out our sponsor's products?"

"The energy drinks?" Brandon asked, feigning innocence.

He couldn't look Blake in the eye either. I covered my mouth with my hand so they wouldn't see my smile.

Blake pulled something out of his pocket and flipped it over to Brandon. He caught it between his fingertips and turned white as he realised it was a condom. I was close enough to see that it was strawberry flavour. Yum.

Brandon closed his eyes and groaned. "Mate, I can explain."

Lexi rushed over and threw her arms around him like a human shield. "It's not all his fault. It was both of us. Please don't be mad at him."

Blake couldn't hold his smile back. "I'm not mad at either of you. But you," he pointed at Brandon, "if you hurt my little sister, I'm going to take out all your spark plugs and water down your fuel."

Brandon let a smile escape.

"And Lexi, if you hurt my best friend, I'm not picking you up when you fall out of a club ever again. Or taking you shopping."

Lexi grinned at him, and her arms tightened around her prize.

"And for goodness' sake, keep it down at night, would you? I'm happy for you, I really am. But I don't want to hear my little sister doing *that*."

First, she blushed, a colour the cosmetics counter would call "mortified magenta." But then she grinned and stuck out her tongue. "I'll wear a gag."

Brandon's eyes lit up.

"Lexi, don't," Blake said. "That isn't an image I want in my head."

"Okay. My lips are sealed."

"They'd better not be," Brandon said.

"Get out of here, you two."

They ran for the stairs.

After what happened in the afternoon, I didn't think I'd ever laugh again, but once more, Blake proved me wrong. We stood side-by-side, shoulders shaking, as a bedroom door slammed upstairs.

"I couldn't bear them having to sneak around any longer," Blake said. "Not to mention, they were gonna wear out the suspension on the car."

"It's always about the car, isn't it?"

"Of course. And it's got suede seats. It's not easy to get stains out of suede."

That set me off again, and I gave a most unladylike snuffle, which made Blake laugh even harder.

"We might as well have dinner," he said once we'd both calmed down. "I doubt we'll see either of those two again tonight."

"I'll cook," I volunteered. "I don't have such a busy week. You relax."

"Really? You don't mind?"

"No, I'm happy to."

"Thanks."

He dipped his head and kissed me on the cheek. It seemed to be on impulse, because when he drew back, he looked as surprised as I felt.

"I'm just going to take a shower," he mumbled, and scurried for the stairs.

I touched my cheek, feeling the warm spot that his lips had left behind. My face wasn't the only part of me that had gone up in temperature. Why had he done it? Was he really that happy about having a night off cooking?

I forced thoughts of Blake from my mind as I prepared the ingredients for spaghetti bolognese. I couldn't afford to think about it. Two weeks with him, that was all I had. Two weeks.

I might have been able to control my waking thoughts, but nobody passed the memo to my subconscious. That night, every dream I had starred Blake, in various degrees of undress. Then, at two in the morning, I came so hard I woke myself up. I was shaking, and I could feel my arousal running down my leg.

Even though I was alone, I knew I was blushing.

I hadn't had an orgasm for years with Antonio. Sex had become something that I dreaded even when it wasn't forced upon me. The most I gave that bastard over the last four years was a convincing fake.

So why was I imagining the soft caress of Blake's hand over my cheek? The soft tickle of his hair against my chest? His sweet words whispered in my ear?

What was in those cocktails Lexi had made me drink this afternoon?

Hours passed before I managed to get back to sleep, and in a bid to stop my thoughts from straying back to Blake, I forced myself to think of anything but. Which was how on that moonless night, the darkness that was Antonio crawled back into my mind. It was his hands that gripped me, his mouth that suffocated me, his weight that pinned me down.

The hot flush Blake had given me turned into a cold sweat as I tried to banish the devil in a tailored suit from my stubborn subconscious.

I only managed to get rid of him when I got too tired to think at all.

When I woke, my flimsy curtains were fluttering in the light breeze coming in through the open window, and through the gap in the middle, the sun blazed high in the sky. I rolled over and looked at the clock on the nightstand. It was ten thirty.

I blinked then shot up as the lateness of the hour registered. Blake had said he wanted to leave for the circuit at nine. I'd overslept by an hour and a half!

I sprang up and ran for the door, forgetting to care that I was only wearing a T-shirt and a pair of knickers. The note only caught my eye as it drifted to the floor in the draft. It had been left next to a glass of orange juice on the dressing table sitting against the far wall.

The piece of paper was folded in half, with "Mia" written on the front in Blake's slanted handwriting.

I checked in on you this morning, and you looked so peaceful I didn't want to wake you. I'll run the gauntlet myself today. Enjoy some time with the horses.
Blake

I should have felt happy. Blake had given me a day to myself. A little taste of freedom. A day in the sunshine to enjoy my two four-legged friends. Wasn't that what I'd always wanted?

So why did I wish I was at the circuit with him

instead?

CHAPTER 18

BY NINE O'CLOCK in the evening, both cars were still missing. I'd had lovely long rides on both horses, exploring the local countryside and popping over a few hedges on the way. Apart from a handful of cars passing on the main road, all French registered, and one old man out walking his poodle, I hadn't seen a soul.

Then, so I wouldn't think about things I shouldn't, I cleaned the lorry inside and out. That took me up to five o'clock. I tried to watch a film, but the love scenes weren't helping my malfunctioning libido. Rather than frustrate myself further, I emptied the laundry hamper and put through a load of washing, growling in frustration when I realised I was holding a pair of Blake's underpants. This was *not* helping my hormones. I flung the rest of the dirty clothes in the machine and slammed the door then vacuumed the whole place from top to bottom.

After last night's alcohol-induced dreams, I wasn't about to risk a nightcap, so once I'd eaten dinner, I made myself a glass of hot chocolate before heading to bed for an early night. No way would I be oversleeping tomorrow.

Except Blake came to me again. Tonight, he wore a pair of tighty-whities and a halo reminiscent of one of his magazine spreads as he flitted in and out of my consciousness, always just out of reach. Gah! I should have tried the wine after all. Like, a whole vat of it. Enough to render me unconscious.

Eventually, the haze cleared and he sat down next to me. I leaned into him as he stroked my hair, pausing occasionally to twirl a lock around his fingers. Dream Blake had even brought me coffee. The bitter aroma drifted into my nostrils, making me reach for the cup.

Wait a minute. Did I usually smell in dreams?

My eyes flicked open, staring up into Blake's baby blues.

"She wakes," he whispered, moving his hand away from my head.

It was all I could do to stop myself from grabbing it to put it back again.

"I missed you." It slipped out before my brain was properly awake. I wanted to take the words back, to pretend I hadn't said them, but I couldn't.

Because Blake gave me a sweet smile and said, "I missed you, too."

Then he reached out and tucked a few loose strands of hair behind my ear, something he seemed to make a habit of doing.

My heart skipped a beat as his hand lingered on my pillow. As well as the coffee, I could smell the underlying scent of Blake. Shower gel and something else, an intoxicating musk that was all man.

"Are you coming with us today?" he asked.

I nodded, my mouth too dry to speak.

"Will half an hour give you enough time to get ready?"

"Mmm hmm."

"I thought it would. Lexi always needs at least two hours. She's already filled the backs of both cars with outfits."

"For the photoshoot?"

"No, she just can't make up her mind what to wear. We've got designers bringing clothes for the shoot."

I giggled, and Blake traced the outline of my lips with his finger while I melted into the mattress. As he rose to leave, I was rethinking the whole half an hour thing. I was pretty sure it would be at least fifteen minutes before my legs started working again.

After a cold shower, I picked out a pair of cute shorts and a halter-neck top. I didn't dare to wear heels, but I did swipe on some mascara and lip gloss before I ran down the stairs.

Blake gave me an approving smile as I hustled past him to the car. "Not bad, beautiful."

Goosebumps popped up on my arms at the sound of his voice. This was getting decidedly tricky. Why was I feeling like this?

Things only got worse as we set off. Once he'd settled at a comfortable speed, Blake twined the fingers of his spare hand around mine and casually rested it on my thigh. Not a word was said, but I was sure he must be able to hear my heart as it drummed a wild tattoo against my ribcage. By the time we got to the circuit, I felt as if the pressure of a thousand oceans was crushing my lungs.

Blake seemed unaffected. He gave my hand one last squeeze as he got out of the car and stepped into...mayhem.

People were running everywhere, clutching clothes, photography equipment, and make-up. For once, Lexi and Brandon had managed to make it to the circuit without taking a detour of the horizontal variety, and they were in the thick of it. Blake gave me a resigned glance as he got swallowed up by the mob.

The good thing was, nobody noticed me. I stayed in the car until I got my breathing back under control, and luckily it was thirty degrees without the air conditioning so at least I had an excuse for looking like a hot mess.

By the time I struggled outside, Lexi was already perching on the bonnet of a car, wearing a pair of tailored shorts and a team polo shirt. She stared into the distance, contemplating the meaning of life as a photographer ran around, snapping away. Occasionally, he paused to bark instructions at an army of hovering assistants, who leapt forward to fluff her hair or touch up her foundation.

The boys were up next, also modelling team merchandise. I'd have certainly bought everything they were wearing. It didn't matter that I was female—I'd have just framed it and put it on my wall.

Then, because it was Aston Martin, they had to do a few James Bond inspired pictures. If I'd drooled at the sight of Blake in a polo shirt with the buttons undone, once he was wearing a tuxedo, my tongue rolled out of my mouth and across the sizzling tarmac.

My fingers itched to pull on the ends of his bow-tie, to undo those buttons one at a time and feel my way down his chest to...

Snap out of it, Amelia.

I couldn't think that way. I only had a week and a half left, and I didn't want to make things any more complicated than they already were.

Just then, a buzz started from my left. The chatter grew louder, and as the crowd parted, a small man with an Afro that added six inches to his height strode through, somehow managing to look elegant in four-inch platform Converse.

Lexi squealed and dashed into his arms. I thought for a second she was going to flatten him, but after a brief wobble, he managed to stay upright.

"Ishmael! You made it!"

He stepped back and gave a little bow. The glitter in his hair twinkled in the sunlight. "I wouldn't miss seeing one of my favourite girls for the world."

Who was he? Judging by the number of people hanging around him, he was quite important.

I soon found out. Lexi took his arm and led him over. "Mia, this is Ishmael. When I found out he was in Paris, I begged him to bring dresses."

Ishmael? I stuck out my hand, but he ignored it and tugged me forward by the arms so he could kiss me on the cheek.

"Nice to meet you," I mumbled into a bouffant of hair.

I must have looked a bit confused when he let me go because Lexi tried again. "It's Ishmael. You know, *the* Ishmael."

I tried to give a subtle shake of my head, but he caught it and hooted with laughter.

"Lexi, darling, she hasn't got a clue." His accent was from New York, his manner confident. He turned to me. "Don't worry; nothing offends me except tattooed eyebrows and moccasins."

He grasped my shoulders and held me at arm's length, eyes critical. "Lex, I can see you've had a go, but the girl still needs help."

Well, he might not get offended, but I did. My face crumpled. True, I wasn't wearing any makeup, but what was wrong with my denim shorts and T-shirt combo?

I barely had time to overanalyse it before I found myself being dragged into the team motorhome. Lexi pushed me onto the sofa while Ishmael called to an assistant dressed in a playsuit printed with skateboarding poodles to bring, "the pink box with the pom-poms on."

When he opened it up, I saw it was a make-up kit, and he started on my face, talking to Lexi as he went.

"Now, you need to use this eyeshadow with the green dress. It matches perfectly. And, Lexi, she needs to pluck her eyebrows, for McQueen's sake. You could hide a tribe of Pygmy warriors in those."

I'd never been able to bring myself to start ripping my hair out. I broke out in a cold sweat just thinking about it.

"And her legs," Ishmael continued.

Lexi nodded, hanging onto his every word. I looked down. What was the problem with my legs?

Ishmael ran a hand over them. "See? Stubble. Razors are bad news. Wax is most definitely called for. And I'm guessing you haven't tidied up your lady garden either?"

Oh good grief, please don't let him look there!

Lexi was making notes now, and I wanted to sink into the floor. I think it was safe to say I didn't need to use blusher.

Ishmael was oblivious to my discomfort as he stacked up more products for Lexi. "This lot's for the other dress."

"The black one?"

"Not black, darling. Black's so last year. It's midnight charcoal."

A few minutes later, Ishmael sat back on his heels. "Right, you're finished. Take a look."

I almost didn't dare as I shuffled over to the mirror that Lexi had set up on the counter. How bad was it? I imagined Barbara Cartland eyeshadow, glitter, porn star lips. But that wasn't what I got.

"Wow," I breathed. "I look amazing."

I wasn't normally one to say something like that, but there really wasn't another word for it. My skin was flawless, and he'd outlined my eyes perfectly with a hint of colour. My lips were lightened to a shimmering beige, and I looked as if I'd been airbrushed. And in all honesty, he was probably right about my eyebrows.

"You like it?" he asked, grinning.

I nodded. "It's...wow."

"Dresses next."

I felt like I could walk down the red carpet in the moss green satin number he made me put on first. It was strapless, but with a little padding, it pushed and lifted until I had cleavage for the first time in my life.

"Perfect," Ishmael declared. "Next."

"How did you know it would fit?"

"Lexi sent an album-worth of photos and described you perfectly."

Lexi gave me an "I know what I'm doing" look. Okay, I had to concede that on that particular point, she did.

I went back into the smaller room to change, and this time, the dress was as black as Antonio's heart. It was also more risqué than anything I'd ever worn, despite the amount of fabric used to make it. Sure, it fell to my knees in elegant drapes, but the V-neck was slashed to my stomach.

"I can't wear this," I whispered as I peeped out. "There's something wrong with the top."

"Come out," Ishmael said.

I took one step then Lexi pulled me and I took two more.

The designer appraised me critically. "Nonsense. That's exactly how it's supposed to look. You'll need to lose the bra, though."

"But if I move, I'll show *everything*!"

"Don't be silly, we'll tape you in."

Blake chose that moment to appear, wrapped in a robe, his hair tousled. "She can't wear that."

"Thank you. See, someone else agrees with me. It doesn't fit."

"Oh, it fits all right," Blake said. "Too well. If you go out like that, I'll end up punching someone before the night's out."

Lexi put her hands on her hips. "She's wearing it. Blake, you'll just have to learn some self-control."

"With Mia in that outfit? How?"

She smiled sweetly. "I'm sure you'll find a way."

"We'll see. Anyway, I'm done parading around in my underwear. It's your turn."

I'd missed it? A groan slipped out, and I tried to turn it into a cough.

Apparently it didn't work because Blake sidled up to me. "Don't worry, beautiful. I'll give you a private show later if you want one."

He disappeared into the other room as my legs gave

way and I landed on the sofa. He'd meant that as a joke, right? Right?

CHAPTER 19

ONCE I'D GOT back into my casual clothes, I went outside to watch a little of Lexi's photoshoot with Ishmael. As well as some beautiful gowns, she ended up wearing one dress that closely resembled a parrot and another designed to look like it was upside down.

"I'm having gymnasts for my next runway show," he told me. "I want them walking on their hands."

"But surely people won't wear the dresses like that?"

"Of course not. I don't care if I sell those crazy outfits or not. I just want the column inches so people see my proper clothes, love them, then buy them."

Underneath all the pink sparkles, it seemed there was a businessman lurking, and after I'd got over his initial bluntness, he wasn't a bad guy.

"Brandon and I are going out clubbing with Ishmael tonight," Lexi said as she tried to rub away some of the glitter that was stubbornly clinging to her skin. "Do you want to come?"

The nosey part of me was fascinated to see what a night out with those three would be like. No doubt it would involve copious amounts of alcohol, and more than likely the gossip pages too. But I couldn't afford to appear in those. It was with some disappointment that I declined.

"Maybe another time, if this mess ever blows over."

"I'm gonna hold you to that," she said as she shimmied into a silver garment that I was sure should have a pair of trousers with it. She put on a pair of stilettos and sorted out her hair before declaring herself ready. Oh, apparently it was a dress, then.

Lexi's night out meant that when I rode back with Blake, it was to an empty house. My footsteps echoed on the flagstones as I walked into the kitchen. I'd never noticed that before, but in the still air, it was like I had baby thunderclaps following me.

"You could have gone out with them if you wanted to," I said to him. "I wouldn't have minded."

"Nah. I've sworn off drinking until after the race, and it's no fun being the only sober one."

"Shall I make dinner?"

"I can help."

I'd been hoping he'd leave me to it, but I should have known he wouldn't. It was one of those rare moments I longed for Antonio's apathy, but instead I got Blake, filling every nook and cranny of the kitchen with his presence.

"You seem nervous," he said.

"I am, a little."

There was no point in lying. I just wasn't going to admit I was nervous about being with him rather than because of Antonio.

"Why don't we take your mind off things?"

In what way? Surely not that private show he'd promised earlier?

"How?" I asked, a touch breathlessly.

"This place has all the movie channels, and there's popcorn in the cupboard. I thought we could watch a film."

"Oh." Was that it? I didn't know whether to feel pleased or disappointed.

"You don't sound very enthused."

I tried to inject some false cheer into my voice. "No, a movie's great, honestly."

In truth, I barely watched what was happening on screen. My whole awareness was focused on Blake's arm, which had found its way around my shoulders. His fingers gently stroked my shoulder, pausing occasionally to twirl my hair. I found myself sinking back into him as his warmth diffused through me. His heartbeat melded with mine, a soothing rhythm that threatened to lull me to sleep right there in his lap. A couple of times I had to pinch my arm to stop myself from drifting off.

As I lay in that limbo between consciousness and dreaming, it struck me how comfortable I was. Not just physically, although Blake's chest managed to be softer than a feather pillow, but mentally as well.

Watching a movie with a man was such a normal thing to do, yet it was a first for me. Antonio had always refused to sit in front of the TV, citing wasted time and media manipulation. Quite ironic, as he was using them to his own advantage now. But tonight, I felt safe. Secure. In my little cocoon of Blake, no one could touch me. No, the only danger came from within—those pesky feelings that threatened to run away with my sanity.

So relaxed was I in my own fantasy world, I didn't notice when the credits started to roll. It was only when Blake yawned and stretched his arms over his head that I realised how late it was.

"Did you like the film?" he asked.

"Yes, it was great." I couldn't even have told him the title.

"The sequel's on tomorrow if you fancy it?"

"Sounds good to me."

If I got to snuggle with Blake again, I was up for it.

He gave me a lazy grin. "It's a date. I think it's time we went to bed, though."

My answering yawn showed I concurred.

Blake pulled me up off the sofa, and in what had become our custom, he led me up the stairs. When we stopped outside my door, I held my breath. Would he kiss me tonight? Properly? My body was taut with anticipation as he dipped his head.

He pressed a sweet kiss to the edge of my lips then drew back.

"Huh?" It just slipped out.

"What?"

"Nothing."

He gave a low groan and leaned forward, supporting himself on the wall with his hands. He may not have been touching me, but he was close enough that I could feel the heat radiating from his body.

"You have no idea how hard this is," he said.

I had a feeling he wasn't talking about his anatomy, although when I glanced down, I could see a promising bulge.

"What is?"

"Keeping my hands off you."

My inner harlot spoke up before I could gag her. "Then don't."

He smiled, but it was tight, pained, and he shook his head. "You haven't spoken about what your ex did to you, but you don't need to for me to know it was bad. So, I'm not going to start anything."

"B-b-but...what if I want you to?"

He leaned closer, his voice husky. "If you want more, you have to ask for it. It's your move." He bent and kissed the opposite corner of my lips. "Think about it."

Then he was gone, leaving me bereft in the corridor. His door clicked quietly as it closed.

Think about it, he said. *Think about it*. Well, I did little else for the rest of the night. I tossed and turned, trying to work out what I should do. The front door slammed and giggles drifted up the stairs as Lexi and Brandon arrived home. I rolled over and checked the time. Three o'clock. At least somebody had been getting some.

Blake said he couldn't keep his hands off me, but what did he have in mind? A day? A week? From what Lexi had told me, short-term was his preference.

And I wasn't sure I could handle that. With every hour Blake and I spent together, my heart slid a little further away from me. Trying to keep hold of it was like attempting to grip a bar of soap with wet hands. And what if I gave in to my feelings? I might as well rip my damn heart out of my chest and hand it over, because if I went to bed with him, I wasn't sure I could stop at just one night.

And he'd given me a choice. Again. When I was with Antonio, there had been nothing I wanted more than to decide my own destiny, but with Blake, I couldn't help wishing he'd make the decision for me. I didn't know what to do.

I was none the wiser in the car the following

morning. From the look of Blake, you'd think last night's conversation never happened. He took my hand in his and casually rested it on his thigh, absentmindedly stroking my palm with his thumb as he navigated around the puddles. We'd had quite a storm overnight. When I'd checked the horses before we left, they'd been huddled together under a clump of trees, looking cheesed off.

"Everything okay?" Blake asked. "You were quiet at breakfast."

"I was thinking."

"Hmm."

What the hell did "hmm" mean?

Lexi wasn't with us today. It was Ishmael's last afternoon in France before he flew home to New York, and they were going shopping. They'd invited me, but when I questioned Lexi, she admitted there had been quite a gaggle of photographers around the evening before. Far safer for me to stay behind. At least, that was the excuse I used. No sense in confessing I'd rather spend a few minutes with Blake than a day trailing around Paris's most exclusive boutiques. Blake had lent me his eBook reader, and I was planning to curl up in the motorhome with a good story while he did his thing.

With no sign of Marianne, he walked me in and left me with a kiss to my hair and a caress of my cheek. I sighed as I nosed through his list of books. He was a thriller fan, but he'd said I could buy anything I wanted, so I downloaded a romance novel, just to torture myself a little bit more.

The rain drummed against the roof as I settled in for the day, pretending to read while thinking about the man who was fast becoming my own fantasy.

CHAPTER 20

BLAKE SPENT FRIDAY doing interviews with a host of reporters the team had lined up. I watched a few, but they were mostly asking the same questions, and half of them weren't speaking in English. With the use of a translator, everything took twice as long, and even Blake looked to be getting fidgety.

In the end, he handed his keys over to Lexi. "Why don't you two go home? I'll hitch a lift back later with Brandon."

"Fab! We can start getting ready for the party tonight."

I looked at my watch. It was only one o'clock. "That gives us six hours."

"Yes, I know. It'll be cutting it fine, but I reckon I can get you in good shape by then. I even picked up some hot wax while I was out yesterday."

Hot wax? Terrific. My mind flitted back to Ishmael's comments about my yeti-legs. I didn't fancy having everything ripped out by the root.

"Maybe I'll just stay here. Marianne could still turn up."

But Lexi was already dragging me to the car. I mouthed "Help!" at Blake, but he only laughed. A lot of use he was.

Oh, how I longed to forgo what Lexi had planned.

I'd been to plenty of snobby parties with Antonio, and I'd never worried about my eyebrows being perfectly shaped back then. But a little voice inside me said, "This is Blake. You want to look perfect for Blake." And I did. Even if it meant a bit of pain to achieve it.

Lexi sent me off to strip to my knickers with just a robe over the top while she prepared her torture instruments. When I returned to her bedroom, she had tweezers, trimmers and a pot of wax bubbling away. Now I knew how prisoners of war must feel.

"You want to try the water boarding first?" I asked.

"Huh?"

"Never mind. Let's get this over with."

She led me into the bathroom and made me sit on the edge of the tub while she smeared wax on my calves. There was only one way it was coming off, and that was...

"Ayeeeeeeeee!" I screamed as she ripped away the first strip. It felt like I'd been attacked by an army of sewing machines.

She ignored me and stroked my fingers up my leg. "See? Smooth."

I had to admit it was. I gripped onto the cast iron bath as she worked her way up my legs, surprised that the tub didn't bend in my hands. Then she made me stand and turn around so she could do the backs. Beads of sweat popped through every pore as I ground my teeth against the pain.

"Now onto your arms."

Soon I was covered in red speckles, and I looked like I had some sort of tropical disease.

"This'll fade, right?"

"Sure. Just give it a couple of hours. Now, get on

the floor and spread 'em."

"Sorry, what?"

"I need to do your bikini line. No point in Blake sliding over the rest of you only to get lost in the jungle."

"What?" I choked out.

"Oh, come on. I'm not stupid. It's going to happen soon. It'd *better* happen soon. I've got a bet with Brandon. If you and Blake do it before the race, he's taking me to Tenerife for a week. So you'd be doing me a favour if you got on with it."

I had no response for that. I stared, open-mouthed.

Lexi just carried on talking. "Brandon doesn't reckon you will. He says Blake's different around you to all the other girls. He respects you." She grinned. "But I know my brother. And you."

I closed my eyes and stared at the blackness. "He said it was my move."

"I knew it! What are you waiting for?"

"I'm scared," I whispered, opening my eyes.

"What of?"

"I've only ever been with Antonio."

Her jaw dropped. "What? One man, ever? But you're, like, twenty-five."

I shrugged. "I always thought when I fell in love, I'd be with one man for life. Then Antonio happened, and I thought I'd be with him until death."

"You're free now. You should enjoy yourself."

"Truth is, I'm not sure I can let myself go like that."

She winked at me. "Come on, give it a try."

"You'll say anything to get to Tenerife, won't you?"

"You know me too well." Her face hardened. "Now, open wide."

I was walking like a cowboy by the time she'd finished. My bits felt as if they'd been set on fire, and every time my knicker elastic rubbed against the sensitive skin, a fresh wave of pain shot through me.

The look didn't go well with the stunning dress, or with the scarily high heels that I'd wedged my feet into.

As always, Lexi had a solution. "Take the panties off."

"I can't do that!"

"Why not? It's a long dress. Nobody'll know."

"I'll know."

"Mia, you know it makes sense. No chafing, no VPL."

"Fine. But if I trip in these shoes and expose myself to the world, I'm going to hunt you down and wax you."

"At least if your bits make the gossip pages, they'll look tidy."

Oh my, that was comforting.

"Who's driving tonight?" I asked Lexi as we walked into the kitchen.

Well, she walked. I waddled.

"How about no one?" Brandon said, his eyes darkening as he looked at Lexi. "I'm not sure I want to go anymore."

As it was a formal event, she'd worn a long dress, but it hugged every curve and left nothing to the imagination.

"Dude, you have to stop looking at my sister like that," Blake said.

"I can't help it."

"Try. And I'll drive."

Blake offered me his arm to walk to the car. I accepted gratefully, still not having come to terms with these shoes.

"You look beautiful," he whispered, as he leaned down to open the back door for me.

I grinned at him.

"Now you look more beautiful," he said.

I wasn't sure whether it was the amount of testosterone emanating from the front seat, or the fact that Lexi had convinced me to take off my underwear, but by the time we arrived at the hotel where the function was being held, I felt more than a little hot and bothered. Thank goodness for the blast of cool air from the air conditioning as we walked into the foyer. At least, that was what I thought until I glanced down and saw the effect it was having on my chest. I pulled Lexi's pashmina around me then carried on at Blake's side.

Up ahead, a photographer was asking each couple to pose for pictures. I stiffened. I couldn't afford to get photographed with Blake, who was undoubtedly the most handsome man at the event. He gave me a slight nod to let me know he understood and nudged Lexi on ahead of us.

She rose to the occasion admirably, distracting the photographer, whose eyes bugged out of his head when he saw her ample assets. While she turned this way and that and giggled, Blake and I slipped past unnoticed into the ballroom.

Now, I'd been to my share of fancy places with Antonio, and although this wasn't a patch on events in say, Cannes or Monaco, someone had obviously gone to a lot of trouble to ensure that everyone had a wonderful night. The mini replica cars in the centre of each table twinkled under the lights, and waiters circulated, handing out glasses of champagne. I snagged one and sipped, trying to calm my nerves.

Our table was at the front of the room with Angus and his wife, a couple of bigwigs from Aston Martin, and some sponsors. Brandon and Lexi were on the next table entertaining a similar bunch. While it was fun, it was also work for Blake, so I made small-talk with the wives while he talked cars with the men. It was a situation I was accustomed to, but somehow with Blake, it didn't seem like the agonising affair it usually was. Or maybe his hand on my thigh was just distracting me from the monotony.

Lexi grabbed me after the starter. "Bathroom break."

I flashed a smile at Blake as she dragged me out of the ballroom, and he shrugged.

"I'm bored already," she said as she touched up her lipstick. "And there are still two courses left."

"Just smile and enjoy the food."

"I'm trying. Did you see that woman on the next table? She's with some old dude, but she can't keep her eyes off Blake. Her tongue's hanging out like the dog she is. And she's had Botox."

I hadn't noticed her, but when I got back, I saw Lexi was right, although the woman wasn't so much a dog as a cougar. There was something fascinating about someone whose facial expression was devoid of all movement, and I found myself glancing back at her every so often. She was ignoring her date completely. How charming.

Not that Blake paid her any attention. When he wasn't talking to the money men, his eyes stayed focused on me. And after dinner came dancing.

"Will you do me the honour?" asked Blake, holding

out his hand.

"Of course."

I wasn't the best dancer in the world, but Antonio had made me take lessons so I wouldn't embarrass him, and I managed to get through a waltz without incident.

"I didn't picture you as a dancer," I said to Blake.

He was surprisingly good.

He grimaced. "My mother really wanted two girls. She was horrified when I quit ballet and started karting."

I gave an indelicate snort. "Ballet?"

He nodded, trying and failing to hide a smile.

"In tights?"

"Unfortunately, yes."

"Are there photos?"

"I think I've managed to burn them all over the years."

"I've still got one or two," Lexi whispered, having crept up behind us.

Blake groaned. "If you show those to Mia..."

"What you gonna do?" she giggled.

Before he could answer, she pulled me away and skipped down the corridor, laughing.

"Do you really have pictures?" I asked as we walked in the direction of the bathroom again.

"Yup. In glorious technicolour. He had a floppy fringe as well. I'll show you if you help me with my hair. Some of the bits at the back have come unpinned."

I fixed her up as best I could, and I thought it looked okay, but my experience of styling hair was limited to plaiting up horses and their hairstyles weren't nearly as fancy as Lexi's.

"Any good?"

"Perfect."

Lexi checked my outfit and pronounced me decent, but on the way back to the ballroom, she stopped and pulled me behind a potted palm.

"That woman's up ahead. The one who looks like a puppet. Fix it."

What woman? Oh, the cougar who'd been eyeing Blake up. I tried not to run people down, but at the sight of her trailing her fingernails up his arm, I may have called her a few nasty names in my head. And when she leaned over to whisper in his ear, I saw red. She knew I was with him—she'd been watching us all evening. Did she have no shame?

I marched over, the unsteadiness from the alcohol somehow counteracting my natural wobble on heels and transforming my walk into something that didn't look like a toddler taking her first steps. Slipping my arm around Blake's waist under his jacket, I plastered myself to his other side and kissed his cheek.

"There you are, darling. I wondered where you'd gone."

He gave me a surprised smile. Surprised but pleased. "I was just talking to... What was your name again?"

His bored tone told me he'd forgotten it on purpose.

"Crystal."

"Well, Crystal, it was nice meeting you. If you'll excuse us."

He detached Crystal's fingers from his arm and steered me away from her. I tossed a smile over my shoulder as she wished me a painful death with her eyes.

"Was that a touch of the green-eyed monster?" Blake asked, lips quirked up in amusement.

"No, of course not." Whoops—I was snapping. I softened my tone. "I was just helping you out. Because...uh...I was worried her facial paralysis could be contagious."

I could deny his suspicions all I wanted, but yes, it definitely was jealousy. Not something I was accustomed to. With Antonio, I'd have gladly gift-wrapped and delivered him to any woman who showed an interest.

He chuckled. "Easy, babe. Don't get your knickers in a twist."

I was glad it amused him. He hadn't exactly been beating her off with a stick. "Well, that would be difficult, seeing as I'm not wearing any."

His smile faded, and his eyes hooded as he backed me against the wall. I was caged in by his arms as his lips stopped millimetres from mine.

"You can't say things like that."

"Why not? It's true."

I knew I was playing with fire. Maybe I wanted to get burnt.

"Because I'm hanging onto my self-control by my fingernails, and if you tempt me, I'm going to lose my grip."

"What if I want you to?"

He leaned forward, just enough for me to feel his hard cock against my hip. "Do you really?"

"Uh..."

"Mia, if you want it, you have to say it."

Oh, I wanted it, but something about the way we

were positioned made Antonio's face pop into my mind. He'd liked to take me like that. He always wanted to dominate. I knew Blake wouldn't do that, I *knew*, but I couldn't help the lump that rose in my throat.

"I can't," I whispered.

He backed off instantly.

"I'm sorry. I'm so sorry," I muttered as I ducked out from under his arms and hurried down the corridor, my heart racing.

I was also positive I hadn't imagined the look of devastation that flashed across his face. I'd done that to him. Me. I'd led him on then let him down. I'd thought I wanted him. Hell, I knew I wanted him. Why hadn't I gone for it?

One answer. Memories.

Damn Antonio. Damn him and the horrors he'd planted in my mind. Would I ever be able to forget him and move on?

Would I ever be free to follow my heart?

CHAPTER 21

THAT EVENING WHEN Blake walked me to my room, there was an invisible barrier between us.

"I'm sorry," I said quietly as we stopped by my door.

"Nothing to be sorry for."

"But... I just ran off. And I hurt you."

"You need time to heal, beautiful. It was too soon. I can wait."

He gave me a soft kiss, but I stiffened on instinct. As he walked off, there was a palpable tension in the air.

He'd said he *could* wait. But *would* he?

It wasn't like we had long left together.

The awkwardness was still there the next morning as we left the house. In the cloying air between us at the breakfast table, in the silence that filled the car, in my arid mouth.

Never having been in that situation, I had no idea what to say. Would words even help? Maybe I needed to let my actions speak. When he settled his hand in his lap after we'd turned onto the road out of River Farm, I reached and curled my fingers around his, trying not to think about how close they were to his...you know.

He squeezed my hand back and flashed me a smile, and I relaxed a notch for the first time since last night's dinner.

Pretty fields and quaint cottages flashed past as we sped along the now-familiar route. How many more times would I get to ride it? I'd come so far in the last two weeks, not just physically, but in my distancing from Antonio.

Hang on. Why had we gone straight past that road? Surely, we should have headed right?

"I think you missed a turning."

He shook his head. "Today's the last chance I've got of any free time. I thought I'd take you out for brunch. Angus told me about a little café in the next village."

It was over coffee and croissants, okay, *pain au chocolat*, that any awkwardness left between us faded away. At a tiny table, one of three in front of a patisserie that also served liquid caffeine so strong you could stand the spoon up in it, we were simply Mia and Blake, two friends who perhaps wanted more.

Blake wasn't a racing driver, and I wasn't an ex-show jumper with a shattered heart.

We were just us.

As Blake chatted about a film he wanted to see and the disaster he'd had decorating his lounge before he left England, I realised that he wasn't Antonio, and he never would be.

No matter how brief things might be between us, the only way he'd hurt me would be through our parting.

Was that a good enough excuse to hold back?

No, it wasn't. Despite the ticking time bomb, I wanted him.

All too soon, Blake looked at his watch, and it was time to leave. The second part of the drive was far more comfortable than the first, full of laughter, and here and there a touch or caress. When we arrived at the circuit, this time I took the initiative and leaned over. Only a kiss on the cheek, but it represented more for me—hope, and a dream of a future where I wasn't alone.

Blake raised his eyebrows, looking surprised yet pleased.

"Thank you," I whispered. "For this morning, and also for just being you."

"Anything for..." he started, but he didn't finish because there was a knocking on the window.

He sighed and rolled it down. "What?"

"Sorry, Blake, but there's a small problem. Well, not so small. I thought I'd better give you a heads up."

The speaker was one of Blake's mechanics, although his name escaped me.

"Is it the car?" Blake's voice held a hint of panic.

"No, it's, er... that."

He pointed towards the next garage but one, miming a large chest.

That garage belonged to a privateer Porsche team owned by a software mogul. Blake had pointed him and his harem out to me the other day—a balding man surrounded by girls half his age who'd forgotten to get fully dressed that morning.

"Buck Wilson. Now, there's a man who wants to win at all costs," he'd said. "I beat him to pole position at a race last year, and overnight, someone stole the fuses out of my tyre warmers. We didn't realise they weren't working until it was too late."

"Tyre warmers? Are they like leg warmers for the car?"

Blake laughed. "That's one way of putting it. They heat the tyres up to the correct operating temperature in advance, so they grip the track. If you start on cold tyres, you end up sliding all over the place. I went from first to tenth by the second corner."

"And you think it was Wilson?"

"He made some snide comment about me not preparing properly. It wasn't so much what he said, but the way he said it."

"What did you do about it?"

"What could I do? We had no way of proving anything. Since then, the mechanics have taken it in turns to sleep in the garage overnight, and I've made it my goal to beat him on the track. So far, I've managed it."

It was clear there was no love lost between Wilson and Blake, and it was out of the Wilson Racing garage that Marianne now walked, dressed in an all-in-one Lycra outfit emblazoned with the team's logo. They were sponsored by a well-known brand of haemorrhoid cream. I stifled a giggle.

Blake saw her and groaned. "Tell me he hasn't given her a job as a promo-girl."

The mechanic shrugged. "I could tell you that, but I'd be lying."

"Bloody hell. She'll scare the punters off."

"We reckon Wilson noticed her stalker-ish tendencies and he's hoping she'll distract you."

"You're probably right."

As the mechanic walked back to the garage, Blake leaned against the headrest, closed his eyes, and groaned. Marianne's gaze zeroed in on his Aston Martin, and she set out in our direction, thighs jiggling as she walked.

That...that harpy!

As at the dinner, I saw red, and it wasn't just in the scarlet lipstick she'd plastered on. No way was she getting my man. Wait a minute... *My* man?

There was no time to think about that as she got closer. Blake was muttering a quiet string of expletives as I leaned over and laid my lips on his, silencing him. His eyes flicked open, widening as I deepened the kiss. He responded by wrapping an arm around me and pulling me tight against his chest. Drinks bottles tumbled out of the centre console as his tongue touched mine, and sparks from my mouth travelled through me like a waterfall, lower and lower.

I wanted to get closer, and I twisted my body, gripping his thigh as I pressed myself against him. Then I slipped on the leather and beeped the horn with my elbow.

Oops.

Everyone in the paddock stopped and stared, and my face turned a shade that matched the Ferrari whose driver had braked next to us to have a look.

On the plus side, Marianne had stopped dead in her tracks. Score one to me.

"Lifesaver," Blake said. "You okay?"

"A little, uh, warm, but yes."

He chuckled and went to get out of the car, but I stopped him with a hand on his arm. He turned expectantly.

"Blake?"

"Yes?"

I closed my eyes and took a deep breath. "I'm asking."

His eyes lit up. "Are you serious?"

I bit my lip, more nervous than ever, but I knew I'd made the right decision. I nodded.

He slipped back into his seat and leaned over to my side, his lips meeting mine in a kiss that started off sweet but fast progressed to ravenous. Then as the audience outside began applauding, he came to his senses and pulled back.

"Better get to work. Although at this moment, I'm strongly considering starting the engine and driving off into the sunset."

"I'll still be here when you finish."

"If you weren't, I'd hunt you to the ends of the earth."

I stiffened at his words, visions of Antonio in the forefront of my mind. He realised what he'd said and looked stricken.

"Shit, Mia, I didn't mean that. I just... I didn't think."

I managed a small smile, although I felt tears pricking. "It's okay. I know you didn't."

Blake hugged me to him. "I'll do everything I can to erase those memories, I promise. I want you to have a future that's only happy."

And I wanted a future with him in it. Sure, he had his faults, but above everything else, Blake was kind.

"I'd like that." I kissed his cheek to show I wasn't mad. "I'll walk with you to the garage."

As the day wore on, Blake's sweetness pushed Antonio further back in my mind. Rather than sitting in the motorhome, I perched on a toolbox at the back of the garage so I could watch what was happening, carefully decked out in a team baseball cap and big sunglasses. When the car went for scrutineering, which Blake had explained to me meant being checked for eligibility and safety by a team of experts, the noise level dropped but the tension rose.

With good reason, it seemed.

Angus returned to the garage and let loose a string of curses. "They're saying the seat fittings don't conform to the regulations. I tried to argue that the regulations are vague and it's a matter of interpretation, but the officials weren't having it."

There was a collective groan from the assembled team.

"What does that mean?" I whispered to Blake.

"It means we're going to have a long night."

He wasn't kidding. It was almost two by the time the designers and the mechanics had gone backwards and forwards and got the problem fixed. Blake yawned as he got into the car, and I followed suit. There weren't enough energy drinks in the world to fight off the weariness seeping through my veins. It would have taken scaffolding to hold my eyelids open, and the entire journey passed in a blur.

Back at the house, Blake paused outside my door. This time, though, the seal was broken, and he kissed me properly. A slow burn ignited as his tongue explored my mouth, and when he nipped at my lips with his teeth, I felt it between my legs. But as I shivered in delight at his touch, my eyes closed, and it wasn't just with anticipation. My breath mingled with Blake's as lust fought with tiredness, a duel to the death. He was fighting the same battle, it seemed, because his kiss turned into a yawn, which turned into an embarrassed apology.

"Mia, hell, I'm so sorry. I just... I can't..."

"It's okay. You're not the only one. We should get some sleep."

"Yeah," he agreed, leaning his forehead against mine.

Neither of us moved.

I needed to sleep, but at the same time, I didn't want to leave his embrace. He was my safe place, my island in a raging river. I inhaled his musky scent and committed it to memory. Who knew how much longer I'd get to experience it first hand? Would he stay the week after the race with me? He'd said he wasn't planning to, but if we...if we...would it change anything?

One thing was certain. Our relationship had an expiration date, and I didn't want to waste any of the time we had left.

"Will you stay with me?" I asked. "Just to sleep, that's all."

He pulled me tighter against him. "Nothing would give me greater pleasure."

I managed a cheeky grin. "Nothing? Are you sure about that?"

"Okay, maybe there is something that would. And when you're ready, I look forward to giving you a step-by-step demonstration."

My subconscious stumbled at the promise those words held, but it was only a trip. When I looked down the mountain I was climbing, I could see Antonio in the distance, a tiny speck at the bottom, getting smaller and smaller as Blake held my hand and helped me clamber towards the summit.

With his help, something that had once seemed

impossible was coming into reach. I just needed to grab it.

CHAPTER 22

THE ALARM WENT off at six, interrupting a delicious dream where Blake had wrapped himself around me from behind, one hand on my stomach and the other tangled in my hair. His breath tickled my ear as he slept through the opening beats of Rihanna's "Shut Up and Drive" playing from his phone, but when I opened my eyes to hit the snooze button, I found the arm resting on my side all too real. Maybe being awake wasn't so bad?

"Ten more minutes," Blake mumbled.

Who was I to argue with that?

Last night, as I'd scurried off to the bathroom to put on a pair of pyjamas, Blake had stripped off everything but his boxers and climbed under the quilt. And right now, I could feel every hot, perfectly formed muscle in his chest and legs as they pressed against me. And that wasn't all I felt. It seemed Blake was a closet rounders fan because he'd brought a bat to bed and sandwiched it between the two of us. Each time he breathed, it nudged my ass in a promise of what was to come.

I snuggled back into him and his arms tightened, claiming me. He didn't need to. I already knew I was his.

"Morning, beautiful," he whispered.

"Good morning, sexy."

I smiled as I said the last word, pleased because I didn't trip over my tongue with nerves. I'd never said that to anybody before.

His lips found the back of my neck and peppered it with barely there kisses. I sighed as he ran a finger down my side, eliciting a shiver from me as he hit a ticklish spot.

"Keep still, Mia. I'm so hard it hurts."

"Sorry."

"Never apologise for making me get that way. It's a good thing. And later, when I've got time to take things slowly and give you what I want to give you, I'll show you how good." Rihanna started singing again, invading our quiet bliss. "But right now, a cold shower's on the agenda."

Bed wasn't the same without him. It felt too big, too cool and most of all, too empty. I no longer wanted to be in it alone, and besides, I needed an icy shower myself.

That antsy feeling didn't subside at all during the day. Each time Blake paused to talk to me, with his fingertips brushing the small of my back and his voice caressing my ears, I melted a little bit more.

When he beckoned me into the motorhome at lunchtime and ravished me against the wall, the puddle inside me turned into steam.

At lunch, when he fed me chocolate mousse and ran a finger along my thigh under the table, the steam became molten lava.

And in the afternoon, when Marianne snuck into the garage and tried to corner him, I grabbed her hair extensions and hauled her right out of there.

"I don't know what came over me," I said,

mortified, once I'd deposited her outside and come to my senses.

The team, who'd been staring open-mouthed, gave me a round of applause. Lexi followed that with a high five.

"I told you that you liked him!" she said, as if that was the sole reason I wanted to throw him onto the nearest horizontal surface and ride him like a prize rodeo horse.

Then Blake slipped his arm around me and whispered, "I think I just fell in love with you."

He was joking. Right?

The end of the day couldn't come soon enough. I was sitting in the car, thighs pressed together to try and relieve the ache that pulsed between them, when Brandon knocked on the window. Once I'd wound it down, he leaned on the door.

"I'm taking Lexi out for dinner. We won't be back until at least eleven. Just so you know."

"Oh, okay."

Did he realise what I was planning for this evening? I sincerely hoped not. That would be more cringeworthy than the Marianne incident. Maybe he was just being thoughtful? You know, so we didn't make extra food or anything.

He lifted the navy-blue carrier bag he was holding through the window and deposited it in my lap. "Our sponsors sent these," he said, before giving me a wink and walking off.

I unrolled the top, peered in, and promptly died.

Brandon had handed me a bag containing six cans of energy drink and what looked like Trojan's entire range. Talk about embarrassing. And yet at the same time, strangely fascinating. I lifted out a couple of boxes and examined them.

Fruit flavoured, one of the packets proclaimed. *Make sure you get your five a day with strawberry, watermelon, raspberry, peach, and apple*. No banana, I noticed. I guess you were supposed to have one of those already.

The biggest box rattled when I shook it. What was it? I fished out what looked like a small silicone donut.

"I hadn't imagined you were the type, but I'm game if you are," Blake said, making me jump as he got behind the wheel.

Mortified, I dropped the fruit bowl back in the bag and hurriedly closed it. "I don't even know what that is," I said, nodding at the donut, which he'd taken off me.

"It's a cock ring. It vibrates and everything."

He flipped a switch and tossed it back to me, but I missed and it landed between my legs.

"Not helping," I squealed, snatching it up and throwing it back at him.

He was laughing as we pulled away.

He wasn't laughing when we arrived back at River Farm. No, he was smouldering. One look at his hooded eyes and the bulge between his legs, and I wasn't sure I'd be able to walk from the car. My legs had turned to jelly.

Not that Blake cared. When I stumbled, he picked me up and carried me into the house.

"One day I'll spread you over the bonnet, but not today. Today, I want to savour you."

I thought he'd put me down once we got inside, but he carried on walking through the kitchen and up the stairs with me clutching the carrier bag as if the fate of the free world depended on it. The thought of what he might look like wearing the donut thing floated across my somewhat hazy vision. I couldn't wait. He wasn't even halfway to the next floor when I started unbuttoning his shirt.

We didn't quite make it as far as the bedroom when he lowered me to my feet, pressing me against the wall while he pulled my top open. Buttons scattered everywhere. His fingertips flitted across my bare skin, and I shuddered at his touch. The catch on my bra proved no obstacle, and then I was exposed to him. The part of me I hated most. I'd always been self-conscious about my size, but as Blake gazed at me from head to toe and back again, slowly and appreciatively, I just felt...sexy. Not something I was accustomed to, but I liked it.

I dropped my eyes to where his shirt was hanging open. I still couldn't quite believe this man was here, with me. Surely I'd wake up soon? I'd have pinched myself if my hands hadn't developed a life of their own and started running themselves over his chest.

My out-of-body experience continued as the crazed, wanton woman who was everything I'd never been clawed at Blake's back and rubbed against his cock, desperate to relieve the throbbing between her legs. She kissed him; she stroked him; she even nibbled him. And then she did something she never thought she'd do. She dropped to her knees and reached for his belt.

I'd never willingly done this before. When Antonio fucked my mouth, it had been a chore or a punishment. I'd always wondered how it could be pleasurable. But as I unzipped Blake's jeans, I wanted to taste him, every last inch. There was a gap in me that needed to be filled, and only his hardness would serve the purpose.

He sprang free as I dragged his boxers down his legs. Oh goodness, it was bigger than I was used to, but what was one more challenge after the past few weeks? I swirled my tongue around the tip, eliciting a long, drawn-out moan from the vision of hotness that stood above me, taking his turn to use the wall for support.

I could only fit half of him into my mouth, but that didn't seem to matter if his grunts of pleasure were anything to go by. I'd just added an extra dimension by stroking his balls when he hooked his hands under my armpits and pulled me up his body.

"Mia, beautiful Mia, I can't hold on much longer, and the first time I come with you, it's not going to be in your mouth."

I was torn. I'd been enjoying myself.

Blake mistook my hesitation for cold feet. "If you want me to stop, you only have to say the word."

I met his eyes. "No, I don't want you to stop. I trust you."

His answer was to pick me up again and lay me on the bed. Luckily, I'd tossed the bag of treasure through the doorway when I sank to the floor outside, and Blake pulled out a condom without looking first. Pot luck.

"Bubblegum flavour?" I asked. "Am I supposed to chew it?"

He gave a mock shudder. "Ouch."

Moonlight washed in through the full-length windows, and I watched our shadows as Blake slowly worked his way down my body, paying particular attention to my nipples. I had no idea they could be so sensitive, and as he sucked one into his mouth then blew across it, a delicious tension spread through me. My head fell back on the pillow and my back arched as the beginnings of something I hadn't felt with a man for a long time stirred deep in my belly.

I hadn't just had a dry patch; I'd spent years camping in the Sahara. But now I'd finally found my oasis.

Blake continued his leisurely descent, pausing to swirl his tongue around my belly button. Impatiently, I pushed his shoulders downwards and he grinned up at me.

"Did you want something?" he asked.

"Uh... Yes?"

"What do you want, Mia?" His voice was low and sexy, and I nearly came from the rumble of that alone.

"I want..."

How was I supposed to say it? I cringed at the thought. Blake looked up at me, his eyes glinting, waiting.

I tried again. "I want you to...you know...with your tongue."

He smiled at me and undid the top button of my shorts, then dropped lower and licked a trail up the inside of my thigh. So near, yet so far.

"This?" he asked innocently.

I shook my head.

"Then what? Say the words, Mia."

I couldn't. I pointed instead.

He chuckled but obliged by undoing the rest of my buttons. "Beautiful, I'm gonna have to teach you to talk dirty."

"Okay, but can you do that tomorrow? About to burst into flames here."

His answer was to peel my shorts and the scrap of lace Lexi called panties down my legs. As his breath hit my sensitive parts, I shivered, but it was nothing compared to the swipe of his tongue I felt seconds later. The rasp of a day's stubble on my thighs contrasted with the ripples of pleasure spreading from my centre, then someone screamed.

It took a second for me to realise the sound had come from my lips as the glow that had been spreading through me detonated into fireworks. I closed my eyes, awash with sensation, my breath coming in ragged pants.

The bed shifted as Blake moved, and as his weight settled on top of me, I felt him nudge my entrance.

"Mia, I need to know you're sure."

I nodded quickly, like one of those dogs on the back shelf of a car driving over a field of speed bumps. I'd never been so sure about anything in my life.

He eased into me slowly, stretching me, filling me. When he was in to the hilt, he stilled then dropped a line of soft kisses along my jawline.

I opened my eyes. "Is everything okay?"

"Give me a minute, or this'll be over far too quickly."

I didn't mind, not one bit. I was only too happy to lie back and enjoy everything he offered me—the cool trail of his tongue over my collarbone, his hands fisting in my hair, searing kisses that made my toes curl.

But when he started to move, wow. I'd come once, and I thought I was done, but with each thrust, he stoked the fire that was building once more. As he moved faster, I wrapped my legs around him, urging him on. I'm sure it wasn't pretty—we were a mess of arms and legs and grunts and moans and sweat—but I'm equally sure neither of us cared.

I muffled my scream against Blake's shoulder as I shattered once more then looked just in time to see his face soften into ecstasy as he followed me over the edge.

Neither of us spoke for a minute afterwards. Blake was careful to support his weight on his elbows as he traced the contours of my face with his eyes. As for me, I felt like I was glowing. I actually glanced down to check. I wasn't, of course, but the sight of us joined at the hips brought a smile to my face.

"What's that for?" Blake asked, lifting a finger and running it over my lips.

"You. That was just...just..."

"I know; it was. When I said the other day that driving the circuit at Le Mans was the most amazing thing I'd ever done, that was only because I hadn't been to bed with you yet."

He kissed me, long and deep, and I could taste myself on him. Far from being the turn off I always thought that would be, it made me feel even hotter.

"You up for another round?" Blake asked.

I bit my lip. Wasn't this the point where the guy rolled over and went to sleep? He wanted more? A thrill of excitement ran through me. He wanted more!

"Mia?" A hint of worry crossed his face.

"I'd never sleep again if it meant more of this."

He chuckled, another sound I'd never associated with sex. "I'd love that too, but I need my beauty sleep. And there's the small matter of a race." He brushed my hair away from my face and met my eyes. "Just you wait 'til next week, though."

"Next week?" I blurted. "You still want me next week?"

A slow smile spread out, a Cheshire Cat in the dim light. "And the week after, and the week after that."

I pulled him to me, not caring how heavy he was. "I can't wait until next week."

CHAPTER 23

THE NEXT MORNING, I floated out to the car on a cloud, my steps light, my face flushed from the orgasm Blake had just given me in the shower. Even though we were running late, and Lexi and Brandon had already left, it was still the perfect start to the day. I couldn't stop smiling.

At least, until we got to the circuit. As we drove in, the paddock, which for the past week had been a quiet hive of activity, was filled with bigger crowds than a football match. Hordes wandered past, pints of beer in hand, even though it was only seven thirty in the morning.

"Keep your head down, there's cameras," Blake warned as he drove up to the garages.

Flashes lit my peripheral vision as I focused on my lap. Blake had switched the car into automatic mode so he didn't have to change gear, which left one of his hands free. I'd claimed it and twined my fingers around his as if that would make everything okay.

"I'll need to hide today," I said.

The idea of being spotted made me sick to my core. I'd never been a huge celebrity, but I'd made the papers a few times, both at home and on the continent, and that was before Antonio started his media campaign. Even with my new hair and make-up, I was still recognisable.

"I have to agree with you." Blake thumped his fist on the steering wheel. "Dammit. I want to show you off to the world. You shouldn't be hidden away like someone I'm ashamed of."

"I know you're not. That's all that counts."

He sighed. "Yeah, I know. But I don't have to be happy about the situation."

Even now, Antonio had so much power. Would it be like this for the rest of my life? Would I always need to skulk around in the shadows, fearful of him catching up with me?

It weighed on my mind as I scurried out of the car to the motorhome, complete with Blake's eBook reader so I could while away the hours. At least the fridge was well stocked and the coffee was good.

And things could have been so much worse. Two weeks ago, I'd had nothing. Now I had *something* with Blake. I wasn't quite sure what it was yet, but my heart had swelled with happiness when he said he wanted it to carry on.

I had Lexi, too. And when she trooped into the motorhome mid-morning, wearing a cheerleader outfit and shaking her pom-poms, she took one look at me and whooped.

"Freaking heck, Tenerife, here I come!"

"What?"

"You totally did it!"

"How can you tell?"

"Ah, she doesn't deny it. It's obvious, anyway. You've got the secret smile of a well-screwed woman."

"Okay, we did. But that's all you're getting."

"That's all I want. Blake *is* my brother. It's bad

enough that I have to listen to his headboard banging against the wall, without hearing the juicy details."

"We weren't that bad!" I'm sure I would have remembered that kind of noise.

"I meant at home." She clapped a hand over her mouth. "I shouldn't have said that."

My mood deflated like a pricked balloon. It wasn't so much the mention of other women—I got that he was no saint—but the mention of his home. Of course, he had one. And he'd have to return to it. I didn't even know where it was, or whether I had any prospect of staying near him.

"It's okay." I paused. "Where does he live?"

"You guys haven't talked about that?"

I'd avoided the subject, and Blake hadn't volunteered the information. I shook my head.

"Can't blame you," Lexi said. "In your situation, I'd have been more interested in the sex too."

"That's not what—"

"We live in Kent, just down the road from Brands Hatch circuit. That's how Blake got into racing. He used to go with Dad and watch the rallycross when he was a kid. I think they just wanted to get away from Mum's nagging."

"You still live near your parents?"

"A couple of miles away. We bought a house together a few years ago. Neither of us is home much, so it made sense to share. Are you coming back with us?"

"I don't know." There was a lump stuck in my throat. "I don't know what I'm going to do. I don't even know how I'm going to get out of France."

Lexi reached over and squeezed my hand. "We'll

think of something. Don't worry."

I only hoped she was right.

As I lay in bed that night with Blake sleeping peacefully beside me, I realised I did know one thing— it would destroy me to let him go. Even in sleep, he demonstrated his feelings, with my legs captured between his and his arms wrapped around me. It was so different to the coldness Antonio had shown me over the years. Blake had brought me into the sunshine, and I had no desire to go back to the shade. After just three days of waking up next to him, it felt normal, like this was my life now.

The next day, I scooted off into the motorhome again when we arrived at the circuit, but by early afternoon, cabin fever had set in. Not only that, but the first qualifying session was due to start soon, and I wanted to see Blake driving.

"Wish me luck," he said as he changed into his racing overalls.

I'd never thought the equivalent of a shiny onesie could look hot, but Blake managed to pull it off. Not only that, I couldn't suppress a giggle at the Trojan logo on his leg, either. They should have centred it over his crotch. It would have been more appropriate.

"Good luck." I could feel his heart racing as I hugged him. "Nervous?"

"Just a lot," he said. "It's only qualifying for the most important race of my life."

On impulse, I stood on tiptoes and kissed him on

the nose.

"What was that for?"

"It's for luck." I went a little pink. "I always kiss the horses on the nose before a big competition."

Yet another thing that Antonio had berated me for. He said it was unbecoming, that they were just animals, and they didn't care.

Blake gave me a lopsided smile. "So you're saying I remind you of a horse?"

Oops. I hadn't really thought that one through, had I? A brainwave struck, and I stepped forward and cupped my hand between his legs. "In some ways."

His smile turned into a grin that stretched from ear to ear. Phew, nice save. I deserved a medal for that one.

"A prize stallion?"

It was my turn to grin. "I'll ride you later."

The session started at one o'clock, and at five past, I stuck my head out of the door. Apart from the cars roaring past on the other side of the garage, all was quiet—everyone had gone to watch the spectacle. I couldn't resist the lure either—after checking both ways for any stray cameras and finding the coast clear, I scurried over to the garage and snuck up beside Lexi.

"Blake's just gone out on track," she half yelled in my ear, pointing at the bank of TV screens. "First lap."

I caught a glimpse of his Aston Martin zooming past, its distinctive green livery a blur at the speed it was going. Please, oh please, let him stay safe.

Lexi took off the team cap she was wearing and squashed it on my head, carefully arranging my hair around my face so it wasn't easily visible. Then she fished around in her bag and came up with a pair of sunglasses, which she pushed over my eyes.

"Keep those on. There's loads of journalists around. They like to nose around in the garages when there's not much going on out there." She jerked her thumb towards the circuit.

"Thanks."

Painted Ladies went to war with Red Admirals in my stomach as the Aston streaked past on another monitor. I never got this nervous during my own competitions. I gripped Lexi's hand, and she squeezed mine back.

Around us, the garage hummed with activity. Mechanics studied the telemetry feed from the car, and the men on the pit wall loaded up information boards with a confusing mass of numbers to tell Blake how he was doing. It wasn't just the guys in France who were busy, either. There was a live video link back to the factory, and Angus told me there were more people crowded around monitors back in England, studying data and comparing it to the team's rivals.

Blake had one hell of a support crew.

An hour into the three-hour session, he'd got the car into seventh place, and it was Brandon's turn to drive.

"Not bad, son," said Angus, clapping Blake on the back as he climbed from the car. "First year for the factory team and we're in the top ten."

My gorgeous racing driver was as happy as Murphy in mud when he came over and gave me a sweaty kiss behind a stack of tyres, well out of sight of prying eyes.

"You must be my lucky charm," he said.

"You're certainly mine."

Brandon went a fraction of a second slower on his fastest lap, but in the dying moments of the session,

Tom got the team up to sixth. It was smiles all round as the mechanics started to prep the car for the evening session.

I thought the laps in the dark would be slower, but that wasn't the case.

"The air's cooler, which makes it denser," Tom explained as he leaned against the wall next to me. "And the denser the air, the more power the engine can put out."

"But surely it's more difficult to see?"

"The headlights are bright, plus when you've learned the circuit, you know where to turn. Once you've settled into a rhythm, you can start putting in the quick laps."

I hoped he was right. My competitive streak was coming back, and I wanted Blake to win.

The temperature difference was noticeable as the sun dropped. I'd forgotten to bring a jumper, so Blake found me a team jacket, and I slipped it on, jamming my hands in the pockets. Once he'd finished his drive, getting up to fourth at one point before slipping back a place, he slipped an arm around me for a few minutes, which worked better than any radiator.

"You okay back here?" he asked.

"Can't think of anywhere I'd rather be."

When the session finished at nine o'clock, the guys were in fourth again, thanks to a sterling effort by Tom.

Blake was frustrated, though. "I missed the turn in at the first chicane on my fastest lap and had to go down the escape road. I can't afford another mistake like that."

I thought back to my own errors over the years. There'd been a fair few of them. Antonio had always made me feel like an amoeba whenever I'd screwed up, and that never helped.

I squeezed Blake's hand. "You get another go tomorrow. You'll get it right; don't worry. Do you want a coffee before we go home?"

He sighed. "Yeah. That sounds like a good idea."

CHAPTER 24

I'D HOPED TO sneak back into the garage the next day, but when we arrived, it was full of TV crew.

"They're filming a documentary," Lexi said as she steered me to the safety of the motorhome. "Unless you want to be on Channel 4, you'd best keep out of the way. They're bored waiting for something to happen, and they're interviewing everyone. I've already had two goes, and they promised I won't end up on the cutting room floor."

Great. I sighed and flopped back on the sofa. I wanted to watch Blake drive. Then I had a thought. Would they be showing today's session live on TV? There was a small set in the corner, and I flicked through the channels until I found Motors TV. The commentary was in French, but I got the idea.

I drew my feet up on the seat and wrapped my arms around my legs as I watched Blake put the car into third place. He didn't miss the chicane today. Could he go faster? Oh dammit, a commercial break. No, I wasn't interested in buying a new Renault or any beer.

When the program came back, drops of rain had started to fall. I saw them peppering the camera lenses at *Tertre Rouge* first, and when I peered out of the door, it looked like Zeus had decided to send a deluge from the heavens. Puddles were already forming, and fat drops of water splashed back up as they hit the ground. The few people out in the paddock were running for cover, sheltering under whatever they could.

What had happened on the track? Was someone still out in the Aston? I looked at my watch and saw it was an hour into the session. Blake had been about to hand over to Brandon before the adverts.

I backed away from the doorway and went back to the TV. It was hazy, another victim of the weather, and above the clatter of the rain on the roof, the commentators talked quickly, managing to sound both grave and excited at the same time. A feeling of dread grew in the pit of my stomach as I tried to make out what was happening on screen. Then I heard a wail from the garage, and I knew instinctively that it had come from Lexi.

The need to stay hidden forgotten, I ran through the downpour for the pits. As I burst in through the door, the team was clustered around the wall of monitors. I couldn't miss the mangled green wreckage on the centre screen. As I watched, a lick of flame showed at the bottom of the car, flickering higher, fighting against the rain to take hold.

Lexi had a death grip on Angus, and I hurried to her side. She loosened one hand and used it to grasp mine instead. It was like watching a horror movie. Orange-clad marshals raced through the gravel trap to where the car lay upside down in pieces, smashed into the tyre wall with debris all around. They were running, but time stilled so it looked like they were going in slow motion. A cloud of powder mingled with the black smoke as they doused the flames.

My heart was beating so fast I was risking a coronary, and the tears falling down my face matched Lexi's. Who had been driving the damn car? I looked around wildly. There was no sign of Blake or Brandon. I could only see Tom, his face pale and his knuckles white as he gripped his crash helmet.

"Lexi, who is it? Who's in the car?" I asked.

Even as the words left my mouth, I wasn't sure I wanted to know the answer.

She turned to me, eyes wide, her cheeks streaked with mascara. But before she could reply, I heard a sharp, "Fuck me," from over my shoulder.

I turned and Blake was standing there, rivulets of water running down his face. I threw myself into his arms, sobbing with relief.

He didn't take his eyes off the screen. "What happened? Mia? Lexi? What the hell happened?"

I shook my head. I didn't know.

Lexi didn't either. "I was speaking to the TV crew. I missed what happened," she sniffed.

Angus filled him in. "Brandon tried to overtake a back marker, but the guy lost control in the rain and slid into our car. Brandon spun and ended up going into the barrier."

"Fuck," Blake murmured again and closed his eyes.

I could only imagine what was going through his head. Brandon had been his best friend for a decade.

I stepped to the side so Blake could hold Lexi as well, and together the three of us watched as the emergency crews arrived and began the slow process of extracting Brandon from the wreckage. They had to turn the car the right way up first—slowly, carefully— then use cutting equipment to free him.

And when the marshals unfolded blankets and held them up to block the view of the cameras, I felt sick.

"I'm going over there," Blake said, stepping back. "I need to know what's happening."

Lexi leapt to her feet as well. "I'm coming too."

"No, you're not. You're waiting here. Mia, stay with her."

I nodded, too worried to speak.

Thankfully, she didn't argue, and I wrapped my arms around her as she sank onto a chair one of the mechanics brought over.

"He'll be okay," I told her, trying to make her feel better even though I had no idea if my words were true.

It was the longest fifteen minutes of my life as we waited for news. Angus paced up and down, muttering, and the mechanics stood around in shock.

The near silence was interrupted by Lexi's phone ringing, and the tinny sound of "We Own It" from the *Fast and Furious* movie cut through the air.

"It's Blake," she said, her voice hollow, her eyes not moving from the spot on the wall she'd been staring at. She passed me the phone. "You answer it. I can't."

My fingers were shaking as I tapped the screen. "It's Mia." I didn't dare to ask how Brandon was.

"Brandon's okay," Blake said. "Bruised but okay. He's awake and he's already complaining."

"Thank goodness." I let out the breath I didn't realise I'd been holding and relayed the message to everyone else who was staring at me expectantly.

"They're taking him to the big hospital in town rather than the circuit's medical centre. Can you bring Lexi? My car keys are in my jacket pocket."

"Of course."

"For fuck's sake, drive carefully. Conditions are horrendous out here."

I got the address for the hospital from one of the race organisers hanging around in the paddock and settled Lexi into the passenger seat. Angus jumped in the back then Tom came out and offered to drive. I relinquished the keys gratefully.

Blake was right—the weather was awful. Cars crawled along a road that was more like a river, and the wipers couldn't keep up. Forks of lightning lit up the sky in nature's fireworks show. Tom stopped by the entrance of the hospital to let us out, and even though the doors lay only a few feet away, Lexi and I were both soaked by the time we got inside. Blake was wearing a furrow in the floor of the waiting room.

"They've taken Brandon off for tests. They're not sure whether he's concussed, and he needs x-rays," Blake said. Then he cracked a smile and eyed up Angus. "He wants to know how the car is."

Angus started laughing. "An accident like that, and he's worried about the car?"

Blake shrugged. "He reckons he's still driving on Saturday."

Lexi set her mouth. "Over my dead body."

Blake stood in front of her and gently gripped her arms. "This is what he does, Lex. You can't stop him from doing his job."

"But it nearly killed him!" Her voice rose to a shriek.

"The cars are built as safely as they can be. Racing's in his blood, and mine, for that matter."

"I don't want you to race anymore either."

He hugged her. "I have to."

"We'll see about that."

She stomped off and plonked herself on a chair. Angus's horrified expression said he'd overheard her outburst, and he backed off into the corner, clearly apprehensive about dealing with an upset woman on top of all the other problems.

Blake went to follow his sister, but I grabbed his hand. "Just leave it a minute. She's upset; you're upset. Don't say anything in the heat of the moment that you'll wish you could take back later."

I thought he was going to ignore me, but then he stepped back. "You're right. I'll let her calm down and talk to her later. She can't stop Brandon from racing, though. It's what he does."

I bit my lip. Lexi wasn't the only worried one. "I know."

And I also knew Blake could never stop racing. The show jumping ring lured me in the same way, like a bloody Siren.

Almost two hours crawled by before we were allowed in to see Brandon.

"One at a time," the doctor said. "Family first."

According to Blake, Brandon's parents had moved to Australia a few years ago and had no interest in motor racing, so they weren't there. Lexi insisted she was next of kin, and the doctor gulped and didn't argue with her.

As she marched off along the corridor, Blake sagged back against the wall. "I hope she takes it easy on him."

I felt so sorry for the poor guy. Having to contend with a heavy accident and a pissed off Lexi on the same day was no walk in the park. Fifteen minutes passed. I fetched cups of coffee from the machine for everyone, more for something to do than because we were thirsty. A nurse went into Brandon's room and came out with a chart. Half an hour crawled by.

"What are they doing in there?" Blake muttered.

"Hopefully having a civilised conversation."

Finally, the door cracked open and Lexi came out. Smiling. Was that a good thing or a bad thing? Had she managed to convince him to give up racing?

Blake gave me a worried glance, and I knew he was thinking the same thing.

"Your turn," Lexi told him as she sat down next to me.

He glanced at Angus, grimaced, and set off in the direction Lexi had just come from.

"How did it go?" I asked.

Angus hovered in my peripheral vision, eavesdropping.

She shrugged. "Okay, so he wouldn't budge on the driving." Then she grinned. "But he told me he loved me, and now we're going to the Caribbean instead of Tenerife."

I gave an inward sigh of relief. "That's not a bad result. How is he physically?"

"Pretty good. No concussion, although I'm kind of disappointed about that. The doctor said if Brandon was concussed, he wouldn't be able to race on Saturday. He's got a hairline fracture in one thumb, but they've given him painkillers and strapped it up."

The car had done its job, then. He'd all but walked

away from a horror of a crash. Thank goodness.

Blake came back into view, striding towards us. "Well, he kicked me out. Said we've got to go back to the circuit and rebuild the car. He wasn't taking no for an answer."

Angus started for the exit. "You heard the boy," he said to Tom. "Let's go."

Blake paused on his way out. "You guys stay." He leaned over to kiss Lexi on the cheek and me on the lips. "I'll pick you up later."

In the end, the hospital relaxed their "one person at a time" rule and let us both in to hide with Brandon. I say hide, because the waiting room turned into a media circus. Men with cameras, digital recorders, notepads... The security guards tried to push them back, but more kept appearing. Nothing brought out the vampires like the prospect of blood.

Brandon was in good spirits, apart from having a rant about the driver who'd run him off the road. "Bloody idiot! He wasn't looking in his mirrors, or at the blue flags the marshals were waving to tell him to let me past. Arsehole just came across into me, and I had nowhere to go but into the barrier."

"At least you're okay," I said.

"Yeah, there is that. I just hope they can get the car repaired. We've come all this way, and it makes me sick to think we might miss out on the race."

"We'll keep our fingers crossed, won't we, Lexi?"

I gave her a pointed look.

"We will," she grudgingly agreed.

Chapter 25

"DO YOU THINK they'll be able to fix the car?" I asked Blake as we lay in bed that night, or rather in the early hours of the morning. He stroked my back softly, and I struggled to keep my eyes open through an orgasm-induced haze.

"I think so. The chassis is intact. We've got spares for everything, and these cars are surprisingly easy to fix. Most of the parts just bolt on. They're designed to fall apart in an accident to dissipate the energy. Quite often crashes look nastier than they are."

"I was terrified when I saw the state of it."

"Me too," he admitted quietly.

His fingers continued to caress my skin, tantalising my sensitive nerve endings as he stared into space, lost in thought.

Finally, he spoke. "How do you feel about me racing?"

"What do you mean?"

"Lexi freaked out over Brandon today. It had me worried."

"Does it matter?" I whispered, voicing my fears. He'd said he wanted a few weeks together, but what then?

His reply seemed to take forever. The dizziness I felt as I waited for his answer told me how much it meant to me. How much Blake meant to me.

"Yes, it matters." He closed his eyes briefly before fixing his gaze on me. "Not all accidents are bad. You destroying the front of my car was the best thing that ever happened to me."

It took a few moments for me to process that. "You see a future for us?" It came out as an embarrassing squeak.

He gave me a heart stopping smile. "I'm not letting you go. Ever."

Those words from Antonio, said with malice, made me quake in fear. But as they left Blake's mouth, I felt a lightness, a happiness that I'd never experienced before. I showed him that with a kiss.

When I pulled back, he was laughing. "I'm glad you feel that way." His face grew serious again. "Now will you answer my question?"

"I'll never stop worrying, but I understand that you have to do it. It's the same reason I spent years clinging on to half a tonne of horse as they flew over fences taller than I am."

"Maybe it's me who should be worried. Do you think you'll compete again?"

"When I was with Antonio, I wanted nothing more than to run away from the whole damn circus and never look back. But I'm already starting to miss jumping a bit."

"You know I'll support you if you want to go back to it."

"I don't see how I can. Antonio'll spot me if I ever set foot near a show again."

Blake hugged me. "One day, we'll find a way."

When he said "we," a tear fell out of my eye and

plopped onto his chest.

"What's wrong?"

"Nothing. Everything's right. That was a happy tear."

Another first for me.

We snatched five hours of sleep before it was time to get up again. Lexi and Brandon were already in the kitchen, with Lexi fussing around as Brandon sat at the table with a snazzy bandage on his thumb and a nasty-looking bruise on his cheek. The doctors hadn't wanted to discharge him last night, but he'd insisted he was fine.

"Does it hurt?" I asked, pointing at his hand.

"I've got painkillers. I'm more worried about the bandage fitting under my gloves."

How lucky he was. I could still hardly believe he'd walked away from that crash. And I got another surprise when we arrived at the circuit. The car looked like a car again. Judging by the yawns from the mechanics, they'd been working all night.

"Who wants coffee?" I asked.

A dozen weary hands went up. I busied myself with a couple of trips back and forth to the coffee machine in the corner, ensuring everyone was fuelled up.

"What are the plans for today?" I asked Blake as I finally sat down with my own steaming cup.

"We've got the drivers' parade in town." He grimaced a little.

"What's that?"

"We all get to ride around in open-top cars while horny women scream at us, then we get hit on by the Hawaiian Tropic girls."

My face reflected his, and I blew out a thin stream of air. "Great. And I'm stuck here."

He cupped my face in his hands. "Mia, there's only one woman I'm interested in having in my bed, and she isn't parading around in a swimsuit."

"What's wrong with women parading around in swimsuits?" asked Lexi as she strutted past wearing, you've guessed it, a swimsuit.

"Nothing, if they're Mia and they're doing it next to our pool."

Lexi turned to me. "Don't worry, if any of them get too close, I'll poke their eyes out."

"Thanks, I think."

I tried catching up on sleep in the afternoon, curled up on the sofa in the motorhome, but each time I closed my eyes, I was accosted by visions of bikini-clad women chasing after Blake. These feelings of jealousy were new, but although I hated them, I was grateful I had something to be jealous over.

Now, a nicer dream would have involved the silicon-enhanced lovelies feasting on Antonio, his screams for mercy ringing in my ears. That would have made me smile.

Blake stumbled in a few hours later, scrubbing at his face. "Have you got anything that'll remove lipstick?"

"I'm not sure I want to know."

"I thought they were going to rip my clothes off me at one point. The organisers had to call security."

Brandon strolled in, looking calm and unruffled.

"You need a Lexi. Did you see when she pulled that crazy blonde's legs out from underneath her?"

"She was going for your lips," growled Lexi, stomping up the steps. "And she called me fat, the little bitch. It's a good thing I was heavier than her. She couldn't get up when I pinned her to the kerb."

Good grief.

Blake wrapped his arms around me from behind as I rummaged in my bag for wet wipes. He stunk of sweat and perfume.

I handed him the packet. "Try these. What you really need is a shower, though."

He sniffed his armpits. "I'll agree with you there. That's the smell of fear."

I sighed. He could be so charming, but I loved him anyway.

Wait.

What?

I loved him? I couldn't love him, surely? No way. I hadn't known him long enough. I backed up in a panic until my legs hit the sofa and I sat down with a bump.

Could I love him? This man who'd sneakily cajoled me into living with him then proceeded to show me what it was like to be respected and cherished.

The answer was yes, and it scared me.

What if he didn't feel the same way?

What if we split because I couldn't live a normal life in public like the thousands of other women who were queued up to take my place? My chest seized at the thought of what the future might hold.

"Mia?"

He was looking at me strangely.

"Er, yes?"

"Are you feeling okay?"

"Just a little faint. I forgot to eat lunch."

He bent and kissed me. "Stay there. I'll go and find you a sandwich. Your blood sugar's probably dropped."

Blood sugar. Yeah.

When we got back to River Farm on Friday evening, our final night at home before the race, both guys were suffering from a bad case of nerves. Sure, they tried to put a front on it, but I could tell by the way Blake bounced his knee under the table as we grabbed a late supper, and the way Brandon started chewing on a nail before snatching it away from his mouth when he realised what he was doing.

They stayed up late to go over strategy as Lexi and I packed bags for the next day. We'd be leaving in the early hours, and we wouldn't be coming back until after the race. I folded up a spare set of clothes, adding a waterproof jacket and boots plus my essential toiletries. Lexi, it seemed, was trying to cram her entire wardrobe into one family-sized suitcase.

"Can you sit on this while I zip it up?" she asked.

I looked dubiously at the contents, piled high and hanging over the sides. "I'm not sure that's going to help. You might have to leave a few things behind."

"No way."

I leaned forward and picked up an evening dress. "Do you really need this?"

"There's a dinner after the race."

"Blake said we were coming back to change."

"What if we're running late? What if we have to go straight there?"

"Then the rest of us'll be going in jeans because none of us are taking formal wear."

She grudgingly hung the sequinned number back in the wardrobe, smoothing out the wrinkles it had acquired. "I guess you're right."

I carried my bag down and left it by the back door then helped Lexi to drag hers next to it. Did Aston Martin make trailers? Because we'd probably need one for Lexi's stuff. I could see me having to give her a lift in the horsebox.

The guys were still sitting in the lounge, a room we'd seldom used. They had telemetry charts spread out on the coffee table as they watched a video of one of the test sessions.

I bent to give Blake a quick kiss. At least it was meant to be quick, but he pulled me down onto his lap and made sure I did it properly. I couldn't say I was sorry.

"I'm going to get some rest," I told him. "I'll see you later."

He nodded and returned to his papers.

I was barely awake when he crawled in beside me, but all he wanted to do was sleep. He tucked the quilt around us, pulled me close, and we dozed off together.

Chapter 26

I CHEWED AT the ragged edges of my bottom lip as I waited for the race to start. Lexi didn't look much calmer as she stood next to me in the Lycra outfit she'd worn for her role as a grid girl.

"The organisers weren't very happy about me being out there," she'd told me earlier. "They wanted all the girls to match. You know, skinny, blonde hair, blue eyes, blank stare. But Blake and Brandon insisted they were having me or they weren't having anybody."

"That's a good thing. Too many girls get the message that you have to look like a Barbie doll to conform. At least in a small way they sent a message."

"And Marianne got pissed because the cameras were on me instead of her."

"Bonus."

Blake was first in the car. The competitors had just set off on their green flag lap, and then they would go for a rolling start. That meant they'd cross the start line at racing speed but they weren't allowed to overtake until they were on the other side.

My eyes were pinned on the TV monitors as I watched the cars cross from one camera to the next. After a few minutes, I heard the roar of fifty sports cars approaching, and my heart threatened to beat out of my chest as they flew over the line, sounding like angry bees swarming around a megaphone.

As they came out of the first corner, Blake held his starting position of fifth. Other cars had overtaken the team in the final qualifying session, but Blake hadn't been too upset.

"It's a long race, babe. A lot can happen in twenty-four hours."

He'd got that right. In twenty-four hours, I'd gone from homeless and hopeless to finding the man I wanted to spend my future with.

And at least Blake hadn't crashed right away, unlike a car near the back, which was parked up in the gravel, wheels spinning as the driver tried to escape but got nowhere.

"The field's already stretching out," I said to Tom at the end of the first lap.

"It's only to be expected. There are four types of car racing, and ours is in the top class. The other three groups will all be slower."

"What are the differences?"

Probably I should have asked Blake about all this before, but I'd had more important things on my mind, like what the hell was happening between us. And when that was clarified, his lips, his abs, his...

"...pole position. It's always going to go to one of the prototypes." Tom seemed happy to explain. "There are two Prototype classes. We're in LM P1, and there's also LM P2. Those cars aren't so technologically advanced, and each LM P2 team has to have at least one amateur driver. Then there are the two GT Endurance classes. They're closer to what you get on the road. There's one class for the pros, another for amateurs."

"How do you know which is which? I mean, how do

you know if a car is slow in one of the LM P classes or fast in one of the GT ones?"

"Look at the numbers. LM P1 cars have red numbers and the P2s have blue. Then the GT Pros are green and the Ams are yellow."

"That doesn't help at night, though."

"You'd be surprised."

"What do you mean?"

"Wait until it gets dark and you'll see. They have different coloured headlights as well—white for LM Ps, yellow for GTs."

Okay, now at least I knew the basics. I wouldn't feel like a complete idiot if someone happened to engage me in conversation.

"How long will Blake drive for?"

"Two stints to start with. A stint is twelve laps because that's how much fuel the car holds. A driver won't do more than three stints in a row because it's hard to concentrate for longer."

I did the maths in my head. Twelve laps at three and a bit minutes per lap was around forty minutes. Double that up to an hour and twenty. I looked at my watch. He'd be out of the car at about half past four, so I had just over an hour to wait.

Lexi interrupted my thoughts.

"Let's watch the next few laps from the grandstand," she said.

She was tugging at my hand before I'd even agreed.

"Okay, where is it?"

"Follow me."

We climbed up into the Tribune grandstand, high above the pits. It was so steep, I felt a touch of vertigo as I peered downwards. Lexi had no such qualms. She rushed to the railing at the front and leaned over the edge.

"There's Blake's car!"

She pointed at a green blur that whizzed by on the track. I gingerly took a couple of steps downwards, but by the time I looked again, it was long gone.

Lexi insisted we stay until we saw the Aston do its first pit stop. I'd finally got brave enough to peer down, and the mechanics looked like little green ants as they scurried around, putting more fuel in and wiping the windscreen. Then she got bored.

"Shall we go and check out the shops?" she suggested. "I heard there's a Hermès boutique."

"I can't even afford a carrier bag from Hermès."

"How about we just get ice cream then?"

"I want to wait and see Blake first."

"Okay, later? And we can go to the funfair. I want to ride on the big wheel."

"Sure."

She had her determined face on—there was no getting out of it. I only hoped I'd manage to talk her into going on something nearer to the ground than the wheel.

I was waiting for Blake as he got out of the car. The second he stepped onto the concrete, Brandon slid in, and Blake leaned back through the door to help him do his seatbelt up. That was how the team worked— everyone had a role to play, and everyone pulled their weight.

As the Aston roared off along the pit lane, a tired but happy-looking Blake entered the garage. I had a bottle of water waiting for him, and he sucked down three-quarters of it before he spoke.

"Fucking amazing! That was a rush." He leaned close to my ear. "Sex with you still takes the prize, though."

I flushed with pleasure. "I'll give you your winnings later."

He squeezed my backside. "How long is this race again?"

"Too long."

A mechanic caught Blake's attention, and he sauntered off, leaving me free to experience Lexi's brand of fun. Hermès was every bit as expensive as I remembered, but we got ice cream, and she press-ganged me into going on the wheel. While she oohed and aahed, I hung on to the edge of the gondola and screwed my eyes shut.

She poked me in the side. "Open your eyes, chicken. You can see for miles from up here."

I cracked one lid open. She was right. You could also see the ground, and it looked bloody solid.

Thankfully, we were soon back on it again, and I ran to catch up with Lexi as she strode over to the shooting gallery.

"Ooh, look at those cuddly bunnies!"

"Aren't they kind of big?" Like, almost as big as Lexi.

She pointed at her chest. "Yes, but I like big."

So did the man standing next to her, it seemed. He rattled off a string of French, picked up a gun, and two minutes later we had a giant pink rabbit wearing a pair of sunglasses parked between us.

"Well done," I said. "Now what do we do with it?"

Lexi scrunched her lips to one side. "If you take one arm and I take the other, we can carry him between us."

"Or we could just leave him here."

"No! Not after that horny dude went to the trouble of winning him for us. He'd be offended."

"Us? This was all you."

"Caring is sharing. And he's soooo cute."

Thirty minutes later, all heads in the pit garage turned as we struggled in with Roger, as Lexi had named him.

"What the...?" Angus asked.

"It's a rabbit," Lexi informed him, quite unnecessarily.

"He'll have to go in the motorhome. We're in the middle of a motor race here." I thought I detected a faint "for Jimmy Krankie's sake" on the end of his sentence.

"That's fine. I'm thirsty anyway." Lexi grabbed Roger and dragged him along behind her. "I want one of those energy drinks. They taste awful, but they're strangely addictive."

We hadn't been back long when Brandon swapped places in the car with Blake. Some of the team guys came with us to the motorhome to eat dinner, keeping an eye on the TV in case anything happened. Even inside, a little way back from the action, the cars going around on the circuit were earsplittingly noisy. I'd become accustomed to it, but there was no point in trying to hold a conversation. I had to make do with sitting close to Blake, our thighs squashed against each other in a show of solidarity.

Just after seven, he picked up his crash helmet. "My turn again. I'm planning to do three stints this time."

That meant I had a longer wait. Lexi and I spent the time sorting out the bunks in the motorhome, ready for the drivers to get some sleep. They were planning to grab an hour whenever they could. When it was Blake's turn to rest, I crawled in next to him. There would be no funny business; I just wanted to be close.

"Thanks for being here, babe," he murmured, just before he drifted off.

By his side? There was nowhere else I wanted to be. Not then, not ever.

Something woke me up half an hour later, and it took me a few seconds to work out it was silence. I shook Blake's shoulder. "What's happened to the cars?"

He sat up. "Safety car must be out."

He rolled out of bed, and I followed him to the TV.

"One of the GT Pro Porsches has hit the barrier. There's debris all over the track."

He pointed at the screen, where I could see shadows littering the tarmac.

"What will they do with it?"

"Sweep it up. The three safety cars'll stay out until the marshals have finished. Means I get an extra couple of minutes in bed."

We waited until we saw the driver was okay then headed back to the bunk. The bed felt cold and empty when Blake went out for his next turn. I didn't want to stay there on my own, so I pulled on a coat and nursed a cup of coffee in the corner of the garage until he'd finished his three stints. As night fell, so did the temperature, right into single figures. Tom was right about the numbers—they shone in the dark, along with the brake discs, which glowed red when the cars slowed for the tighter corners. The effect was hypnotic.

When Blake came back in, we didn't go to bed right away. My fingers were icy in his heated grip as we watched Brandon drive off, then Tom. The team was hanging onto fourth when a groan went up from the mechanics in the early hours.

"What's wrong?" I asked nobody in particular.

"Tom's just radioed in. He got a puncture going round Mulsanne corner."

That left him half of the circuit to drive at a snail's pace before he could get back to the pits for a replacement.

Blake cursed under his breath. "We're in eighth now. This is the part I hate, when luck comes into play and we end up going backwards."

I squeezed his hand. "Like you said, it's a long race."

By the time the glow of the sun showed over the horizon, two cars ahead of us had experienced their share of mechanical problems. One retired completely —gearbox failure, according to the commentator. I'd been relieved to find a commentary available in English via Radio Le Mans, so at least I could find out what was going on without constantly having to ask people.

I stood my vigil back in the garage while Blake took another turn on the track. As I urged the sun to rise faster, my breath misted the air. How could this be summer? I'd borrowed an extra coat, but even then, I was still shivering.

Angus put a coffee into my hands. "Hold this, lass; it'll warm you up."

I smiled gratefully, even though there was only one thing that would heat me properly, and he was currently barrelling through the twists and turns of Indianapolis at the far end of the circuit. I crossed everything and willed him on.

Blake's tiredness was showing as he handed over to Brandon. "That was a long night. There's something magical about being out there at that time in the morning, though. Everything's still except the cars."

I knew it from early morning rides on the horses back before I'd met Antonio. My heart sang at the thought of being able to share that with Murphy and Harley again soon. And Blake. Who knows, maybe I'd even get him to swap his thousand or so horsepower for one on occasion?

CHAPTER 27

AS BLAKE GOT into the car for his final stint, the team lay in sixth. Two Audis, a Peugeot, a Nissan, and Marianne's sugar daddy were ahead of them.

"The Audis and the Peugeot, now that's to be expected," said Brandon, who had dark circles under his eyes but claimed he couldn't sleep. "I'm not even upset about the Nissan. But the arsehole in the Porsche? That stings."

Blake must have been having the same thought. As the lap counter ticked up, he was getting closer and closer to the car in front.

Lexi jumped up and down every time the pair crossed the line, shouting for her brother to drive faster. She was certainly making her bra work hard—every time she bounced, the pit lane came to a standstill. Nor had she escaped the notice of the cameraman hovering outside—the whole world was getting an eyeful.

Blake was on his last but one lap when he finally overtook the asshole by slipstreaming the Porsche on the run from Mulsanne to Indianapolis. When Wilson braked late and drifted wide, Blake squeaked past on the inside.

The cheer that went up in the garage was deafening, and I barely noticed I was dancing around like a madwoman until Brandon picked me up and swung me around. "We'll get fifth if we can keep this up," he said, eyes sparkling.

Blake was grinning from ear to ear when he climbed out of the car. Brandon high-fived him as they swapped, and Tom clapped him on the back.

"That was for those bloody tyre warmers," Blake said.

"And Marianne," I added. "I saw her on the monitors, and she looked like she was sucking a bag of lemons."

"Even better."

Brandon held the position, and despite the Wilson's best efforts, the Aston Martin opened up a comfortable gap.

Then the drama happened.

The safety car shot out of the pits, and everyone crowded around the monitors.

"I don't believe it!" said Angus his Scottish accent getting even broader. "The Nissan's only driven into one of the Audis. What was he thinking?"

I didn't know either, but judging by the way the two drivers were squaring up to each other by the side of the track, they were going to be having words about it. The Audi driver pulled off his helmet and threw it down in the gravel as the pilot of the Nissan yanked off his gloves.

The marshals were soon on site to referee, and as we watched the video replay, it seemed that the Nissan came up alongside the Audi going into Tertre Rouge and the Audi turned into him. The result was two mangled cars smoking next to the barrier.

"Much as I hate to be unsporting..." Blake said.

"We're in a podium position."

He finished up with the same demented footwork Lexi had been doing earlier. Maybe it was genetic?

In the last hour, Tom climbed back in the car. He'd take the chequered flag, and everyone agreed he deserved it. He'd put in some awesome times over the last day.

Meanwhile, Blake and Brandon were glued to the monitor. "Come on man, bring it home," Blake urged him. "I want to be spraying that champagne."

Angus stepped between them and tapped a notepad filled with his untidy scrawl. Old-fashioned, but he'd told me that even in this world of technology, he still liked to keep a pencil in his hand.

"You might be a step higher, laddie, if my calculations are correct."

Blake turned to him. "What do you mean?"

"The Peugeot's got another stop to make, by my calculations. Either that or he'll run out of fuel."

Blake gripped my hand and resumed watching the monitor. "Angus must have been wrong," he said, as the Peugeot started what would be its final lap without pulling into the pits.

But as the car came around Arnage, the tightest corner on the track, it didn't seem to be going as fast as it had on previous laps.

"It's slowing," I said, pointing at the blue vehicle on the screen.

"Well, I'll be damned. The old man was right."

The Peugeot ground to a halt on the kink halfway to Porsche curves. Tom flew past twenty seconds later and drove into the stadium amid a rainbow of waving flags.

"Second. Bloody hell, we came second," Brandon

said, as if it had come as a complete surprise to him.

"Not bad for our first time out," Angus said, putting an arm around each of their shoulders. "I'll be breaking out the Macallan tonight, lads. Nothing like a wee dram to celebrate beating the big boys."

As Angus walked from man to man, shaking their hands, Blake leaned down to me.

"I know how I want to celebrate, and it doesn't involve alcohol. I want you crystal clear as I make you come all night."

My stomach clenched at his words. "Maybe we could take a bottle of champagne to bed with us. I've heard the bubbles can be an interesting sensation."

His eyes lit up. "I'll make sure I get a magnum."

Blake seemed to be wearing most of a bottle when he made it down from the podium. He and Brandon had sprayed it everywhere at first then poured the rest over each other's heads.

"I'm going to lick you," Lexi told Brandon. "That's Veuve Cliquot. No sense in letting it go to waste."

And she didn't.

I knew which pictures would be making the papers the next day, and thankfully, they weren't of me.

As Blake was whisked away for interviews, I felt strangely hollow. The whole week, I'd been on tenterhooks waiting for the big event, and now that it was over, I felt lost. All that stretched before me now was uncertainty.

Sure, Blake had said we'd be together, but we'd put no thought into how or where. Now the hard work would start. I still had to find a way to get the horses home and work out how to evade Antonio for the rest of my life.

Was there any chance he would give up, call it quits? I couldn't see it. By leaving him rather than the other way around, I'd wounded his pride. And not only did he have a mean streak, he liked to get revenge on people he perceived had wronged him.

Like the time a business rival pipped him at a charity golf day. In the clubhouse afterwards, the man made a crack about Antonio spending too much time at the nineteenth hole, and he did it in front of some of Antonio's clients. It was meant as a joke and everybody laughed, but Antonio saw red.

He ranted for two days, and I ended up in hospital, having acquired a fractured cheekbone by "walking into a cupboard door." Finally, he calmed down. I'd thought it had all blown over, but the next month, the front page of the local paper showed the golf guy standing with his distraught family in front of the remains of their house, which had burned to the ground while they were on an outing to an amusement park. Antonio framed the article and hung it in his study.

No, he wouldn't let me go easily.

While Blake clutched his trophy, posing for photographs and talking into the myriad of microphones that were thrust in front of him, I was hit with a cold dose of reality. What would happen now? We'd have to leave our bubble. We couldn't hide at River Farm forever.

"Lexi, can I borrow your phone?" I asked as she strode past on Brandon's arm, beaming.

Her teeth were so bright, I could have done with borrowing her sunglasses as well.

"Sure." She handed it over.

I logged on to the eventing forum where Alyssa had

left me the last message. Would she have any updates for me? My fingers shook as I tried to type my username into the tiny box. I had to erase it three times and start again.

Sure enough, the envelope in the corner had turned red. I had mail from MyLittlePony.

Antonio knows where you are. You're still in France, right? At a hospital near some car race? One of his men spotted you on TV, and he's on his way. He just left for the Eurotunnel, and he's furious. You need to get out of there, like now. A.

Her message was timed late last night. Shit! I looked over at Blake. He was still talking, this time to a statuesque brunette wearing a T-shirt a size too small and hair two sizes too big.

Dammit, this was his day. His big moment. No matter how much I was freaking out, I couldn't interrupt him. I retreated to the motorhome and peered out of the window. The security guards were milling around, but they didn't seem to be doing much to stop people from coming in. Now that the race had ended, it appeared the paddock was fair game for avid race fans and autograph hunters.

A bead of sweat ran down my spine, and it wasn't from the heat. In fact, I felt chilled to my core.

As the team started packing up the garage, I got kicked out of the motorhome and herded over to the Aston Martin hospitality unit with the others. Blake only had time to give me a quick peck on the cheek before he went to hobnob with the sponsors. I hid in a corner as best I could, hoping to avoid curious eyes. As darkness fell, the shadows were my friend as I waited for the moment we could escape.

Finally, I saw Blake looking around for me and scurried over.

"What's up, beautiful? You look like you've seen a ghost."

"Antonio..." I choked on my words then tried again. "Antonio's on his way. His sister sent me a message."

"What? When?"

"She sent it last night, but I only saw it after the race. He saw me on TV, and apparently he's on his way here."

Blake didn't hesitate. "Get in the car. I'll tell people we're leaving."

"What about all the journalists? The sponsors?"

"You're more important. I'll meet you at the car."

Five minutes later, he strode out, with Brandon and a worried-looking Lexi in tow.

"They don't have to leave, too," I said.

"I don't want Lexi anywhere near that man, and Brandon agreed. Lexi's had quite enough champagne, anyway."

"You haven't drunk any, have you?"

I hoped not, not if he was about to get behind the wheel.

"I had a mouthful on the podium and that was it. Brandon's the same. We've got a couple of bottles back at the house that we were hoping to have a reason to drink."

I laid my head against the window and closed my eyes. "And I've ruined it, haven't I? This was supposed to be your big day."

"It still is. And when we get you safe as well, then

we'll really have something worth celebrating."

He started the engine and pulled away, Brandon following suit in the second Aston Martin. Eyes followed us as we drove out of the paddock, everyone no doubt wondering why two of the golden boys were leaving before the end of the party. Guilt ate away at me. I'd have to make this up to them, but I had no idea how.

"Mr. Hunter? Can you sign this?"

We paused at the exit for Blake to lean out of the window and scribble on the tabard of the guy manning the gate. Blake smiled and said a few words, and the man jabbered back in French, too fast for me to understand. *Please, for goodness' sake, hurry up!*

A horn tooted in the queue behind. *We're trying, okay?* I swung my head round to have a look, maybe offer some kind of platitude.

Only to stare straight at Antonio as he drove past us into the paddock.

CHAPTER 28

I DON'T KNOW who was more shocked, Antonio or me, but it was him who reacted faster. While I froze in fear, he was already throwing his Porsche into reverse.

He'd got halfway through a three-point turn when I came to my senses and jabbed Blake in the side.

"What, babe?"

"It's him."

"Who?"

"Behind us. It's Antonio."

Blake glanced into the rear-view mirror, and thankfully he kept his wits about him better than I did because he didn't hesitate. He laid on the horn and accelerated as the shocked crowd scattered. I turned to check behind us and saw Brandon on our bumper. Lexi looked confused as the pair of Astons sped out of the gates.

Antonio wasn't far behind, and not only that, there were two SUVs following him. His men. He didn't like to do his own dirty work, so that shouldn't have surprised me.

"What do we do now?" I squeaked. My voice was so high I was surprised we didn't have a pack of dogs heading towards us as well.

Blake grinned at me. "We outrun them."

"But he's driving a Porsche."

"What do you think this is? A shopping trolley?"

He had a fair point. At that moment in time, I was beyond delirious that I'd reversed Antonio's bloody horsebox into a racing driver and not, say, an investment banker or an actor.

The Aston shot off, and I gripped the sides of the seat and said a quick prayer to whoever might be listening. Blake was smiling. How the hell could he be smiling?

He tossed me his phone. "Call Lexi get her to put it on speaker. I want to talk to Brandon."

I did as he said.

"W-w-what's going on?" Lexi asked.

I wasn't sure whether the wobble in her voice came from fear or from alcohol.

"The man in the car behind us is Antonio."

In the mirror, I saw her turn to look. "Uh oh. He doesn't seem very happy."

Even when things were going well, he was never very happy. Now, he was murderous. "No. No, he isn't. Can you put the phone on speaker?"

Brandon's voice soon came through. "Dude, is there a reason why we're driving round the countryside at three times the speed limit? Or was twenty-four hours of racing not enough for you?"

"Mia's ex is chasing us. We need to lose him before we can go back to the farm."

Brandon didn't even question the craziness of it. "Bro, you sure know how to show a guy a good time."

It was then that Blake mashed his foot to the floor and really went for it. Thank goodness I hadn't eaten dinner that evening because I surely would have lost the lot. I thought he'd driven fast on our other trips between the farm and the circuit, but this adventure made it seem as if he'd been pedalling on those journeys.

When I glanced across, his eyes were fixed on the twists and turns of the road ahead, his face a mask of concentration. I risked a glance behind.

"The SUVs are dropping back."

Their lights were visible in the distance, but barely.

"Good. Where's the asshole?"

"Still with us."

Antonio had often disappeared on track days with that bloody car, and now it seemed the time he'd spent thrashing it around Silverstone was paying off.

"It's easier to follow," Blake said, as if he'd read my thoughts. "You've got the lights up ahead, showing you where the road goes, plus if you get close enough, you can slipstream." He took his hand off the wheel long enough to squeeze my hand. "Don't worry, though. We'll lose him."

"Maybe he'll run out of petrol," laughed Brandon over the speaker. "Good thing we've both got full tanks."

How could he joke? We were in a bloody car chase.

"Nah, we'll flick him off before that."

"You know what we need? Music."

"Judas Priest, 'Breaking the Law?'" Blake suggested.

"I was thinking more Bruce Springsteen, 'Born to run.'"

Lexi's voice came through. "Brandon! Concentrate on the damn road."

Blake threw the car around the bends, and I couldn't help squealing in terror as he wove in and out of traffic. Where were the police when you needed them? I'd gladly have been arrested if it got me out of Antonio's sights.

"He's still behind us," I said.

Brandon spoke up. "But he nearly lost the back end on that last corner."

Blake tried to make me feel better too. "That Porsche has got traction control, four-wheel drive, electronic stability control, ABS, the works. But it doesn't have us. He'll stay close for a while, but he'll make a mistake. Trust me."

We turned off the main road and onto a narrower one, but still Blake didn't slow down. Then, as both Astons sped around a tight bend in convoy, Lexi's shriek was followed by Brandon's chuckle.

"Annnnnnd... He's gone."

"Gone?" My voice cracked. I didn't dare to hope.

"Over in yonder field," Brandon said, in his best impression of a Somerset farmer.

Blake only had one word to say on that. "Good."

"Can we slow down now?" Lexi asked. "I think I'm gonna puke."

Blake heeded her request, and thankfully no retching came from the car behind. While he seemed perfectly calm, I couldn't stop shaking. Even my teeth were chattering, and it was still over twenty degrees outside.

"Won't be long until we're back, babe. Hang in there."

Rather than parking in his usual spot outside the back door at River Farm, Blake tucked the car behind the barn out of sight. Brandon pulled up next to him.

"Sit tight," Blake told me, before coming around to

open my door.

He helped me up and gripped my waist to steady me as we walked back to the house. I don't think I could have made it on my own.

"Do you think he knows where we're staying?" I asked, as my legs buckled underneath me and I collapsed onto a seat at the kitchen table.

"Probably not at the moment. We didn't broadcast we were staying at the farm, but it wasn't a huge secret either. If he wants to find out, I reckon he will, but it'll take him a few days."

Heart pounding, I tried to get up. "I need to leave. I need to get the horses and get out of here."

Blake pushed on my shoulders so I sat down again. "No, you don't. *We* need to leave. And we will, in the morning. I've had hardly any sleep, and I need to get some before we go driving across the country."

The race. The dinner. "What about your party tonight?"

"Fuck the party. You're more important than poncing around in a suit."

"I hate wearing suits, anyway," Brandon said.

Tears started to fall, and I wiped them away with the hem of my T-shirt, beyond caring that anybody might see my underwear as I lifted it up. "But where will we go? What about the horses?"

"We'll sleep on it," Blake said, his voice firm. "We'll think of something in the morning."

Sleep, he said. Like that was easy. I lay awake with his arms wrapped tightly around me, my tears soaking the pillow under our heads. This was my fault. I'd brought this on all of us. Why hadn't I run when I had the chance? Yes, Blake would have needed to deal with

Marianne, but there was no way she could have caused as many problems as Antonio.

"I'm so sorry," I whispered. I wasn't even sure Blake was still awake.

He was. "Nothing to be sorry about."

"But all this...this mess. It's not fair that you should have to deal with it."

He hugged me to him, stroking my hair. "It's our mess now. I'm not letting you go. I've told you that."

"Well, you should," I said stubbornly. "You could go back to your life and be happy."

"I won't be happy unless you're with me. Something was missing before, and I didn't know what it was until I met you. So you're stuck with me. It's not your fault your ex is an arsehole. You can't help it. Just like I can't help it that I've fallen in love with you."

He'd *what?*

My eyes flicked open and I could see his in the moonlight, blue and clear, but with a hint of worry.

"You love me?"

"Why do you sound so surprised?"

"Because... Nobody's ever said that to me before."

"You were with that man for what, five years?"

"Six."

"And he never told you he loved you?"

I shook my head.

"Then he's an even bigger prick than I thought."

Somehow, that made me laugh and cry harder at the same time. My body shook with great racking sobs that could probably be heard on the next continent. I tried to stop, but they kept coming.

Blake held me until I could breathe again, stroking my hair. What had I done to deserve him? He was my anchor, and without him, I'd be adrift, heading for the edge of a whirlpool with no prospect of escape.

"What did he do to you, beautiful?" he asked, so softly I barely heard.

"I can't." How could I tell him? I wanted to die every time I thought about it. "I feel so stupid for letting it happen."

"You shouldn't. He was the one doing it. Never, ever beat yourself up over the things he did. If you do, he'll keep winning."

He kissed me softly, chastely, and I felt myself warming inside as my own love for him unfurled like a rose on a spring day.

"What are we up against, Mia? I know you don't want to talk about him, but I need to know. Please."

So I told him. I cried and talked and talked and cried as I told him about the years of abuse, mental and physical. About the rape, the broken bones, and the jagged barbs from his tongue. I told him about my isolation and the constant pressure to win to make ADS Enterprises look good. I told him about what a cold-hearted, vicious bastard Antonio was, and how he'd stop at nothing to get his own way.

And when I'd finished, Blake held me to him, and I felt tears running down his cheeks as well.

"I knew it had to be bad, but that...that... I'm going to kill him."

"You can't. I dream of doing it. I have for years, but if one of us ends up in jail, then that's no life either."

His fists clenched behind my back. "Well, I'm going to do something. He won't get away with it, I promise you."

This was what love felt like. It was having someone

who believed you and believed *in* you, no matter what. It was having someone who took your back. It was having someone who wanted to be with you, no matter how screwed up or broken you might be.

"Blake, I love you."

"You just made me the happiest man in the world."

And then we both laughed because it was either that or cry again.

CHAPTER 29

THE NEXT MORNING, I found another message from Alyssa.

Antonio's crashed his car, and he's got a broken rib and concussion. Were you involved? What happened? Are you okay?
   A

I showed it to Blake. "Do you think I should reply?"

"Will she tell Antonio?"

"Not unless he makes her somehow. She doesn't like him either."

"Then you might as well. She sounds worried. Just don't tell her where we are in case he does get it out of her. Plus, she might send us some info back, and fuck knows, we could use that."

"It's good news about the broken rib, isn't it?"

"It's a shame it wasn't his neck."

I was in a car with someone else and Antonio crashed as he was chasing us. Is he still in hospital? Do you know what he's planning to do next?
   Amelia.

I almost typed Mia, I'd got so used to my new name.

Hopefully I wouldn't have to use the old one for much longer. I wanted to be Mia more than anything.

At the breakfast table, Lexi was tucking into a family-sized bar of milk chocolate. "I eat chocolate when I'm stressed," she explained, offering it to me.

"You eat chocolate all the time," Blake said.

"Not for breakfast. On a normal day, I hold out until at least ten."

I shook my head. I wasn't hungry. All I wanted was coffee, preferably intravenously. Funnily enough, I hadn't slept well.

"So," Brandon said. "What's the plan?"

"We've got six weeks until the next race. I need you to take Lexi somewhere safe while I try and find a place for Mia."

Lexi looked up hopefully. "The Caribbean?" she asked, in a small voice.

"Yeah, sweetheart, we can go there if you want," Brandon said, smiling down at her. Despite their rocky start, it was clear they adored each other.

"The further the better," Blake agreed. "And if she talks too much, you've got the advantage of being able to leave her there."

Lexi scowled at him, and judging by his "Ouch," he got a swift kick under the table as well.

"Any ideas for Mia?" Brandon asked.

"I'm working on it. I need a can of that energy drink to wake me up first."

Brandon passed him a couple, but it was going to take more than a jolt of caffeine and a ridiculous amount of sugar to come up with a plan. I'd been racking my brains over what to do for weeks and come up with zilch.

"It's the horses that are the problem," I said. "It's hard to hide something with four hooves that weighs three-quarters of a tonne."

"Shame you can't put them in the back of one of the car transporters," Brandon said, his mouth full of cereal. "They could go back with the team."

"That's it!" Blake leapt up.

"What? I was kidding."

"I need to make a couple of calls."

Late that afternoon, we stood back and studied the horsebox with a critical eye.

"If you look closely, you might realise," Brandon said. "But you'd have to know what you were looking for."

"What if they check the registration plate?" I asked.

Blake shook his head. "They won't. Not when the rest of the vehicle doesn't look like what they're expecting."

I had to admit, the Aston Martin mechanics had done an excellent job. The lorry, once royal blue with a red stripe along each side and emblazoned with my name and sponsors now sported the green livery of the racing team. The manufacturer's famous winged logo graced the body, and the windows had been covered so it looked more like a car transporter. Not ideal, but the horses would have to put up with it being a little dark on the way back.

Thanks to another message from Alyssa, we knew we had at least a day before Antonio came looking for us personally, although his goons were still around.

Antonio's still in hospital. They want to keep him for another night, and he's moaning about everything. But I heard father telling Jerry to stick around at the Eurotunnel terminal in Calais until they work out what to do next. Are you staying in France?
A

I gave her an honest answer.

Not sure where I'm going yet, especially with the horses. I'll let you know when I find somewhere safe. Can you tell me if you hear any more news?
Amelia

Blake climbed out of the horsebox, hands on hips as he glared at his team. "Okay, who put the rabbit in here?"

They all looked at each other, shifting from foot to foot until Lexi stepped forwards. "We can't leave Roger behind. He's got sentimental value."

"How can he have sentimental value? You've only had him two days."

"Memories of a fun night out with Mia."

"I almost threw up on the big wheel and then we got all sweaty carrying Roger back to the pits," I said.

"But we were still laughing while we did it."

Brandon held his hands up, the voice of reason. "There's plenty of room in the horsebox, and it's not like we can take him to the Caribbean. We'd have to buy him an extra seat, and besides, he's got the wrong complexion for the beach."

Lexi grinned, triumphant, and Blake rolled his eyes.

"Fine," he said. "But when me and Mia get our own place permanently, he's not sharing it with us."

Permanently? My heart gave a jolt. Things were moving so, so fast, but at the same time, it felt so, so right.

Blake slung an arm around my shoulders. "Anything from Holly yet?"

"I'll give her another call."

With nobody else in England to turn to, I'd called Holly earlier and given her a brief outline of the situation, asking if she knew somewhere, anywhere, that could take two horses at short notice. Us humans could camp out in a bed-and-breakfast, but they couldn't. Trooper that she was, she'd promised to call around.

Now, I picked up the phone again, keeping my fingers crossed.

"Holly? It's me."

"I was worried you wouldn't ring back."

"You're stuck with me now. Did you have any luck?"

"I think so. I mean, it's not as posh as you're used to, but..."

"I don't care about posh, Holls. Remember when we used to sleep in the back of my old horsebox when we went eventing?"

She giggled. "Oh yeah, and we took it in turns to get up in the night and re-inflate the air mattress because neither of us could afford a puncture repair kit."

"And that time we left the side window open and it rained, and we woke up soaking wet and hungover?"

More laughter. "Those were good days. Uh, you might get to relive the whole rain experience."

"What do you mean?"

"I know a girl from eventing. Her horse is only at novice level, but she's been around for a couple of years. Anyway, her family's got this holiday cottage in Northamptonshire, but they've been having problems with the roof so it's empty at the moment. She reckons you can use it for six months for next to nothing."

"What about the horses?"

"There's a DIY yard half a mile down the road with two vacancies. I'll be honest—it doesn't sound great." I imagined her wrinkling her nose in the way she always did. "But it's got individual turnout and an arena, and there's plenty of hacking."

"Is it a big place?"

"Twenty-five boxes. But if you're not working, you could skip the busy times. Everywhere else I tried was chocka."

"No, that sounds great."

"Shall I let them know it's a definite yes?"

"Please. And thanks, Holls. You don't know how much it means to have a friend like you."

"Aw, shut up before I cry, you daft mare."

Blake was standing at my elbow when I hung up, one eyebrow raised. "Anything?"

"She's found us a cottage and space for the horses. Not ideal, I mean, the cottage has a leaky roof, but..."

He silenced me with a kiss. "If we're together, it'll be perfect. Now, we need to get the rest of this stuff packed up."

Clearing up River Farm took us the rest of the day, and Lexi looked longingly at the pool before Blake threatened to shove her in it if she didn't get a move on and sort out her crap. We piled everything up by the back door. Two bags for me, two for Lexi to take to the

Caribbean, and another five of hers to come back to England with us.

"What the hell did you put in these?" Brandon asked as he dragged them out to the lorry.

She shrugged. "Just a few outfits."

"Do I need to get the floors in my house reinforced?"

"You've got a spare room, haven't you? I thought I could use it as a wardrobe."

Blake patted him on the back. "She's all yours now, mate. Best of luck."

I shed a tear as Lexi insisted on me taking half of her make-up and several pairs of shoes. These weeks had turned out to be the best of my life, and I wished I could turn the clock back and relive them, over and over again. And now there were only ten hours left before Brandon and Lexi flew to the Bahamas to relax in all-inclusive luxury, while Blake and I headed for a two-bedroom bungalow with a dodgy roof and slightly unreliable heating. Holly had texted me with the details.

Blake cooked our last supper, steak and chips, and as we sat down, I wondered whether we'd get the chance to eat together like that again. If Antonio got his way, I'd be making my dinner reservations with Hades.

"Never did drink that champagne," Brandon said.

Blake pulled me closer to him. "Better stay sober today, just in case. We'll take it back across the channel with us and save it for a special occasion."

My fork clattered down on my plate, my fledgling appetite lost at the thought of having to run in the middle of the night again. "I'm sorry."

Blake gave me a squeeze. "Don't be. We'll be

drinking it soon enough, you'll see."

I wished I shared his confidence. I couldn't see how we'd get out of this situation, short of me being carried away in a body bag.

Our final night in France was bittersweet. Blake made love to me, and he poured that love out with every murmur, every breath, every stroke. But every tick of the clock took us a second closer to an uncertain future.

The horses didn't want to go, either. Murphy protested about being made to leave his sweet green paradise by standing up on his back legs and waving his front ones around. The people watching leapt back while I hung onto the lead rope and waited for him to behave himself. I'd learned over the years that once he'd made his point, he'd settle down and give in.

Blake had gone pale by the time I'd finally got the little git loaded. "Does he always do that?"

"Quite often, yes. Don't worry, I'm used to it."

"Rather you than me."

An overly rotund Harley gave one last, longing look at the field as she waddled up the ramp.

"Don't worry, sweetie. You'll be back on the grass in no time."

I got a soft whicker in response.

After a last, tearful hug with Lexi and Brandon, we set off up the driveway in the lorry with Blake driving. One of the mechanics followed in Blake's Aston, baseball cap pulled low over his head. If you only gave a quick glance, it would be easy enough to confuse the two of them.

I hid in the back, sitting on the sofa with my knees drawn up to my chest. The journey to the tunnel seemed to take forever. Every so often, I'd catch a glimpse of one of the other team trucks through the front windscreen as they changed lanes on the péage.

"Nearly at the terminal, Mia."

"Have you seen any of Antonio's men?"

"One of the guys spotted a black SUV parked in a layby half a mile back and messaged through."

As we approached customs, I shut myself into the tiny toilet cubicle. I'd never known customs to be tight. With my rosettes and Antonio's charm, we usually sailed straight through. On one occasion, an official had insisted on peering into the horse compartment, but after Murphy snapped at him and he caught a whiff of the *eau de* poop, he'd backed right out again. But today, it would be just our luck if they decided to pull the lorry apart on a whim.

I held my breath while Blake wound down the window. We'd hung air fresheners in the cab so today it smelled lemon fresh. I could hear him having a conversation with someone, but too quietly for me to make out the words.

Then we were moving again, and we didn't stop until we were on the train. Blake opened up the door, and I knew from his grin that we'd done it.

"Did they say anything?" I asked.

"Just congratulated me on the team's result. Word's spreading. I signed an autograph, and I don't think he even realised we had horses in here."

I grabbed him and kissed him. "Did I tell you how much I love you?"

"Once or twice, but I'll never get sick of hearing it."

I felt like singing when we were finally back driving on the left-hand side of the road. The three-hour journey to our new temporary home seemed to go a lot faster than our last three hours in France.

"I take it we're dropping the horses off first?" Blake asked.

"Please."

I wasn't sure I wanted to see the cottage, anyway. Holly's description hadn't exactly been glowing.

And neither was the yard. I realised right away why they had vacancies. Muck was strewn all over the place in front of the rickety stables and tools had been left carelessly in the way of the horses. I wrinkled my nose as I climbed out of the box. A good yard smelled of horses. This one had the acrid stink of urine mixed with doggy poop. Not a good combination.

Blake picked up on it, too. "Will they be okay here?"

"We'll manage for a few weeks. I'll be looking after them myself, so I'll make the best of it."

As I led Harley down the ramp, a crowd of whispering onlookers gathered to watch. I could tell by the sneers it was going to be one of "those" yards. The ones where everyone had a clique, and if you weren't a member, it was time to look forward to a life of misery. Oh, and just to make things worse, the group was already eying up Blake.

Harley didn't seem too thrilled with her new digs either. Her filthy look said, "You lied about the grass."

"Sorry, sweetie. But you do need to diet for a couple

of weeks."

Murphy followed, and I turfed the pair out in a scrubby field. Harley pulled a face while Murphy rolled in the muddy gateway. At least he was doing his bit to disguise himself—he didn't look very grey anymore.

Blake wheeled over musty-smelling straw bales from the barn, and I set about putting beds down. The bucket sitting in one corner of Harley's stable suggested it wasn't only the cottage suffering from roofing issues.

"What else do you need?" Blake asked.

I pointed at the hay bales stacked in a shelter outside. "Can you bring a barrow full of that?"

Yuck. The hay was dusty too. At least at Antonio's, they'd had top-quality grub, even if they did spend life with one hoof in the dog meat factory.

"Sorry, guys," I whispered.

Once we'd got the stables ready, I brought the horses in. At least, I brought Harley in. Then I followed Murphy around the paddock for half an hour until he gave up and let me put his head collar on.

"Little sod," I muttered when I finally bolted his stable door with him on the right side of it.

He sniffed the hay, sighed, and stood in the corner. At least we were free, that was what I kept telling myself. We were free. Now to find Pond Cottage.

"It must be this one," Blake said.

I stared up at the overgrown hedge. "Unfortunately, I think you're right."

Holiday cottage my arse. It was one step away from

being condemned. We stared at the cracked front window and the sagging porch, and my spirits sagged with it.

"I'm so, so sorry," I whispered to Blake.

"I'm not. Not at all. I'm back in England with the woman I love, and that's one step further than we were yesterday. Did you know that when we first started racing, Brandon and I used to share this shitty tent when we needed to stay at the circuits overnight? We went to Snetterton one weekend in a hurricane and the thing blew away, and after that, we had to sleep in his Ford Escort."

A giggle escaped. "Really?"

"Yeah. And he snores. Go on, open the door."

I retrieved the key from its hiding place under the mat, but in reality, there was no need to lock it. The inside was every bit as bad as the outside, from the mildewed walls to the rickety couch. And the small roof issue looked to be a little bigger than we thought, judging by the array of buckets in every room. The smaller of the two bedrooms even had an old baby bath at one end.

"Tell me we'll be out of here by winter?" I said.

"We will." Blake stared at the flowery wallpaper. "This seventies shit is fashionable again, right?"

I fingered the frayed cord on the kettle. "I'm not sure I want to use the original appliances."

He wandered through to the bedroom. "Bed looks all right." A crash followed. "At least, when I unscrew the three legs it's got left, I reckon the mattress'll be okay."

Laugh or cry, right? I took one look at him propped on the lopsided remains of the small double and let the laughter take over. Blake joined in, catching my hand and pulling me down on top of him. Then we stopped laughing and got on with the very serious business of christening our new wonky bed.

That took an hour, and much as I longed to go to sleep, we still had work to do. Unpacking, for one thing, plus the small matter of the lorry wedged at the side of the road outside.

"Where are we taking the horsebox?" I asked Blake.

"I've got a mate who restores cars. He owes me a favour, so he's gonna let us park that brute up in his workshop for a few weeks until we figure out what to do with it."

"How will we get back here?"

"Jeff'll have something spare kicking around that we can drive."

After we'd hauled the cases inside and propped Roger up on the sofa, we trundled off to an industrial estate on the edge of a nearby town. Jeff turned out to be a wiry guy dressed in overalls and thick-rimmed glasses.

"Working late?" Blake asked.

"Helping out a buddy. He had a coming together with a tyre wall at Silverstone last weekend."

"So did Brandon at Le Mans."

"Saw that. Congratulations on the result, though. You gonna go one better next year?"

"Hope so. I sure hope so."

Jeff rolled up a shutter door and waved Blake into a space in the corner of the cavernous warehouse. I'd expected a grubby workshop, but inside, the place was spotless and sports cars gleamed under rows of strip lights. I even spotted a vintage Ferrari.

"Nice cars, huh?" Blake rested his chin on my shoulder. "Jeff's one of the best restorers in the country."

"And still I've spent half my life fixing up Blake's cars after he's pranged them."

"We went to school together," Blake said by way of explanation. "Then Jeff moved up here after a girl."

"Who was a big mistake."

"But now he's got a whole bunch of beauties to spend his days with."

Jeff chuckled. "Never thought I'd see you settle down with a woman either, but it looks like you've found a good 'un."

"Yeah, I have. And I need to get her home. You got a car I can borrow?"

Jeff waved at a gaggle of vehicles parked against the far wall. "Take your pick."

CHAPTER 30

I STABBED AT Murphy's bed with a fork, wishing it was the girl who'd "borrowed" a sack of my feed without asking me. I knew exactly who it was—the miserable-looking brunette with the badly put-together pony that tried to bite everyone who walked past its stable. Her feed bin had been empty yesterday evening, and now, magically, it was full.

But it wasn't just the petty thieving and the bitching behind my back driving me nuts. Yesterday, I hadn't been able to resist popping Harley over a small fence, and a group of girls had stopped to watch us, leaning on the arena fence.

"You need to push her forward more," one of them said.

"And sit up a bit. You'll never do any good if you keep riding like that," another put in.

Considering I'd watched her demolish half a course on her own horse yesterday, I didn't feel she was qualified to offer advice. Oh, how I wished I still had some of my rosettes so I could stuff them in her mouth and shut her up. I'd taken to going to the yard at odd times to avoid them, but at the weekends, it was difficult. They tended to hang around all day, gossiping and bitching.

But despite the awful yard and the sorry state of the

cottage, my new life wasn't all that bad because I had Blake. I'd put up with any amount of childish spite and clanking pipes as long as I got to fall asleep next to him at night. Well, maybe less of the sleeping part.

While I rode, he'd gone out to work. Still riding high on the placing at Le Mans, he needed to attend several interviews and a photoshoot at Silverstone, as well as a test session in the car ahead of the next race in Germany. We'd already decided I wouldn't be going anywhere near his races for the foreseeable future. As long as Blake wasn't seen with me, we hoped that Antonio would assume our liaison had only been temporary and leave him alone.

But at the moment, the goons were still watching. Blake's mother called to say a man in a black SUV came to her house looking for him, and one of Brandon's neighbours phoned the police when she spotted a stranger in his driveway. A friendly constable called Brandon in the Caribbean to let him know.

"Wish I didn't have to drive today," Blake had said over breakfast this morning.

Porridge again for both of us. The cooker didn't work, so we mostly lived out of the microwave.

"I do too, but this is your job. And…and we need the money."

"I've got some savings."

"I hate this. I hate that I can't contribute."

Blake put down his spoon and got up to give me a hug. "Mia, we're not living off my income because you're lazy. You're anything but, and one day, if you want to, you can get a job. But for now…" He shrugged. "This is what we have to do. And usually, I love my job. It's just that right now I'd rather be in bed with you."

"I'll be here when you get back."

"You'd better be. Naked."

And every time Blake came home, he took the long route. He thought he'd seen vehicles following him once or twice, but he'd managed to lose them, even in the Ford Focus he was now driving.

"They keep trying to lend me another Aston," he told me yesterday. "But it's too noticeable at the moment, so I've been putting them off. At least Jeff's given the engine in the Ford a bit of grunt."

The lack of Aston was another thing I felt guilty about, even if Blake assured me it didn't matter. How long could we keep living like this?

I looked at my watch. It was just after ten. I'd already ridden Murphy, whose general unhappiness with his new home had translated into a tantrum when he didn't want to go through a gate. After a quick check to make sure nobody was watching, I'd given up and jumped him over it instead. Blake wasn't due back until late afternoon, so I had plenty of time to exercise Harley then walk into the nearby village and pick up something for dinner. Cash only, of course.

"Ready for a ride, girl?"

Oddly enough, she didn't answer, just snuffled at my pockets looking for treats. She was still portly after her holiday, but as the grazing here was so poor, her belly would soon disappear. At least with the crappy food and all the worrying I'd lost weight myself. Antonio would have been thrilled. The irony was, Blake didn't seem to care whether I was carrying a few extra pounds or not.

Even if the stables were horrid, the same couldn't be said for the surrounding countryside. Once I'd tacked up and climbed on board, the network of bridleways and quiet lanes was a joy to explore, and Harley had her ears pricked forwards as I urged her into a canter. She settled into a steady pace as I thought about what to cook this evening. I'd downloaded *Fifty Dishes to Make in Your Microwave* onto Blake's eBook reader, and I was up to number thirteen. Risotto primavera. Hopefully, it would taste a bit better than the soggy pizza Blake had attempted yesterday.

"What do you think, Harley? Risotto? Or should we skip that and go onto the tuna sweet potato— Woah!"

Harley swerved to avoid the loose horse bolting around the bend, and I clung onto her mane to save myself from being ejected. With us blocking the path, the newcomer had no choice but to stop, and he backed up a few paces, snorting suspiciously.

He was black, or in Ishmael's words, midnight charcoal, a little smaller than Harley but with a wild look in his eye.

"All right, boy. Steady."

I hopped down and approached him quietly, hoping I didn't startle him and cause him to run off again. His reins trailed along the ground, broken at the buckle, and he snapped at me as I tried to take hold of them.

"Easy, easy."

He didn't look like a friendly sort.

And where was his rider?

I snagged the reins on my second attempt and set off in the direction he'd come from with both horses in tow. Harley didn't like him either. She kept firmly on my other side, using me as a buffer. Thanks, Harley. Still, at least it wasn't Murphy. If he'd seen the bastard snap, he'd have tried to sort it out, and that would have ended in tears and a bloody big vet bill.

Half a mile along the track, I saw a figure limping in the distance. The missing rider? It had to be, surely. As we got closer, I saw it was a girl, in her early twenties at a guess.

"This is yours, I take it?" I asked when we got within speaking distance.

She nodded and grimaced. "Unfortunately, yes."

Her jeans were muddy, and the headscarf she was wearing under her crash helmet had bits of twig stuck to it.

"Are you all right?"

Even under her dark skin, she still managed to look pale.

"I don't think anything is broken, but I twisted my ankle when I landed."

"Do you want me to call someone?"

She shook her head. "No, my father will flip out and send the helicopter. I'll manage."

Helicopter? Okay then.

The girl took a step towards me and winced as she put weight on her ankle.

"I'm not sure you should be walking. How about I give you a leg up onto your horse? I could tie the reins together, and then you'd be able to ride back."

Another shake of the head, more emphatic that time. "He's already thrown me three times this week. I don't want it happening a fourth."

"How far have you got to go?"

"Two miles. Three, maybe."

Harley gave me a nudge as well as an idea. "Then why don't you ride my horse? She won't do anything bad, I promise."

"Are you sure? She's very big."

"She's a gentle giant, and she's tired as well. We've been for a long ride already." And she wasn't Murphy, who liked to test out new riders to see how good they were at sticking on.

The girl went quiet, weighing up her options. Finally, she nodded. "Okay. If you're sure?"

"I'm sure."

I helped her on board, careful not to touch her sore ankle, and shortened her stirrups a hole. She looked tense, but I knew Harley would take care of her.

"Can I ride your horse back?" I asked because I didn't fancy walking either.

"I'm not sure it's a good idea. What if he gets you off as well?"

I was used to Murphy and his attempts to join the UK gymnastics team. "He won't; trust me."

"Well, you're welcome to him."

Sure enough, when my bum touched his saddle, the black monster launched into a series of handstands before trying a vicious spin. But it was all to no avail because I'd learned from the master. Thanks, Murph. I booted the git in the sides and hung on until he gave up.

The girl stared at us, wide eyed. "How did you manage to stay on him?"

"Practice, unfortunately. Come on, you sod. Walk on."

He did so grudgingly, dragging his feet, unhappy at having lost his game. Well, at least we were going forwards. On Murphy, we'd have been in reverse.

"What's his name?" I asked.

"Alvarez. And I'm Nurah Mansoor al-Qatari. What's

your name?"

Good question. What was I supposed to introduce myself as? As she'd used her surname, it would sound a bit odd if I only gave my first. So I opened my mouth, and what fell out was, "Mia. Mia Hunter. And my horse is Harley."

Nurah smiled for the first time, and it transformed her face. She had a mysterious look about her, like a princess from an old painting.

"Then thank you, Mia, for rescuing me and for helping me."

"It's no problem, honestly. Does Alvarez pull stunts like that often?"

"I'm not sure. Probably. I've only had him a fortnight. I begged and begged my father to let me have my own horse, and he went out and bought that monster. But if I tell him I've fallen off already, he'll sell him straight away and never let me have another."

"Do you know where he got him from?"

She named a dealer I unfortunately knew all too well.

"That guy's a shyster. He sells badly bred horses for a fortune then blames their behaviour on the new riders. I met someone who used to work for him once, and she said he used every trick in the book for viewings."

"What kind of tricks?"

"Lunging the horses beforehand until they're exhausted, restricting their food and water so they have no energy, and there's been rumours that he drugs them as well, but nobody's ever managed to catch him."

"My father got taken advantage of, then. He won't be happy about that if he finds out."

"You should tell him. There's no sense in carrying on with a horse you don't connect with."

"I'll have a think about it. Your horse is lovely. Have you had her long?"

"Since she was two, and she's eleven now."

We started chattering about horses, and I learned Nurah had learned to ride in Qatar, where she was from, before moving to the UK two months ago. Alvarez was supposed to be a show jumper, although I wasn't convinced. While he had the right breeding, he also had an attitude problem. I predicted he'd either be brilliant in the mould of Murphy or just plain awful.

"Do you keep him near to home?" I asked as we clattered along a narrow lane.

"I keep him at home. We have a couple of paddocks."

Well, didn't that turn out to be the understatement of the decade? When we rounded a bend, an imposing gateway lay ahead of us, complete with CCTV cameras and a guard hut. She waved to one of the men on duty as they opened up the gates for us.

Nurah and Harley led us down a long driveway before turning right into a stable complex I could only have dreamed of. Pristine boxes surrounded a paved courtyard, lush green fields rolled into the distance, and she even had an Olympic-sized arena. Rather than the stench of manure, the air was filled with the smell of money. Whoever owned this made Antonio look like he earned minimum wage.

A man wearing spotless white breeches rushed out to take Alvarez from me, confusion crossing his face as he tried to work out who I was and where the second horse had come from.

Nurah did the honours. "Rashid, this is Mia. I had a little mishap, and she helped me out."

"You are all right?"

"Yes, I'm fine." She turned to me. "Would you like to stay for lunch before you ride back?"

In this place? Hell, yes. It wasn't every day I got to visit a virtual palace, and I bet they didn't cook out of a microwave, either. The last time I'd been somewhere so posh was when Antonio dragged me to a castle in Italy for one of his business meetings. He'd ignored me all weekend before complaining my dress was too short, even though he'd chosen it.

But today, I could enjoy myself. "That would be lovely."

"Rashid, could you take Mia's horse and make her comfortable?"

"Of course, Your Excellency."

Sorry, what? Your what?

CHAPTER 31

I TRAILED AFTER Nurah as she walked towards the main house, waving off a uniformed man in a golf buggy who tried to give us a lift. It looked as if her ankle was feeling better.

"Did Rashid just call you 'Your Excellency?'"

"Yes. It's a bit embarrassing, really. I do wish he wouldn't, but father trains them like that."

"Who's your father?" I blurted.

"He's just a sheikh," she said, waving it off as if it was nothing. "And I'm only minor royalty on my mother's side."

Royalty? Sheesh. I tried to act as casually as she did, but I couldn't help being overawed by the amount of gold on display when we got into the house. Mansion. No, palace. The staff must spend half of their life polishing things. Lunch was served by a butler, who presented us with an array of crustless sandwiches and pastries arranged on delicate china.

"I couldn't even imagine living here," I said, finally giving up on trying to play it cool. "It's every little girl's dream."

"I would gladly swap with you. I don't have anyone to talk to all day apart from the staff. At least you can keep your horses at a stable with other people."

I told her some of my stories from the past week,

and she soon began laughing. "The yard owner actually told you that you had to pick the mud out of your horse's feet then put the bits back in the paddock it came from?"

"Yes, that honestly happened. Bonkers, isn't it?"

"What's bonkers? I'm not familiar with that word."

"It means crazy. I keep forgetting you're not from here. Your English is so good."

"Crazy, yes, that makes sense. I had an English tutor almost as soon as I began talking. Father said it was important to learn another language."

"I can just about order a meal in French. School wasn't really my thing. I spent most of my teenage years at the stables."

"It shows. Not many people could have stayed on Alvarez earlier. I know I couldn't. In fact, I'm not sure I ever want to ride him again."

"I'll have another go if you like." Monster or not, I was curious about him. "And you could try Harley. She'll take you around a course quite happily."

Sunshine flooded the room as Nurah smiled. "Oh, that would be lovely! Do you want to come over tomorrow?"

The chance to ride in her pristine arena without catty comments following me around? Yes, please. "I'm free all day."

"Then come in the morning. We can have lunch again too."

"Dammit!"

I stared at the bowl in the microwave. Somehow, the risotto was both crunchy and overly squidgy. Too much time? Not enough?

"Should I pick up a takeaway?" Blake asked from behind me.

I stopped what I was doing to throw my arms around him. "Missed you."

"Same, babe." He dropped a couple of carrier bags and peered at my dodgy dinner attempt. "What is it?"

"Not edible, that's for sure. What's in the bags?"

"Shirts, Trojans, pens, energy drinks, hair gel, keyrings, tiling grout. There's more shit in the car."

"Tiling grout?"

"New sponsor." He wrinkled his nose. "I'm not sure about that one."

"How was testing?"

"Good. Really good. I knocked half a second off my best time. How was your day? Those bitches at the yard still getting you down?"

"It was...interesting."

Blake let out a low whistle when I told him where I'd ended up. "You'll be ditching me for the rich and famous soon, then?"

"No chance! I'm not going to say no to borrowing Nurah's show jumps, though."

Blake gave me a hug. "I'm glad you've found a friend. And I can't say I'm upset that they've got decent security. I worry about you here by yourself when I have to go out."

My heart did a little flip. It was nice to have someone who cared. Not to mention someone who gave me at least two orgasms every night and looked hot in a pair of boxer briefs. I was well and truly spoiled.

Blake picked up a fork and prodded dinner. "Shall I go out for fish and chips?"

"I'll love you forever if you do."

He grinned. "Babe, you'll love me forever anyway."

He was absolutely right about that.

The next week brought a new routine. I headed to the yard early each morning and rode Murphy, then while he spent the day in the field, I took Harley over to Nurah's. Blake was right about her too—it was good to have a friend. Although we came from different backgrounds, she was only a few years younger than me, and we had plenty to talk about. Each morning, I'd give her a lesson on Harley, we'd eat lunch, and in the afternoons, I tackled the problem that was Alvarez.

He was a grumpy sod, but there was more to it. Once I'd spent a bit more time with him, I was sure of that.

"Have you had the vet check him?" I asked Nurah.

"He passed a vetting when father bought him."

"Who did it? Your own vet?"

"No, the seller suggested one."

And he was probably crooked. It wasn't unusual for dodgy dealers to have connections to a number of equally dubious characters. "I think you should get your own vet out to give him a look over and maybe scope him for ulcers."

"Ulcers?"

"In his stomach."

He often flinched when I touched his back and

sides, and his hatred of everyone and everything spoke of underlying discomfort.

"I'll get Rashid to make an appointment right away. Do you want to stay and watch a movie? We have a movie theatre."

Of course they did. And, it turned out, a chef who served popcorn in a gold-plated bowl. Nurah preferred rom-coms against Blake's thrillers, and we settled back for a nice dose of cheese and giggles.

"Thank you for staying with me," Nurah said when the credits rolled. "I've been a little lonely."

"Thanks for inviting me. Do you miss Qatar a lot?"

"In some ways. I miss my friends, and I miss the rest of my family, but I was glad to come and support my father in his new business venture. The cooler weather is a nice change as well. And in the future, I hope to make more new friends."

I held up my glass of cola. "To new friends."

She clinked it with her own glass. "I agree, to new friends. Maybe we could go out together one day? To one of the big horse shows?"

I was trying to think of a way to politely decline when she carried on.

"What about Olympia? My father will get us a private box to watch from."

"He doesn't mind paying for things like that?"

"Not at all. And I'm lucky he's quite liberal. As long as I don't do anything that will cause him shame, he lets me choose my own hobbies."

The chances of Antonio spotting me in a private box were slim, and he'd never expect me to be hanging out with Qatari dignitaries. "In that case, I'd love to go."

When I arrived at Nurah's palace the next day, she rushed up and hugged me, holding her headscarf on in the wind. "You were right! Alvarez does have ulcers. The vet's given him some medicine."

"That's good news. Not that he's got ulcers, but that he's getting them treated. You might find he turns out to be a different horse."

"I do hope so. He's so difficult as he is." She gave Harley a pat. "Can I jump her again today?"

"Of course."

Nurah was a sympathetic rider, and she listened. It was a pleasure to teach her because I could see it was making a difference. As she went around the course I'd set up for the second time, I noticed a dark-haired man leaning on the fence nearby, watching us. Another man hovered behind him, wearing a suit and tie accessorised with an earpiece.

As Nurah cleared the last fence, she squealed with joy. "Father, did you see?"

The dark-haired man broke into a grin. "I did. You looked very impressive."

"Harley's amazing. She's my dream horse."

He turned to me. "How much to buy her? Name your price."

"She's not for sale."

"Everything is for sale."

I shook my head firmly. "Not Harley." Not when I'd fought tooth and nail to keep her for so many years. First when I'd put up with Antonio, then when we'd escaped from France. "Nurah's welcome to ride her, though."

"In that case, why don't you keep her here? It will save you from having to bring her every day."

"Murphy could stay here too," chipped in Nurah. "Couldn't he, father? He's Mia's other horse."

He gave his daughter an indulgent smile. "Of course. Whatever makes you happy."

"You'll come, won't you?" she asked me.

"I'm not sure I'll have enough money for livery here."

Her father scoffed. "We don't need your money. Seeing my daughter smile is payment enough."

I really didn't like the other yard, and neither did the horses. Keeping them with Nurah would be a dream come true. "I could offer lessons on Harley in return and help with Alvarez."

"Then we have a deal."

Nurah let out a whoop that made Harley skip sideways. "That's awesome! We'll have so much fun. How soon can you come? Tomorrow? Please say you'll come tomorrow?"

"I can send men to help," her father offered.

But I didn't want to be beholden to him any more than I had to. "How about I bring Harley tomorrow and Murphy the day after? My boyfriend will help me bring my equipment."

"I'll ask Rashid to prepare two stables for you."

When I got home and explained the new development to Blake, he was only too happy to assist.

"Thank goodness you'll be out of that shitty place. You sure you're okay riding over? I can fetch the lorry if you want to take both horses together."

"Best not." I was still worried about Antonio's eyes everywhere. "I reckon we'll fit everything into the car if we make two trips."

"Shame I didn't borrow a car with a bigger boot, eh?"

I was just grateful we had a car at all. "Nurah's place isn't that far away."

"I've got to admit, I'm curious about it. The way you've described it, it's like a palace."

"That's what I call it: The palace."

"Kind of appropriate for you, princess."

"Oh, don't get all gushy on me."

He picked me up and threw me over his shoulder. "Don't worry about that. I've got other plans, and they don't involve talking."

Nurah was waiting the next morning when I clattered up the drive, Blake following slowly behind in the Focus. We'd managed to fit a surprising amount of gear into the back, although it would need a good vacuum out afterwards.

As soon as we got close enough, I hopped off to do the introductions.

"Nurah, this is Blake."

Her blush didn't escape me as she held out her hand. He kissed it á la Angus, the smooth git. Thank goodness her father wasn't around.

"I'm... I'm uh... Nurah Mansoor al-Qatari."

He grinned. "Lovely to meet you."

She gave her head a small shake and smoothed her

headscarf down. "Well, yes, let me show you through to the stables."

Rashid ran out and helped Blake to unload the car while Nurah followed me into Harley's new home.

"He's hot and very sweet." She sighed. "You're so lucky."

"You'll find your Prince Charming one day."

"All the princes I've met are anything but charming," she replied, totally serious.

"Have you met a lot of princes?"

"Enough. Father wants me to marry one someday."

"Like an arranged marriage?"

"I'm not keen on the idea, but he doesn't want me to stay single for the rest of my life. Unless I can find someone suitable by the age of twenty-five, he and mother will step in."

I lifted Harley's saddle off and hung it on the rack outside. "How long does that give you?"

"Three years."

"That's quite a while."

"Not when I'm in a new country. I'm not so great at meeting people."

"You met me."

She choked out a laugh. "Maybe I should try riding Alvarez again? See if I can fall off in front of a man this time."

"That's a little drastic."

"Do you have any better ideas?"

"I'll have a think about it."

Harley settled in straight away. Her new stable was twice the size of her old one, and after she'd had a roll, she tucked into her hay. Alvarez gave a dirty look from the stable next door before he went back to his dinner.

Grumpy sod. He'd been on Gastrogard for his ulcers for two days now, and although it was too early to see much improvement, at least he hadn't tried to bite me today.

"That place is a bit of a step up for them, isn't it?" said Blake as we drove back to Pond Cottage.

"Yep. All we need now is a house where it only rains outside and we'll be sorted."

"I was thinking I might start having a look around. See what else there is to rent. If the horses are happy, we could stay in this area. Brandon doesn't live too far away, when he's home, and Lexi's always moaning that the house in Kent doesn't have big enough bathrooms. We could all have a fresh start."

"Are you serious?"

"About you? Always."

Things were finally, finally coming together. That night, as Blake held me in his arms and his warmth seeped through me, I finally allowed myself to dream of a future with him.

CHAPTER 32

"MURPHY, WILL YOU get on with it!"

First, he didn't like coming to the yard by Pond Cottage, but now it seemed he didn't want to leave it.

The lady who owned the place looked on with a scowl. She hadn't been impressed when I announced we were moving on so soon, but I hadn't been impressed by her using Murphy's water bucket to weed her garden, so I figured we were even.

"I'm so sorry!" I called to the girl whose wheelbarrow he'd just backed into, which caused him to leap forward as if it had attacked him.

At least he went in the direction of the gate.

"It's for your own good, you idiot," I told him as he finally condescended to walk down the lane. "A palace awaits you. You get better grass and a bigger bed."

I left out the part about Alvarez and his grumpiness. Even though Murphy probably couldn't understand a word I was saying, I didn't want to take the chance. Sometimes animals were smarter than we thought.

A quick glance at my watch said that despite Murphy's escapades, we weren't running too late. Nurah was expecting us at ten thirty, and Blake would be over later with the last of my stuff once he'd finished a call with the PR lady at Aston Martin.

"Murphy, walk on. It's a flipping leaf."

Killer leaf, more like. It flapped in the road and Murphy leapt over it. Good grief, horse.

A car sounded from around the bend, going too fast, and I squashed Murphy against the hedge. *Dammit, slow down, you idiot*. There wasn't anywhere for me to go—the steep banks at the side of the road were lined with trees, and I'd passed the last driveway fifty yards back. At least we were on a straight bit, which would give the wannabe racing driver time to see me and stop.

And he did.

The gleaming new Mercedes slewed to a halt across the road, and its driver got out and stood with his arms folded, glaring at me. Oh, shit! I looked behind me for an escape route, but Antonio's men had already covered that. An SUV parked at an angle blocked the way.

How was I supposed to get out of here? Unless I could fly, all the exits were blocked. I briefly thought of Nurah and her helicopter, and the absurdity of getting plucked from Murphy by a dangling bodyguard made me smile for a second.

"I don't know what you're laughing at, Amelia," Antonio said. "Nothing about this is funny."

I sobered up right away. "I'm well aware of that."

I couldn't help being a little snarky. He brought out the worst in me, and over the past few weeks with Blake, Antonio's power had diminished. While he still scared the crap out of me, I'd started to find my personality again.

"You stole from me, you little bitch."

"I borrowed. And it was partly my money that paid

for that horsebox."

My words might have been strong, but I was trembling inside. Murphy felt that and started fidgeting. He'd always been overly sensitive.

"Not just the horsebox, Amelia. What about my fucking wallet? I need it back, and I need it back now."

His wallet? What wallet? "I didn't take your wallet. Wait—was it in the horsebox?"

"Don't play dumb, Amelia. It doesn't become you. You know perfectly well it wasn't in the horsebox. If you give it back now, I might let you live."

"But I don't have it!"

"You never used to be a liar, Amelia. Is that *his* influence? That racing driver you've been fucking?"

"It's not like that."

"You mean you didn't spread your legs for him before my bed was even cold? If you'd shown that slutty side before you took off in the middle of the night, I wouldn't have had to turn elsewhere."

"You're blaming your adultery on me?"

"Oh, don't be so touchy, Amelia. You know none of those women meant anything to me. It was always you I came home to at night, at least until you betrayed me. I'll ask again, where's my damned wallet?"

He started to advance, but when Murphy stood on his back legs and waved his front ones around, Antonio paused.

"One request, Amelia, and it's such a straightforward one. If you can't manage to accommodate that, you're even more of a traitor than I thought."

It wasn't a request. He never requested; he ordered. And I really didn't have any idea what he was talking about. We were in a stand-off, Murphy wouldn't keep still, and I was freaking out. I looked at the banks again, searching for a gap in the trees big enough to fit a horse through.

"No point in trying to escape, Amelia. I'll hunt you down like the bitch you've become. And I'll always find you. You're running out of friends, and it's easy enough to find somebody who'll sell you out."

I tried to stop the tears that threatened, but it felt hopeless. I was trapped, by circumstances as well as two vehicles. A cruel grin spread across Antonio's face, the one he always used to show before he did something really nasty. I thought he was going to try and hurt me with his words again, but he climbed into his car instead.

"I'll give you a taste of what's to come. It'll be worth a dented bonnet to break that bloody nag's leg." He slammed the door and started the engine.

Murphy shot backwards at the noise, and I'd only just got him under control when Antonio accelerated.

Surely he wasn't going to...he was...he was bloody going to hit us! It would be a battle of one horsepower against hundreds, and I had a split second to make a decision.

So I made the only one I could.

"Canter!" I screamed at Murphy, digging my heels into his sides.

He was surprised enough to do what he was told, and a second later we hurtled towards Antonio's car in a crazy game of chicken. But I had a trick that he didn't.

I just caught the look of shock on Antonio's face as Murphy took off, then the car was underneath us and we were clear. The narrow lane gave us a further advantage as Antonio couldn't turn around easily. I galloped Murphy a hundred yards, two hundred, praying he didn't slip, then made a sharp turn onto the nearest bridleway. A couple of tree-trunks across the entrance to stop fly-tippers left Antonio unable to follow.

We slowed to a canter as I fumbled in my pocket for my phone. Blake answered on the second ring.

"Get out! Get out!"

"What? Mia, is that you?"

"Yes, it's me. You need to leave. Antonio's in the lane by the stables and if he knows about the cottage, he could be there any second."

"Where are you? Are you okay?"

"I'm on Murphy, and I'm heading to Nurah's. I'll meet you there."

I almost dropped my phone as Murphy dodged a fallen tree, so I stuffed it back into my pocket and concentrated on riding. Now that Murphy had got over his initial reluctance to do any exercise, he'd decided to make the best of things. Or perhaps he was just humouring the woman bouncing around on top of him because she was clearly mad.

I smelled burnt rubber in the air as I neared Nurah's, and I knew Blake would be waiting for me, having driven like a lunatic to get there. He was parked just inside the gate, and I steadied Murphy to a sensible speed as I approached the gatehouse. The guard outside looked a little concerned.

"Are you all right, ma'am?"

"I am now." How much of the truth should I tell? "Some idiot with road rage couldn't get past me in the lane, and he tried to run me down."

"Should I call the police?"

"I expect he's long gone, and I didn't get his registration number, so I'm not sure there's much point."

As the gates closed behind me, the guard resumed his watch, and I slithered off Murphy into Blake's waiting arms. He held me tight, and that was the only thing that stopped me from falling all the way to the ground.

"What the hell happened? You scared the shit out of me with that phone call."

"Can we get out of sight? Please?"

He kept his arm around me as we walked up to the stable yard, and I put a sweating Murphy into the box Rashid had prepared for him. I'd only just got his saddle off before he was down and rolling.

"What happened?" Blake asked again.

"Antonio was in the lane. He threatened to kill me, and then he tried to do it."

"What? How the hell did he do that? Did he have a gun or something?"

"No, he tried to run me over with his car. Murphy jumped it."

Blake's mouth dropped open, but it was Nurah who spoke. She must have walked in without us noticing. "You did what? You jumped a car? No way!"

"I didn't have a lot of choice. Murphy was a star, but he's going to be stiff in the morning, the poor thing."

"Why was the driver trying to hit you?"

I sank down onto the ground outside Murphy's stable. Blake sat next to me and gathered me into his arms while Nurah remained standing with an "I'm waiting" expression on her face.

I had to tell her. I couldn't risk putting her in danger, and no matter what Antonio thought of me, I couldn't lie to her either. Not when she'd been so kind to me. I started at the beginning, glossing over what Antonio did to me, but finishing with his attempt to break Murphy's legs.

"That... that... I don't even have words for him. Well, I do, but I'm not supposed to use those ones."

"Don't worry, I'm thinking them."

"What are you going to do?"

"I'll have to give the horsebox back and hope he doesn't make good on his threat to hunt me down. I don't know why he thinks I've got his wallet. I didn't take it, so I can't give it back."

"Then I wonder why he thinks you do?" Blake asked. "Maybe he left it in the lorry somewhere and forgot?"

"I don't see how he could have. He always kept it in his pocket."

His pocket... I thought back to the night I left. Antonio had been asleep on the bed when I'd snuck out to the stables. I'd pulled on my jeans and a sweater, and then because it was cold, I'd picked up a jacket. I pictured the scene. Two team jackets, lying next to each other on the sofa in the hotel room...

"I need to get to the horsebox," I said.

"Why?"

"I've got an idea about the wallet, and I need to check something."

"Do you think he knows what car I'm driving?" Blake asked.

"I don't know."

"We can take mine," Nurah offered. "It has tinted windows."

She forgot to mention that it also came with a chauffeur-slash-bodyguard. He held the door of the limousine open as Nurah led us over.

"Hassan, this Mia Hunter and her boyfriend Blake... I'm sorry, I never caught your surname."

Oh, please. Kill me now.

Blake gave me a sideways glance. "Hunter. Blake Hunter."

Nurah paused, one foot in the car. "I didn't think you were married?"

"We're not. Yet," Blake added under his breath.

Did he really say that? I was shaking as we climbed into the car behind Nurah.

"Uh, I didn't give you my proper name when we first met," I confessed. "Because of the situation, and I didn't know you, and..."

She waved a hand. "I understand. I've done it myself back home when I've got sick of people bowing at my feet. So, what is your real name?"

"Amelia Stanbrook."

Her eyes widened. "As in *the* Amelia Stanbrook? Who won the show jumping final at Olympia last year?"

"I got lucky when one of the Whitakers knocked a fence down."

"Oh my goodness! I should have recognised you, but your hair... It's so different. Usually it's long and red, right? And Harley is Harlequin's Heart?"

I nodded.

Nurah clutched at her chest. "I can't believe I've been riding her!"

"You've done a good job of it too."

Nurah bombarded me with horsey questions while Blake shook his head in bemusement, and for a moment I forgot about why we were there and where we were going. But all too soon, the driver buzzed on the intercom.

"We're ten minutes away, ma'am."

Safely behind the privacy screen, talk returned to the subject of Antonio.

"How did he know where to look for us?" Blake asked.

My conversation with Antonio had happened so quickly, I'd barely processed anything but the death threat. Now I went over it in more detail. "He said there was no point in us trying to run because he'd find me. He said there would always be someone willing to sell me out."

"Only if there's a bastard like him willing to pay." Blake paused and turned to Nurah. "Excuse my French."

"What French?"

I rolled my eyes. "He means excuse his bad language."

"Ah. If you want to say that in French, you should say *salaud*."

"I thought you didn't swear?"

She pressed a finger to her lips. "Not in front of my parents."

Blake chuckled. "Okay, back to the conversation. Who told Antonio where we were? Hardly anybody knew."

"Lexi and Brandon knew, but surely it wasn't them?"

"No way."

"Antonio's sister?"

"She didn't know about the cottage." But that reminded me—I did need to message her.

"I didn't say anything," Nurah said. "I promise."

"I didn't think for a minute that you had."

With the amount of money Nurah had, she'd never need to take a bribe. But Holly... She was always short of cash. Could I have been sold out by my oldest friend? That idea left me cold.

The driver buzzed through again. "We've reached our destination."

I got the jitters as we drew to a halt outside Jeff's warehouse. If the chauffeur hadn't got out and opened the door, I might have been tempted to stay in the car. What if my guess was wrong?

But Nurah was already climbing out, looking out of place in perfectly fitted jeans, jewelled ballet pumps, and a colourful tunic.

"How do we get inside?" she asked.

I gripped Blake's hand as he knocked on the small door at the side. Jeff opened it a minute later, wiping his hands on a rag, and smiled wide.

"You lucky sod. Two pretty ladies this time?"

Blake gave him a man-hug. "Must be the aftershave."

"Didn't think I'd be seeing you for a while. You come to take the lorry?"

"We just need to pick something up from it."

Jeff opened the door wider and waved us inside. "Well, you know where it is."

Blake fetched the key from a box on the wall while Nurah and I picked our way over amid half-built cars. The Ferrari was gone, replaced by something equally sleek and sporty looking.

"I should learn to drive," Nurah said. "Sometimes having a chauffeur take me everywhere can be so embarrassing."

"At least you don't need to worry about finding a parking space."

"I suppose."

As soon as Blake opened the door, I climbed on board and switched on the lights. Where had I left the jacket? I certainly hadn't worn it since the day I left. I hadn't wanted another reminder of Antonio. In fact, if I'd been thinking straight in France, I would have burned the damn thing. I rummaged through the storage lockers and eventually found the offending garment stored in a bench seat under one of Harley's rugs. Now, was it mine or Antonio's? He was only one size bigger, so it was hard to tell.

I held my breath as I dipped my hand into the inside pocket then released it as I came out with a black leather wallet.

"This is what he wanted," I said.

Blake peered over my shoulder. "Well, there's a stack of cash in it."

I quickly counted it. "Two thousand euros and another grand in sterling. But that's nothing to Antonio. He paid for most things in cash. Always said he hated the idea of big brother tracking his purchases."

With hindsight, I suspected a chunk of that cash probably found its way into the hands of hookers.

"If it's nothing to him, then why was he so bothered about it?"

"I don't know. He could have just cancelled his

credit cards and got new ones. Maybe it was a matter of principle? He can be a total aresehole about things like that."

"Even so... Are you sure there's nothing else?"

I shook the contents out onto the table. A business card for a car dealer. A couple of receipts. I squinted at them—one for a haircut and another for a meal for two where the second person certainly wasn't me. Then...what was that? I held it up.

"A memory card?" Blake said.

"It looks like the one out of his camera."

"Maybe that's what he was so worried about. I wonder what's on it?"

"I've got no idea. We'll need a computer to find out. Is yours still at the cottage?"

"Yes, and we can't go back there at the moment."

Nurah clapped her hands together. "No problem. I have a laptop. Let's go!"

CHAPTER 33

BACK AT THE palace, Nurah brought her brand-new, state-of-the-art laptop into the lounge.

"I don't know how it all works. I only use it for chatting with my friends back home and surfing the internet."

Blake lined the card up with the correct slot in the side. "I hope there's nothing dodgy on this. No viruses or anything."

Nurah waved a hand. "Doesn't matter. If it breaks, I'll just buy another one. This is so exciting! Nothing interesting ever happens to me, unless you count the time my friend Hameed's yacht broke down and we got rescued by the navy."

I'd much rather have her brand of excitement. I was sure I could put up with being stuck on a yacht for a few days, especially if it had music and a sun deck, which Hameed's undoubtedly did.

Blake pushed the card in, and the three of us crowded around the screen.

What a letdown.

"It's just photos of me," I said. "And they're not even very good ones. Why on earth would Antonio care about them? It's not like he's my biggest fan."

Blake nodded. "Yeah, it's odd. Maybe he put the card in there and forgot about it, and he only wanted the wallet back because he's a prick. The card's so small; it could have been in there for months without him noticing."

"I don't think so." I pointed at one of the photos. "That one's recent. He took it at the show in Cannes. And the shot next to it is from the trip before when we went to Germany. He seems to have one from each place we've been for the last couple of years."

I could follow the timeline by my face. I looked more miserable with every venue we visited.

"What if he just wanted to have a reminder of you with him? I know I would."

"But why these particular photos? You can't even see my face in some of them, and the one on the end's out of focus."

"Maybe there is something else on the card?" suggested Nurah. "A hidden file, perhaps?"

Blake closed down the image browser and looked at the list of files, then fiddled with the settings so hidden files were shown. Nothing more appeared.

"There must be something on here. There just has to be," I said.

Antonio was petty, but he'd seemed more worried about his wallet than the horsebox. And the horsebox was worth thousands.

Blake fished out his phone. "I've got an idea. I need to make a call or two."

Well, I was glad he had an idea because I was all out.

"Can I borrow your laptop for a bit longer?" I asked Nurah. "I need to let Antonio's sister know I'm okay."

"His sister? Isn't it dangerous to contact her?"

"She doesn't like him either."

"Then please, go ahead."

The red message icon was flashing when I logged onto the Show Jumping World website. Alyssa's message was short and sweet.

Do you know why Antonio's car has a horseshoe-shaped dent in the back?
A

I typed back an equally brief reply.

Murphy. But we got away safely.
Amelia.

The less said at the moment, the better. I trusted Alyssa, but I didn't trust Antonio not to find her computer and go through her internet history.

"Poor girl, having to live with those vile people," Nurah said.

"I feel so awful for leaving her there."

"Maybe in time you'll be able to see her again."

"I hope so. I really hope so."

Blake came back a few minutes later, smiling. "I've found someone to take a look at this memory card. Any chance we can borrow the car again?"

"Of course. But can we just wait while I have the chef pack some lunch for us to take along?"

I stifled a giggle. Nurah really did live in another world, but you know what? I was enjoying being a part of it for the afternoon.

"Lunch sounds wonderful," I said.

An hour later, we were back in air-conditioned luxury with a basket of snacks spread out on the fold-down table between us. I sank back into one of the leather seats and tried not to sigh.

"This might even be better than the Aston," Blake said.

"So who's this person we're going to see?"

"Some dude Brandon went to school with. He's a computer genius. I remembered Brandon telling me how he got suspended from school when he got caught hacking into the police database to erase his brother's speeding ticket."

"He can't be that good if the police caught him."

"The police didn't catch him, the teacher did. He looked over Aidan's shoulder and wanted to know where the pie chart he was supposed to be drawing was."

When we got to Aidan's nondescript bungalow in Brackley, he was as excited as Nurah.

"It's not often I try to solve a computer-related problem. Usually, I'm the one creating them."

"You're still a hacker?" I asked.

"Mostly white hat now. I get paid to find the flaws in big companies' networks."

Mostly? I didn't want to know.

Aidan led us into his dimly lit basement, which had more computers whirring away than a branch of PC World. Judging by how pale he was, he didn't get out much.

"Let's see it, then."

Blake handed over the memory card, and Aidan held it up between his thumb and forefinger, studying it as if it would tell him the meaning of life. "Did you scan it for viruses?"

Three blank looks answered his question.

He gave a long, drawn-out sigh. "People like you are why I can cause so much mayhem."

He inserted the card into his laptop and got to work while the rest of us cleared old takeaway boxes from a sofa so we could sit down.

"This is so exciting!" Nurah whispered.

Really? I could think of a thousand other things I'd rather have been doing. Mucking out, sweeping, cleaning tack...

"It's clean, no viruses," Aidan announced a few minutes later.

"Is there anything hidden?" Blake asked.

He worked away for a bit longer. "Not on the card itself, but there's something odd about these photos."

"What do you mean odd?"

"You ever hear of steganography?"

"Is that some sort of dinosaur?"

Aidan rolled his eyes. "It's the art of concealing data within other data. It started out in Ancient Greece, where they sent secret messages by shaving the head of the messenger, tattooing his head, then letting his hair grow back. When he got to where he was going, they'd shave his head again and voila, all would be revealed."

"What have head tattoos got to do with our files?" Blake asked.

"Because in the same way as the writing was hidden then, you can hide information now in computer files. By replacing some unused parts of a file with different data, you can send messages."

My heart started thumping. Could this be the answer we were looking for? "And you think those photos might have hidden data?"

"I'd say there's a good possibility. Some of the file

sizes are too large for the image quality."

"Can you find out what they say?"

"I'll do my best, but it won't be instant. If someone's gone to this much trouble, then I'd put money on the files being encrypted as well."

"So now we just wait?"

"*You* just wait. *I* work like the under-appreciated genius I am."

"Is there anything we can do to help?" Nurah asked.

"I could do with some energy drinks. And a couple of family-sized bags of Wotsits."

"Certainly. We'll get those right away. No problem."

Once we were back in the car, she gave Blake and me a panicked look. "Where do we buy energy drinks? And what are Wotsits?"

Oh, Nurah.

"We can buy energy drinks in a petrol station or a supermarket, and Wotsits are delicious crispy nuggets of empty calories, coated in orange cheesy powder that stains your fingers," Blake explained.

"I don't think we have those at home."

No, she probably didn't. Her chef would no doubt have a heart attack if he found those in his kitchen.

"Then we need to go to a supermarket."

"Okay." She buzzed on the intercom. "Hassan, please take us to a supermarket."

Blake choked back a laugh.

"What?" she asked.

"Nothing."

We drove around until we found a Sainsbury's, and all heads turned to stare at the limo when Hassan pulled up outside the front door. I got that. Probably it wasn't every day a guy who looked like an extra from a

James Bond film arrived to buy groceries with royalty, minor or not. Thankfully, the gawkers got distracted by his smart suit as he shepherded Nurah inside, leaving Blake and me to slink in after her.

"Now what?" Nurah asked.

I headed for the trolleys. "Have you ever been to a supermarket before?"

"Our housekeeper does that."

I passed the trolley to Blake and steered her towards the produce section. "What about clothes shopping?"

"People bring things to the house for me to try on. Oh, but we go to Harrods occasionally. Does that count?"

"Sort of. When you said you wanted to find your own husband, what type of man did you have in mind?"

"I don't know. Someone normal, I guess. A man who respects me for who I am, not because of what my father's money can buy."

"I hate to tell you this, but normal men don't hang out in Harrods."

"You think I should go out more?"

"It might be a good start."

She managed a small smile. "Could you help me?"

"Of course. Let's start with the supermarket and work our way up, okay?"

"How does this work?"

"Just pick what you want from the shelves and put it into the trolley."

Her head swivelled from side to side as she took in the delights of the dairy aisle and the bakery.

"Anything?"

"Anything."

While Blake and I rounded up Aidan's requests, Nurah made her own selections. I wasn't sure what her father was going to say about the fizzy cola bottles or frozen pizza.

"Who's birthday is it?" I asked, seeing the cake she'd added to the trolley.

"Nobody's. I just thought it looked nice."

"Fair enough."

When we got back, Aidan was engrossed in his screen. His mother let us in, and he gave us a thumbs up when we laid his goodies next to him.

"I'll give you a call when I find something, yeah?"

Blake opened a can of energy drink for him. "Thanks, mate."

We reversed out quietly. There was nothing more we could do for the moment.

Back at Nurah's, we gathered in one of the lounges while a maid looked in horror at the carrier bags full of junk food we'd brought back with us.

"I will hide this from Mr. Mansoor, ma'am."

Nurah held up a hand before the maid disappeared. "Please could you bring a knife for the cake?"

I wasn't in the mood for cake. Now that the excitement over the memory card had simmered down, my mind was reeling at the thought of Holly betraying me.

"It must have been Holly," I blurted.

Blake wrapped an arm around me. "I had the same thought."

"Who's Holly?" Nurah asked.

"My oldest friend. We used to live together before I met Antonio, but when he came onto the scene, we grew apart. He wasn't keen on me being close to anyone." I screwed my eyes shut. "But *Holly?* She doesn't even like Antonio."

"Could she have changed?"

"I don't know. Maybe. I don't see who else it could have been."

"Do you feel up to calling her?"

About as much as I felt like running the Marathon de Sables wearing an antique diving suit. But I knew I had to do it anyway. It was another piece of the jigsaw puzzle we were trying to put together.

Blake handed me my French phone, and I dialled reluctantly.

"Holly?"

"Amelia! How's the cottage?"

"It was great until Antonio came to visit."

"He what?"

I told her about being trapped between Antonio and his men in the lane. "Murphy got me out of it, though. He took off at exactly the right moment, and Antonio drove right underneath him."

She laughed, but it sounded forced. "That was some going. It's not every horse that can clear a Mercedes."

"Who said anything about a Mercedes?"

The last time she had seen Antonio, I was bruised in the passenger seat, and he was driving his Porsche. He'd only bought the Mercedes after the crash in France. There was silence at the other end of the line, and I knew then that it was her. The friend I'd once shared everything with had betrayed me.

"Amelia, I can explain," she said.

"Oh good, because I'm dying to hear it. Quite literally, if Antonio catches up with me again."

"He came to see me. He said you'd had a breakdown. That you weren't thinking straight, and he wanted to get you the help you needed."

"That's bullshit. You know what he did to me. I didn't need any more of his help."

I thought back to Antonio's comment about selling out. Nurah's father had said it too—everything is for sale. And everyone, it seemed.

"How much did he pay you?"

There was silence again. Then, finally, so quietly I could barely hear, "Enough."

And I'd heard enough. I hung up and burst into tears.

"Babe, I'm so sorry," Blake said, hugging me.

Nurah's arms wrapped around me as well. "What she did wasn't right. How can I help to make things better?"

"I don't suppose you know of a hotel around here?" I choked out.

"We have a guest house. You and Blake will just have to pretend you're sleeping in separate rooms."

"You've done too much already."

"I insist. Besides, then we can ride in the morning. It will be fun." She smiled her radiant smile, trying to cheer me up.

I hated to take advantage of her, but the thought of driving around and trying to find somewhere else to stay when Antonio was looking for us made me sweat. If he could bribe Holly, surely he'd be willing to fork over a few quid to a hotel receptionist.

"I don't even have a change of clothes."

"You can borrow some of mine. And tomorrow, we can go normal shopping, yes?"

"We'll need to be careful I'm not seen."

"I can have father clear out the store."

I raised an eyebrow at her, and she shrunk an inch.

"That's not normal, is it?"

I shook my head.

"Okay, how about we drive to a different town?"

"That could work."

Nurah's guest house turned out to be almost as big as Antonio's home, and ten times as blingy. I needed sunglasses as I walked into the lounge.

"At least if it rains, we won't need to empty buckets," I said to Blake, trying to make light of things.

"And at least if Antonio turns up, the guards can deal with him."

There was, of course, that too.

Chapter 34

I FELT A little out of place the next morning, dressed in one of Nurah's sparkly tunics, a headscarf, and a pair of jeans, but Blake assured me I looked pretty and there was no way Antonio would recognise me. Even if he did, the bodyguard Nurah's father had provided for our trip to London would have squashed him like a bug.

Her father had visited over breakfast, and I'd worried he might object to us staying there, but once he realised that Blake was Blake Hunter, racing driver, his eyes lit up.

"Some associates and I are building a new racing circuit out in Qatar. I don't suppose you'd have a few hours to give me a driver's perspective on the matter?"

Blake shrugged. "Sure. I was planning to take the girls shopping today, but tomorrow I'm free."

"Shopping?" He raised an eyebrow at his daughter.

"Father, I want to try going by myself."

"There is no need for that."

"I know, but it'll be a new experience, and Mia said she'd come with me."

"Fine. As long as Hassan drives you in the limousine. And you'll need to take Khalid too. Do you remember the PIN number for your credit card?"

"Yes, father."

The sheikh dug a roll of cash out of his pocket. "And

take this in case you get hungry."

What did he think we were going to eat? Solid gold burgers?

"And Blake, if my men are escorting the girls, you'll have time to talk about my race circuit, no?"

I sensed the relief in Blake's eyes at his narrow escape. He was terribly patient, but trailing around boutiques would have been a chore, even for him.

"I'll have all day."

Shopping with Nurah turned out to be an interesting experience. The car dropped us at the door of each shop, and Khalid glowered as we giggled our way through clothes, make-up, toiletries, and jewellery. I tried to spend my own money, but Nurah wouldn't hear of it.

"Father pays my credit card bill anyway, and he won't even notice the extra."

"Are you sure?"

"Back home, my friend Fatemah bought an airplane one month and her father didn't say a word."

"Are you serious?"

"Yes! And you know what was really funny?"

"What?"

"She's scared of flying."

We both dissolved into laughter, but mine was partly due to incredulity. I didn't know what planet Nurah and her friends lived on, but it sure was entertaining to take the occasional trip there.

And when we stumbled in late that evening,

groaning under the weight of our bags, I found Blake had got an invite of his own.

"Did you buy enough stuff?" he asked.

"This is only part of it," Nurah told him.

His eyes widened as Hassan and Khalid staggered in with the rest.

"Do I have any money left?"

I put a finger to my lips. We'd discuss that later.

Blake nodded his understanding. "Have you eaten?"

"We got dinner out."

"In Harrods," Nurah added.

Okay, so we'd taken a small break from "normal."

"Then how about we all have an early night?"

Nurah took the hint. Actually, I don't think she realised it even was a hint. She yawned, covering her mouth delicately with her hand. "Good idea. I'm so tired after real shopping. Can we ride tomorrow morning?"

"Of course."

Sweet though Nurah was, it was lovely to be alone with Blake again. We mussed up the sheets in one room then fell into bed together in the other. Luckily, he'd had a couple of Trojans stashed in his wallet when we ran from Antonio, and we made good use of them.

"Gonna have to take a trip to the chemist tomorrow for supplies, Mia Hunter."

My cheeks went pinker than they already were. "I didn't mean to call myself that. It just slipped out."

He dipped down and kissed me on the nose. "Keep the name, babe."

I didn't know what to say to that, so chicken that I was, I snuggled into Blake and changed the subject. "How did it go with the sheikh?"

He hesitated a long while. "Okay, I think. Looks like I'm going to Qatar."

"You're *what?*"

"Not to live or anything," he added hastily. "Just for a week. Maybe two, as long as it fits around my other commitments. He wants me to act as a consultant."

"That's great! I take it he's paying you?"

"An obscene amount of money."

"Then what's the problem?"

"He wants it to happen soon, and the thought of leaving you behind here…"

"I'll be okay. I can stay here behind the gates, and Antonio won't be able to get to me."

Blake shook his head. "I don't like it."

"Maybe we'll get lucky? Maybe Aidan will find something?"

"Better hope so, Mrs. H."

The call from Aidan came four days later. Since the shopping trip, I hadn't left Fortress Nurah, and I had to admit, I liked having a butler. Blake had snuck out once, late at night, to stock up on condoms for him and chocolate for me. My darling boyfriend had his priorities right.

Murphy settled in, and he was as happy as Murphy ever got. I rode with Nurah each morning and after that, I worked with Alvarez. Now that his stomach wasn't so sore, he lost some of the attitude. He was still difficult, but in the same way Murphy was rather than out-and-out unbearable. And boy could he jump.

Murphy could jump a car, but when Alvarez got going, it felt like he could jump the moon.

"He suits you," Nurah said after she'd watched him try to buck me off before going clear around a one metre forty track.

"I didn't think he would, but you're right. He kind of does."

"Harley's much more my cup of tea. That's what you say, isn't it? Cup of tea?"

"Yes, that's right. You look good on her. Maybe you could take her to a show one day and try a round?"

Her eyes lit up. "I'd love to!"

Before Rashid could alter the show jumps for us to try another course, Blake jogged up to the fence. "Aidan's found something."

An hour later, we were knee-deep in empty drinks cans and Wotsit packets as we crowded around Aidan's computer screen.

"What does that all mean?" I asked.

It was a spreadsheet; one of twelve Aidan had managed to recreate.

"I'm not entirely sure, but if I had to guess, I'd say some kind of money laundering," he said.

"Like crime?"

"Yeah, exactly like crime. Where the hell did you get this shit?"

"Uh, from my ex-boyfriend."

"Seriously? You were dating a crook?"

"I don't know. I mean, I don't think so."

"What does Antonio do for a living?" Blake asked gently.

"Imports and exports, mainly. At least, that's what he told me." But he'd never elaborated on exactly what he imported or exported. And every time I'd asked how work was going, he gave me some hazy answer. "He works for his father's company. They've also got a property portfolio."

Was the whole family involved?

Aidan nodded as he opened another can of energy drink. "Doesn't surprise me. The imports and exports thing, I mean. I did a project once for an accountancy firm, and the firm they were investigating would over-invoice whatever goods they were exporting and get paid in fraudulent funds. If it's going across borders, it's hard to prove."

"You really think they could be criminals?"

"This spreadsheet talks about huge cash transactions, plus loads of smaller ones that look like they're washing the money through to make it look legit. Did you ever see this bloke of yours with large amounts of cash?"

"He paid cash for most things. He always carried a couple of thousand around."

"No, these amounts are bigger."

"Like you might find in a casino? His father ran one as part of their investments."

"Yeah, exactly like you might find in a casino. And I bet if you dug down into its books, you'd find a lot more cash lying around than punters brought through the doors. Smoke and mirrors. It's all smoke and mirrors."

We all looked at each other before Nurah asked the question on everyone's lips. "What do we do now?"

Aidan let out a sigh. "Much as I hate the Old Bill, I'd say it was time to go to the police."

"What if they don't believe us?" I asked. "Or worse, what if they think I was involved? I dated this guy for six years. Six years!"

Blake wrapped an arm around me. "Not voluntarily. You should tell them what he did to you. He shouldn't get away with that either."

"But there's no evidence."

"There's a hoof dent in the back of his car," Nurah said.

"I don't know…"

"And at least if he tries anything else, everything will be on record."

I gripped Blake's hand. "Will you come with me?"

"I'll always be by your side."

When Blake and I walked into the local police station with the files from Aidan on a memory stick and a promise to keep his name out of things, the cops were far happier to see us than I thought they would be. So happy, in fact, that they immediately called up several of their buddies from the Serious Organised Crime Agency and invited them over to join the party.

"Detective Superintendent Box." The older of the two introduced himself and shook our hands. "And this is Detective Sergeant Crichton. I understand you've got some information about the di Stefano family? We've had our eye on them for a while."

"You have?"

He nodded. "We noticed you disappeared off the scene a few months ago. Been waiting for your body to turn up."

I shuddered. They didn't know how close they were

to the truth with that. So I told them. I sat in an interview room for two days and answered every question they asked me. By the time they finished, I was raw. Every detail of my life had been raked up, pored over and torn apart.

Blake stayed with me the whole time, passing me tissues and offering silent support. The police didn't like him being there, but as I refused to talk unless he stayed, they gave in. And while I talked, police experts analysed the files. Once they'd looked at them, they had even more questions.

"This data talks about laundering counterfeit money into the UK financial system. It fits with what we've been seeing for the past few years—a flood of high-quality fake notes, mainly tens and twenties. By the looks of it, the notes are being paid for out of ADS Enterprises, the company run by—"

"Antonio."

"Precisely. And they're laundered through the casino. But what we've never been able to work out is where they're being printed."

"Antonio has a warehouse in West London. Have you tried looking there?"

"Off the record, yes, we have," Box said. "We didn't find anything. It's more likely the notes are being shipped in from abroad, Eastern Europe most probably, but we haven't been able to find the route."

"It's getting across the channel that's the tricky bit," the other man added.

Didn't I know it? It was a problem I'd struggled with myself. Thank goodness Blake had thought of hiding the horsebox in the way he did.

Hmm... Hiding. Horsebox. Hiding... Horsebox...

How many trips had we made back and forth across the channel in that thing? And it was Antonio who'd pushed me into the European tour when I was quite happy on the UK circuit. Antonio who'd kept me on the European tour when my career took off and I got invites to compete in America and the Far East. Bloody hell.

"I think I might have your answer."

Chapter 35

THE POLICE ALLOWED Blake and me to be present as they ripped the lorry apart. They'd retrieved it from the dark corner of Jeff's warehouse and transferred it to their own brightly lit workshop before they started. Oh, and when I told Detective Box that Roger wasn't anything to do with Antonio, he proudly handed the bloody rabbit over without removing his stuffing.

"Seems a shame to take the fella into custody. You can take him home and get him a lettuce leaf."

"Thanks." Hurrah.

I didn't shed a tear as they stripped the horsebox down, panel by panel. That box had once represented my hopes and dreams, but then it came to symbolise my nightmares. It had turned into a prison on wheels.

"Got something, boss," one of the men called out.

I peered into the back as they peeled away the rubber matting in the horse compartment and hit pay dirt. Cash. Cold hard cash stored in a secret compartment under the aluminium floor. Antonio didn't give a shit about me or the horses. He'd just wanted his money back.

Eight million quid, it turned out two days later when they'd counted it all. My "bloody nags," as Antonio loved to call them, had been riding around on eight million pounds' worth of the finest counterfeit notes money could buy. Even Detective Box was impressed by their quality.

And after that, it didn't take long for the police to build their case. A week later, we watched Antonio being led from his house in handcuffs on the big screen in Nurah's movie room. He made the headlines on every news channel. Not only did we have popcorn, we'd pushed the boat out with three different kinds of ice cream, luxury truffles courtesy of the household staff, and Nurah's new favourite food—Wotsits—which the butler served up in a crystal bowl.

The only things missing were Lexi and Brandon, but they were flying home tomorrow, and Alyssa. I'd caught a glimpse of her tear-streaked face next to a policewoman as her entire family got arrested. I'd made sure to tell the police that she had nothing to do with her family's empire, but when she'd just lost everyone, I didn't suppose that meant much. And worse—when I turned my old phone back on, I realised the bust had come just a day after her eighteenth birthday.

"Should I call her?" I asked Blake. "What if she hates me?"

All the di Stefano's assets had been seized. Not only Alyssa's inheritance but the money she needed to live on right now.

"From what you've said, it's Antonio she hates. She could probably use a friend."

"I don't know what to say."

Blake stroked my hair in that comforting way of his. "Just speak from your heart. You can't do more than that."

Every time I picked up the phone, my mouth went dry. In the end, I took the coward's route and sent a message.

Alyssa,

I hope you're okay. I'm so sorry about the way things turned out, but I couldn't sit by and do nothing. Antonio already tried to kill me once, and if I hadn't acted, he would have done it again.

I know how difficult your life must be right now, and I hope in time you'll forgive me. If there's anything I can do to make things easier, then tell me and I'll do it.

Amelia.

While I stewed over Alyssa, Lexi phoned me from the airport. It had been so long since I'd heard her voice, I almost cried. Blake had spoken to her and Brandon while I was riding and caught her up on the situation.

"I've missed you," I said.

"We've missed you too. And Blake a little bit. You're not gonna believe this—we're in the departure lounge, and there's a sale on in duty free. It's like bloody Christmas."

Brandon spoke in the background. "Lexi's saved a hundred and eighty quid on the shopping, and we've just paid out two hundred in excess baggage charges."

"That's my sister," Blake muttered.

Nurah was standing close by too. "Only two hundred?"

"Who's that?" Lexi asked.

"Nurah. I think you two will get on very well."

We were still staying in the guest house at Nurah's. Her father said it was ours until we found our own place. I'd been nervous of him at first, but it turned out he was human after all, and when I met Nurah's mother, I found out where Nurah got her sweetness from.

"We should all have dinner together," Mrs. Mansoor said. "It'll be nice to get to know you. I'm so glad Nurah's meeting new people. When we decided to leave Qatar, it was hard on her. Nasser bought her that horse, and he does tend to spoil her, but it's no substitute for friends."

"Friends are everything."

"And Blake mentioned his sister's coming back from vacation soon. You should invite her as well."

"Okay."

"And Blake's friend? The other racing driver? I think Nasser would like to talk to him too."

Then Nurah insisted on inviting Aidan as he was part of the whole shebang, and Mrs. Mansoor began muttering about party planners. Yep. A whole other planet.

Although Brandon offered to take Lexi and all her luggage back to his place, Nurah wouldn't hear of it.

"We've got plenty of space. Four more bedrooms in the guest house. Does Lexi like riding too?"

Not of the horse variety. "Show jumping's not really her thing."

"Never mind. Maybe she'd like to watch movies with us?"

Nobody batted an eyelid when Lexi turned up with seven suitcases, but everyone did a double take at her attire. Brandon had dressed up, for him, anyway, in a pair of Dockers, and Lexi was wearing a rhinestone-encrusted abaya. She looked around at everyone else, including Nurah's father, who'd covered his mouth with his hand in an attempt to hide his laughter.

"Blake told me you guys were from Qatar, and I had to wear something appropriate, but I feel a bit overdressed."

She stared daggers at her brother.

"Jeans are fine," Nurah told her. "We only wear traditional outfits on formal occasions."

"I think I need to change."

When Lexi came back, she looked more like herself, and despite the fact that they came from completely different backgrounds, she and Nurah got on as well as I'd expected them to.

The three of us spent the next day doing all the girlie things I'd missed out on for so many years. Who knew how much I needed my nails to be painted with little hearts on? I sure didn't until I met Lexi. And after lunch, she dyed my hair back to its original red, and the aftermath of Antonio faded a little more from my mind.

The day after, the boys had another test session at Silverstone, and Mr. Mansoor insisted we all go in the helicopter. It was the first time I'd been able to be with Blake as myself, and with the drama over Antonio, my new relationship hadn't escaped the notice of the press. But the scrutiny was different to before. I couldn't stop smiling with Blake at my side, and I even posed for a few snaps with his arm tight around me. And when one sports reporter asked me when my next show jumping competition would be, I could honestly answer, "Soon."

As long as I could borrow a horsebox, that was. The other one was currently locked up as police evidence and looked like it had been attacked with a can opener.

"You should get one of those couple's names," Lexi said. "Blelia. Miake. Dammit, those don't work."

"You and Brandon could do that instead," I suggested.

"Landon. Brandi. Hey! Brandi—that works."

I burst into laughter at Brandon's horrified expression, while Blake patted him on the back. "Bad luck, mate."

It was a good day, no, a great day, until I got home and saw the red envelope icon blinking on Show Jumping World. I had a message.

Could we meet up this week? For coffee?
   A

That was it. No indication as to her mood, but I quickly agreed to her request. I couldn't do anything else.

Any day you want. Just let me know when and where.
   Amelia

Her reply came almost immediately.

Tomorrow? Eleven o'clock? The coffee shop in the high street next to the church?
   A

I confirmed then spent the rest of the night tossing and turning as to what she was going to say. Would the meeting be pleasant or painful?

Blake stroked my back, his touch soothing. "It'll be okay. She has to know this wasn't your fault."

"That's not much comfort when she's probably homeless, is it?"

"I guess not. Just listen to what she's got to say,

though. She might surprise you."

Well, she certainly did that.

Blake had finally got a new Aston Martin, another four-door, and he dropped me off in my old home town with a kiss.

"Sure you'll be okay? I can come with you if you want."

"Thanks for the offer, but I have to do this on my own."

I got there first and picked at a blueberry muffin while I waited for Alyssa to arrive. As soon as she saw me, she rushed over and threw herself into my arms.

"I missed you," she said, biting back tears. "I hated being in that house without you."

"Are you okay? I mean, they said on the news that the whole family had been arrested apart from you."

"It's the best thing ever to happen. So many nights I fell asleep wishing I'd wake up and they'd be gone, and then finally, it happened. I'm free. They can't hurt me anymore. And it's all thanks to you."

I felt bile rise in my throat. "Hurt you?"

The awful story came out over hot chocolate with whipped cream in a quiet corner of an imitation Starbucks. It turned out Alyssa had been better at hiding things than I was. And Antonio's father had been better at hiding things than his son. Donato's nocturnal visits to Alyssa's room had gone unnoticed by the family for years, me included. We were both in tears by the time she finished her tale, beyond caring about the odd stares the other patrons were giving us.

"Why didn't you tell someone?" I asked. "You could have talked to me."

"I couldn't. Dad said if I did, he'd kill you."

I went lightheaded for a second, and when the cafe came back into view, Alyssa was still sobbing in front of me. "You kept quiet to protect me?"

She nodded. "You were my only friend. If I didn't have you... But then you left, and I wanted you to be happy."

That girl... Barely eighteen years old, and she was stronger than I'd ever been.

"Where are you staying at the moment?" I asked her. "At home?"

"It's not a home. It's never been a home. I'm never setting foot in that house again unless it's with a can of petrol and a match. The police found me a bed-and-breakfast to stay in."

"Do you want to stay with us?"

She nodded, tears falling once more.

Blake didn't say a word when I walked back to the car with Alyssa in tow. He just opened the door, made sure she had her seatbelt on, and set off for our temporary home.

As I watched him, his eyes focused on the road ahead, and my heart swelled with love for the man sitting next to me. I'd be forever grateful for the day I forgot to use my mirrors and reversed into his car. That day had been the start of my life.

And I was determined to help Alyssa with a new start to hers.

She had the same reaction as me when Blake turned into the palace's driveway and she saw the house and gardens for the first time. The neatly manicured lawns. The perfectly trimmed trees. The white columns flanking the front door. Her jaw dropped.

"You live here?"

"Just for the moment."

"And the horses?"

"They're here too."

"Thank goodness. I used to lie awake worrying about Antonio's threats."

"You and me both."

Lexi and Nurah were decorating the lounge with balloons when we got in, while Brandon slept on the sofa. He cracked an eye open as we walked past.

"Jet lag. Shh."

"We thought we'd have the party in here..." Lexi began, then spotted Alyssa behind me. "This is Antonio's sister?"

I nodded, and she ran over and gathered Alyssa into a hug. "I'm sorry you're related to such a prick."

That got a smile out of Alyssa, the first one today.

"So am I," she whispered.

"Do you want to celebrate his downfall with us? We've got cake."

"I think I'd like that."

Lexi linked her arm through Alyssa's and gave me a wink. "Then I'll start by doing your hair. And then your nails. Every girl should look pretty, okay? And I've got plenty of clothes you can borrow."

Good old Lexi. She knew exactly what to do. She'd worked her strange brand of magic on me, and she'd no doubt have the same effect on Alyssa.

Blake slipped his arms around me. "She'll be okay.

We'll both make sure of it."

I took his hands in mine, needing that connection between us. I never wanted to let him go, and now I didn't have to. He was the man I loved, my future husband, and my home.

Epilogue

I WAITED IN the collecting ring, a few unruly butterflies unsettling my stomach. The last time I'd ridden in the European Championship Tour in Cannes it had changed my life.

I wasn't anticipating such a dramatic outcome this year, but I quite fancied going home with a rosette.

My support crew was lined up along the fence, ready to cheer me on. Brandon and Lexi were there, with Lexi wearing a sparkly top from her new fashion line. Nurah stood next to her, clutching the trophy she'd won on Harley earlier in the day. It was her first, and I wasn't sure she'd ever put it down. The professional photographer her father had hired hovered nearby, ready to capture every moment for the family album.

Alyssa was to her right, a grin plastered on her face. We might have moved out of the guest house now, but she spent most of her time at the palace, hanging out with Nurah when she wasn't helping me with the horses.

Mr. Mansoor and his wife came next, both smiling. Whether that was at me or their daughter, I wasn't sure. And finally, there was Blake, number one card-carrying member of my fan club. He blew me a kiss when he saw me looking in his direction.

A crackle came from the loudspeaker as I heard my name being called. "Amelia Hunter on Alvarez to the main ring."

That's right, Alvarez. We had an understanding now. He didn't try to kill me, and I fed him carrots. Oh, and he jumped. He jumped big.

I'd already been around the course on Murphy, and I was lying second to one of the Whitakers, just pipped on time. I had one chance to beat him.

Alvarez, it turned out, was a show-off. He pranced into the ring, his black coat gleaming under the lights. Rashid had brushed him until he shone. When the bell rang, he swished his tail, pranced sideways for a couple of steps, then took off for the first fence. He flew. And when it came to the final obstacle, a replica of Blake and Brandon's Aston Martin, he outdid Murphy with his car jumping skills. I looked up at the clock as we crossed the line then punched the air. We'd done it! First place and the rosette to go with it.

Blake caught me as I slithered off Alvarez, and when he kissed me, I knew which photo would be making the papers the next day.

I'd get a trophy, too, but it would go under the lights in the cabinet Mr. Mansoor had built in one of the living rooms at the palace. He liked to keep the cups around to show his visitors, and I was only too happy to let him.

When he'd heard I needed a new sponsor, we'd come to an agreement. He'd pay all my costs as long as I continued to teach Nurah. That was a deal I could easily live with. Plus, it meant I got the ride on Alvarez. I loved Harley dearly, but Alvarez had the talent and Harley could help Nurah to realise her dreams as well.

And as one half of Team Mansoor, she'd certainly done that today.

Not only did I have a sponsor, but I'd also landed a modelling gig. That's right—me. I was the face of a new line of equestrian clothing, which meant I got free riding gear and money too. Between that gig and the show jumping clinics I was teaching, I could afford to put all of my prize money into Alyssa's university fund.

She was planning to study philosophy at Oxford in September. Nurah was going with her, only she'd be taking a master's degree in political science. And because Nurah was going, so were Hassan and Khalid, and Mr. Mansoor had already bought a luxury flat for them to live in. We could never make up for what Alyssa's family had done to her, but at least going forward, her life would be a comfortable one.

And Antonio's new digs wouldn't be quite so cushy. Along with his father, he'd been sentenced to life in prison for his crimes. Including attacking me, because although I didn't realise it at the time, Alyssa had witnessed one of the incidents. I'd been horrified when she told me, and there'd been tears and hugs, but he couldn't hurt either of us again.

The family who'd made our lives a living hell were gone.

But before the girls went off to university, we were going to take a holiday, all of us, the horses included. River Farm was ours for the next two months, and this time we planned to spend more time relaxing by the pool and less time hiding from demented ex-boyfriends. There would be no car chases, apart from the small matter of the Le Mans twenty-four-hour race. Blake, Brandon and Tom were going back for another crack at it. Angus was heading up the team again, and he was as determined as the rest of us that the Aston Martin was going to finish one place higher this year.

"I've already won, though," Blake whispered to me one evening. "I won you."

After six months of calling me Mrs. H, Blake had finally put his money where his mouth was, and his ring too. We didn't want a fuss, but Lexi and Nurah weren't about to let us get away with that. After a quiet ceremony, we'd arrived back at our new home expecting to spend a quiet evening with a bottle of champagne and an economy pack of Trojans, only to find the limo waiting. When we arrived at the palace, we found that our friends had decked the place out in streamers and balloons, hired a rock band, and organised a banquet.

As for our new home, we'd spotted the perfect house just down the road from the palace, and only half an hour from Lexi and Brandon. It wasn't big—it didn't need to be—but it had a little cottage in the garden so Alyssa could have her own space when she was home.

Back in Cannes, Rashid led Alvarez away as the press shouted out questions.

"Amelia, you've had a dramatic year. How does it feel to be back where it all started?"

At Antonio's trial, my entire story had come out. The whole world knew why I'd legged it with the horses in the middle of the night. Embarrassing, but it had also raised the profile of domestic violence, and I'd received several messages from other women saying that my story had given them the courage to report their own troubles.

"It feels a lot better than it did last time," I told the

reporter.

"And, Blake, how do you feel about your second attempt at the big race?"

He put an arm around me, one hand resting on my belly. "Le Mans can never give me a bigger prize than my wife."

As I twined my fingers in his and thought about what was growing inside me beneath our palms, I wondered when to break the news to him that in fact, it could.

WHAT'S NEXT?

If you've enjoyed 24 Hours of Trouble, why not try another of my romantic comedies?

Life: A Brush with Love

At twenty-eight years old, the only men in lawyer Cate Jenkins' life are her two cats, Thor and Loki, unless you count her not-so-secret love affair with Ben & Jerry.

Escape comes in the form of art classes, where life drawing model, Joe, provides a welcome distraction from the monotony of her job. Each Thursday for five weeks, she gets to lose herself in a world of twinkling blue eyes and chiselled abs.

Meanwhile, next-door neighbour Dane is determined to win Cate's heart. Can his gifts of coffee and kitty treats win out against muscled perfection?

And more importantly, what secrets are both men hiding?

For more details: www.elise-noble.com/life

If you're in the mood for some darker humour, why not try my Blackwood Security series, starting with *Pitch Black*?

Even a Diamond can be shattered...

After the owner of a security company is murdered, his sharp-edged wife goes on the run. Forced to abandon everything she holds dear—her home, her friends, her job in special ops—assassin Diamond builds a new life for herself in England. As Ashlyn Hale, she meets Luke, a handsome local who makes her realise just how lonely she is.

Yet, even in the sleepy village of Lower Foxford, the dark side of life dogs Diamond's trail when the unthinkable strikes. Forced out of hiding, she races against time to save those she cares about.

Pitch Black is currently available for FREE:
www.elise-noble.com/pitch-black

If you enjoyed 24 Hours of Trouble, please consider leaving a review.

For an author, every review is incredibly important. Not only do they make us feel warm and fuzzy inside, readers consider them when making their decision whether or not to buy a book. Even a line saying you enjoyed the book or what your favourite part was helps a lot.

WANT TO STALK ME?

For updates on my new releases, giveaways, and other random stuff, you can sign up for my newsletter on my website:
www.elise-noble.com

Facebook:
www.facebook.com/EliseNobleAuthor

Twitter: @EliseANoble

Instagram: @elise_noble

I also have a group on Facebook for my fans to hang out. They love the characters from my Blackwood and Trouble books almost as much as I do, and they're the first to find out about my new stories as well as throwing in their own ideas that sometimes make it into print!

And if you'd like to read my books for FREE, you can also find details of how to join my review team.

Would you like to join Team Blackwood?

www.elise-noble.com/team-blackwood

END OF BOOK STUFF

I've known for ages that I had to write a book about a racing driver. Motor racing has been a big part of my life since I turned eighteen, and as a track marshal, I've been lucky enough to see behind the scenes. For me, Le Mans is the best race in the world, hands down, which is why I've been fourteen times now! There's no luxury farmhouse for me, though—I camp right next to the circuit with my marshalling team, a crew made up of many different nationalities who have become great friends.

And when I say camping, we've refined the experience over the years—thanks to the wonders of German engineering, we even have satellite TV and a hot shower :)

So, why does Blake drive an Aston Martin and Antonio drives a Porsche? Simple. Because my boyfriend and I are always ~~arguing about~~ discussing which is best. For me, there's no contest—I've been lucky enough to drive a few supercars over the years, and the Aston was the one I fell in love with. The V8 engine, the sportshift gearbox, the awesome sound system... If it's good enough for James Bond, it's good enough for me. The worst supercar I've driven? A Lamborghini Diablo. It was bloody uncomfortable and hard to see out of.

And the horses? Well, I thought of the idea for the story while riding my own horse. Trev's more of a dressage horse than a show jumper—put a tiny fence in front of him and it's pot luck whether he trips over it or leaps in the air like it's going to kill him—but I've been to plenty of shows. That world looks glamorous from the outside, but behind the scenes, it's not as posh as people think. Most riders, like most racing drivers, compete on a shoestring budget, and would rather buy shoes for their horses than themselves (and those are flipping expensive)!

But for me, cars and horses are addictive. Both have a buzz about them that gets into my soul, and I'll always be chasing that extra little bit of horsepower...

OTHER BOOKS BY ELISE NOBLE

The Blackwood Security Series
Black is my Heart (prequel)
Pitch Black
Into the Black
Forever Black
Gold Rush
Gray is my Heart
Neon (novella)
Out of the Blue
Ultraviolet
Red Alert
White Hot
The Scarlet Affair
Quicksilver (2019)
The Girl with the Emerald Ring (2019)
For the Love of Animals (Nate & Carmen)

The Blackwood Elements Series
Oxygen
Lithium
Carbon
Rhodium
Platinum
Lead (2019)
Copper (2019)

Nickel (TBA)

The Blackwood UK Series
Joker in the Pack
Cherry on Top (novella)
Roses are Dead
Shallow Graves
Indigo Rain (2019)

Blackwood Casefiles
Stolen Hearts (TBA)

Blackstone House
Hard Lines (TBA)

The Electi Series
Cursed
Spooked
Possessed (2019)
Demented (TBA)

The Trouble Series
Trouble in Paradise
Nothing but Trouble
24 Hours of Trouble

Standalone
Life
Twisted (short stories)
A Very Happy Christmas (novella)

Printed in Great Britain
by Amazon